'Madeleine, this cannot go on.'

'What cannot go on, my lord? The ride? The Marquis of Risley taking an actress in his carriage?'

'You do not have to be an actress.'

'No, but that is what I am. It is how I earn my living.'

'I could change that.'

'Why do you want to change it? If you are ashamed to be seen with me, why did you ask me out?'

'Because I want to be with you every hour of the day and—'

'I will not become your paramour, Lord Risley. I do not know why it is that everyone thinks all actresses are harlots…'

'Madeleine, how can you accuse me of that?'

'That's what you have in mind, is it not? That is what the flowers and the presents have been all about, to get into my bed. Deny it if you can.'

Born in Singapore, **Mary Nichols** came to England when she was three, and has spent most of her life in different parts of East Anglia. She has been a radiographer, school secretary, information officer and industrial editor, as well as a writer. She has three grown-up children, and four grandchildren. You may find that some of the characters in this story are familiar to you, as *A Lady of Consequence* follows on from Mary Nichols's recent novels *Lady Lavinia's Match* and *The Incomparable Countess*.

Recent titles by the same author:

THE HONOURABLE EARL
THE INCOMPARABLE COUNTESS
LADY LAVINIA'S MATCH

A LADY
OF CONSEQUENCE

Mary Nichols

MILLS & BOON®

First published in Great Britain 2003
Large Print edition 2004
Harlequin Mills & Boon Limited,
Eton House, 18-24 Paradise Road, Richmond, Surrey TW9 1SR

© Mary Nichols 2003

ISBN 0 263 18180 4

Set in Times Roman 15 on 15½ pt.
42-0104-81105

Printed and bound in Great Britain
by Antony Rowe Ltd, Chippenham, Wiltshire

A LADY
OF CONSEQUENCE

Mary Nichols

Prologue

1817

Maddy was alone in the kitchen, the last of the domestic staff to finish her day's work. All the other servants had done their allotted chores and left her to it. The last to go had been Cook who had told her to 'Look lively or you'll not be done before it's time to get up and start all over again,' which did little to make her feel any less exhausted.

There had been a dinner party upstairs and the amount of washing up a dozen people could create was beyond her comprehension: a mountain of plates, tureens, platters, glasses and cutlery, not to mention all the pans in which the food had been cooked. The guests had all departed—she had heard their carriages going over an hour ago—and the family, Lord and Lady Bulford, the Honourable Henry and the two young ladies, Hortense and Annabel, had all gone to their rooms, uncaring that one of their servants still toiled in the nether regions of their London mansion.

The washing up finished, Maddy set out the breakfast trays ready for the ladies in the morning, filled the kettles with water and went to bank down the fire, her last task before retiring. She would never have been slaving here at all, if her mother had not been killed so tragically, she told herself a dozen times a day. Mama had been run down by a horse and carriage in Oxford Street when she was shopping for ribbon for a gown she was making. She had been a seamstress and a very good one and Maddy herself might have followed in her footsteps if it had not been for the accident.

That's what everyone called it, a tragic accident for which no one was to blame. But the day of the funeral she had overheard two of their neighbours talking and they said the young dandy who had been driving the curricle had been racing it and he ought to have been horsewhipped for driving so dangerously along a busy thoroughfare; but then he was an aristocrat and drunk into the bargain, which seemed to be excuse enough for leaving a nine-year-old child without a mother.

The trouble was she had had no father either, at least not one she knew of, and so she had been sent to an orphanage in Monmouth Street that took in the children of soldiers orphaned by war. She supposed someone had told them her father had been a soldier, which was something she had not known for her mother never spoke of him. She had been sent from the orphanage to Lady Bulford when she was twelve and considered old enough to work.

The kitchen of Number Seven Bedford Row had been her world ever since; two long years with each day merging into the next, nothing to vary the routine, no one to talk to but the other servants who all treated her with contempt because of where she came from, though that wasn't her fault, was it? She rarely left the house, except for two hours on a Sunday afternoon, which she spent walking in the parks, pretending she was a lady and had nothing at all to do but look decorative and catch the eye of some young beau who would whisk her away to a life of luxury, such as the Bulfords enjoyed.

She was too fond of dreaming, Cook was always telling her, but what else was there to do to enliven her day but dream? She was doing it now, she realised, squatting in front of the fire, gazing into the last of the embers and wishing for a miracle…

Startled by a sudden noise, she looked round, to see the Honourable Henry standing in the doorway with a quilted *robe de chambre* covering his nightshirt. Scrambling to her feet, she dropped him a curtsy.

'Who are you?' he asked.

'Maddy, sir.'

'That's an unusual name.' He smiled suddenly and his dark eyes lit with humour. He was, she decided, a very handsome young man. 'Are you mad?'

'No, sir,' she said emphatically. 'It is short for Madeleine.' She had been Maddy ever since she arrived. 'That's a high-stepping handle for a no-body,' the other servants had said when she told them her name. 'Can't have you putting on airs and graces here.' And so Maddy she had become. She was too bewildered by a second upheaval in her life to care what they called her.

'How long have you been working here?'

'All day, sir.'

'No, I meant how long have you been working for the family?'

'Two years, sir.' She paused. 'Is there something I can do for you?'

'Oh, yes,' he murmured, looking her up and down. 'Oh, yes, indeed.'

'What is it?' she asked.

He seemed to come out of a trance and laughed suddenly. 'I came down for a glass of milk. I don't seem able to sleep.'

She walked past him into the pantry where the milk was kept in a jug on the cool floor. 'Could you heat it up?' he asked. 'It would be better warm.'

She put some milk in a pan and stirred up the fire again to heat it, while he stood and watched her.

'You are a very pretty girl, do you know that?' he said.

'No.' Standing over the fire had made her face red, but now she felt an extra warmth flood her cheeks. 'You shouldn't say things like that, sir.'

'Why ever not? It's the truth. I'll wager there's many a young blade dangling after you.'

'No, sir. I'm not old enough for young men to dangle after, even if they were allowed, which they are not.' Lady Bulford had made that quite clear when she first arrived and though she hadn't known what her ladyship meant at the time, she had found out since and a great deal more about the ways of the world and young men in particular, which would have shocked her mother if she had been alive to hear it.

'How old are you?'

'Fourteen.'

'My goodness, you are well grown for your age. My mother must feed you well.'

She did not feel disposed to tell him that she lived on leftovers, not only from the family table but from the servants' table. She was a drudge and only one step up from the dogs and cats who lived in the yard and were the last to be fed. She poured the milk from the pan into a glass and handed it to him. 'There you are, sir. I hope you sleep better for it.'

'Oh, I am sure I shall. Will you be going to bed soon?'

'As soon as I have washed up this pan and banked down the fire, sir.'

'Goodnight, Maddy.'

'Goodnight, sir.'

He disappeared, carrying his glass of milk, and she turned back to the fire. Fancy the master's son noticing her and calling her pretty! Was she pretty? Her mama had always said she was and made her beautiful dresses and brushed her dark hair until it shone like velvet, but that had been a long time ago and now her clothes were a skivvy's uniform and she was too tired to do more than rake a comb through her hair to get the knots out. If only…

If only Mama had been alive, she would be living with her in the small apartment over the dressmaking establishment that she had set up and which provided a decent living for them both; she would be learning how to create gowns and pelisses and pretty underwear and hats. Mama said they would make a name for themselves as the foremost modistes in London and that the upper crust would all flock to be dressed by Madame Charron and her charming daughter. Their name wasn't Charron, of course, it was Cartwright, but Mama said the French name sounded grander.

She pulled herself out of what was becoming another of her fantasies and dragged her exhausted feet up the back stairs to her tiny room in the attic, one of a row that housed all the female servants in varying degrees of comfort according to their status.

She was climbing into bed five minutes later, when she heard footsteps on the stair. She paid little attention at first, assuming it was one of the maids coming back from fetching a glass of water, but when they stopped outside her door, she sat upright, her heart in her mouth.

The door opened and the master's son, wearing nothing but a night-shirt, stood facing her. He was smiling. 'Don't be alarmed, my dear,' he said, shutting the door behind him and quickly crossing the room to the bed where she was so startled she could do nothing but sit and stare at him. 'I still can't sleep.'

'You want me to go down and fetch you some more milk?' she asked, her only thought that she would never get to sleep at this rate.

'No, my dear Madeleine,' he said, sitting on the bed beside her and taking her hand; it was red raw from the all the washing up she did, but he did not seem to notice. 'I think I could go to sleep if I could cuddle up to you.'

'Sir!' She was astonished and confused and, in some way, strangely excited. Her heart was beating in her throat and that one strangled cry was all she could utter.

He smiled. 'You are so warm and so beautiful. You have the body of a goddess, don't you know, and I cannot sleep for thinking of it. I want to touch you, touch your warm, pink flesh, feel you, kiss you.' He leaned forward and, taking her head in his hands, bent his mouth to hers. His lips were soft and moist and his breath smelt of the wine and brandy he had consumed. His hands began to roam over her body, pulling up her nightgown and forcing her legs apart.

She realised suddenly that what he was trying to do was wrong. Hadn't the women at the orphanage told her all about men's carnal desires, hadn't she been warned time and time again, against allowing her maidenhood to be taken before she had a wedding ring on her finger? It was, she had been told, the worst of sins, and they cited examples of children whose mothers had never been married. Bastards they were called. It was what happened if you lay with a man before the wedding night.

Some of them had called *her* a bastard, saying her mother had never been to church with her father, whoever he was, but she had furiously told them of her hero father, who had died fighting for his country, simply to shut them up. Now, in a sudden flash of insight, the servants' talk began to make sense. This was no fantasy, no wished-for miracle, but a nightmare.

'No!' she cried, trying to wriggle out of his grasp. 'You mustn't.'

'Mustn't?' he queried, throwing himself on top of her so that she was effectively imprisoned under the weight of his body. 'But, my dear Madeleine, it is not up to you to say what I mustn't do. I do as I please. You are a servant and must do as you are told. You would not want to be turned off without a character, would you?'

'You wouldn't do that?' she asked fearfully.

'I could, but I won't, if you are a good girl.' He buried his head in the valley between her breasts.

'I am a good girl,' she said, struggling to free herself. 'Please let me go.'

He looked up. 'When I'm done with you.' He was not smiling now, but grimly determined and in a way that stiffened her will to resist. Had he continued to ply her with compliments, to whisper endearing words and been gentle, who knows if she might have succumbed? Such was her longing to be loved by someone, to be seen as a human being with feelings, to be treated with tenderness, she might have given up struggling. But, unused to being denied anything, he was angry. And that made her angry too.

She used the last of her strength to push her knee sharply into his groin and heard him yelp with pain as he leapt off her. She rushed for the door and, pulling it open, fled along the corridor and down the stairs in her nightgown, making for the safety of the kitchen. But she never reached it. She ran slap into Lord Bulford, who had left his bed and was coming along the landing, tying the cord of his undress gown, to see what all the commotion was about.

'Where's the fire?' he roared.

'Fire? I don't know anything about a fire,' she said.

'Then what's to do?'

'Your son is in my room,' she said, without stopping to think of the consequences such an accusation might have. 'He tried…he shouldn't have…'

'My son? Don't be ridiculous, you impertinent baggage. What would my son want in your room?'

'George, what's going on?' Lady Bulford, having hastily donned a peignoir, joined her husband.

'This ill-bred chit has accused Henry of going to her room.'

Her ladyship looked Maddy up and down, her lip curled in distaste. 'She is clearly demented. Been having a dream, I shouldn't wonder. Or mistook one of the footmen. If she has been entertaining them in her room, there is only one thing for it…'

'I have not been entertaining anyone in my room,' she retorted, forgetting that it was simply not done to answer back. 'Your son came uninvited. Do you think I don't know the Honourable Henry when I see him? He came down to the kitchen for milk and I gave him some, then he waited for me to go to bed and came to my room…'

'Good Lord! The effrontery of it,' Lady Bulford said to her husband. 'As if Henry would look twice at a misbegotten nobody like her.' She turned back to Maddy. 'What were you hoping to gain by this Banbury tale, money?'

'No, my lady, all I want is to be allowed to go back to bed and not have people coming to my room uninvited.' She spoke very clearly, enunciating her words as her mother had taught her. 'Will you please tell your son his attentions are not welcome.'

'By God! I've heard it all now,' his lordship said, his face growing purple with indignation. 'Go back to bed, is it? And who with, may I ask?'

'No one. I am tired, I have been working all day…'

'Oh, well, if it's overwork you are complaining of, that is easily remedied,' Lady Bulford said. 'You may pack your bags and leave this instant. Your services are no longer required.'

'But I've done nothing wrong.'

'Making false accusations against my son is wrong and impudence to your betters is wrong and complaining about your work is wrong, when everyone knows I am the most benign of employers.'

'And so is rushing about the house in your nightwear in the middle of the night,' his lordship put in, eyeing her appreciatively from top to toe.

'I only did it to escape.'

'Then you may escape. Permanently. You may go back to bed, but I want you gone by the time I come down for my breakfast.'

'But, my lord, where will I go?'

'That is no concern of mine. Back where you came from, I suppose. And do not expect a character…'

'My lord, I beg of you…'

'Enough. I am not going to bandy words with you. Get out of my sight before I throw you out here and now.'

Maddy went back to her room, relieved to find her unwelcome visitor had gone, and flung herself on the bed, sobbing her heart out. Why didn't they believe her? It was so unfair. Where could she go? How could she live? Who could she turn to? She couldn't go back to the orphanage, she was too old for that now. Must it be the poorhouse?

If Henry Bulford had an ounce of shame, he would admit what he had done and exonerate her. But she knew he would not. He was one of the upper crust, people with more money than they could spend in a lifetime and they thought that meant they could do as they liked, just as the young dandy who had run down her mother thought he could do as he liked. People like her were the lowest of the low and didn't matter.

But gradually her misery turned to anger and anger made her strong. She would not be cowed. She was as good as they were, better than they were, and one day she would prove she did matter. One day she would beat them. One day they would have to acknowledge her as their equal; if she trampled on a few aristocratic toes to get there, so be it. And if one of those aristocratic toes turned out to belong to the Honourable Henry Bulford, so much the better. She did not know how she would do it, nor how long it would take, but nothing and no one would stand in her way. She would make her dreams come true; she would be a lady.

Chapter One

1827

The curtain came down on the last act to thunderous applause. The cast took several curtain calls, but everyone knew it was really Madeleine Charron the audience wanted. She had the theatre world at her feet; all the young men of the *ton* and several who were not so young were raving about her, including Duncan Stanmore, Marquis of Risley.

'I don't know which I admire more, her looks or her acting ability,' he said to his friend, Benedict Willoughby, as he rose with everyone else to clap and call bravo. 'Both are bang-up prime.'

'If you've got your sights set on her, you will come home by weeping cross, don't you know?' Benedict said. 'Unlike most of her kind, she is very particular.'

'You only say that because she refused to go out to supper with you last week.'

'Not at all,' Benedict said huffily, as they made their way towards the exit. 'I'm not the only disappointed one; she's turned everyone down, though I did hear she went for a carriage ride in the park with Sir Percival Ponsonby last week, so she can't be that fastidious.'

'Sir Percy is a benign old gentleman who wouldn't hurt a fly.'

'I didn't say he would, but you must admit he's an old fogey. He must be sixty if he's a day and those ridiculous clothes!'

'He's well-breeched and he knows how to treat a girl. And he has always had a liking for actresses, you know that. They appreciate his gallantry and they feel safe with him. It won't last. Percy is a confirmed bachelor.'

'Good God! You aren't thinking of betting on the marriage stakes yourself, are you?'

'Don't be a fool, Willoughby. It is not to be thought of. My revered father would have a fit. But I will take her out to supper.'

'Yes, you have only to wave your title and your fortune under her nose and she will fall at your feet.'

'I'll do it without mentioning either.'

'When?'

'In the next se'ennight. I'll put a pony on it.'

'Done.'

They wandered out into the street. A flower girl stood beside her basket, offering posies to the young men as they escorted their ladies to their carriages. Duncan stopped beside her, fished in his purse for a couple of guineas and rattled them in his palm. 'I'll buy the lot,' he said, throwing the coins in her basket. 'Take them round the stage door for Miss Charron.'

She gave him a wide grin. 'Any message, sir?'

'No. Just the flowers. And do the same tomorrow night and the night after that and every night for the rest of the week.' He found some more coins and tossed them in with the others, before turning to Benedict. 'Come on, Willoughby, I'll buy you supper at White's and we can have a hand of cards afterwards.'

'Aren't you going round to the stage door?'

'What, and stand in line with all the other hopefuls, begging to be noticed? No fear!'

Benedict, who was used to his friend's strange ways, shrugged his shoulders and followed him to their club.

At the end of the week, a small package was delivered to the theatre, addressed to Miss Madeleine Charron. It contained a single diamond ear drop and a note that simply said, 'You may have its twin if you come out to supper with me on Monday. My carriage will be waiting outside the stage door after the performance.' It was unsigned.

It was meant to intrigue her and it certainly succeeded. Maddy was used to being sent flowers, but they usually arrived with their donors, anxious for the privilege of taking her out, or accompanied by *billets doux* or excruciating love poems and definitely not penned incognito. But a whole florist's stock, every night for a week, followed by a single ear drop of such exquisite beauty it brought a lump to her throat, was something else again. This latest admirer was different.

'And rich,' Marianne said, when she saw the trinket. Marianne Doubleday was her friend, an actress of middle years, but a very good one, who had once, not many years before, fooled the entire *beau monde* for a whole season into believing she was a lady and a very wealthy one at that. 'Are you sure you have no idea who it might be?'

'None at all.'

'And will you go?'

'I don't know. He is undoubtedly very sure of himself.'

'So what is that to the point? No doubt it means he's an aristocrat. That's what you want, isn't it?'

Years ago, when she had first joined the company as a wardrobe seamstress, Marianne had befriended her and later, when Maddy had been given small parts, had taught her how to act, how to project her voice so that a whisper could be heard in the gods, how to move gracefully, how to use her hands and her eyes to express herself and still conceal her innermost thoughts, how to listen and understand the undercurrents in a conversation, the innuendo behind the way a word was said, the ways of the worldly-wise, everything to bring her to the standing she now enjoyed.

In return Maddy had confided her secret ambition to be a lady. Marianne had not mocked it; after all, noblemen sometimes did marry actresses, but she had told her how difficult it would be, how they were usually ostracised by Polite Society and that being a lady was not all it was cracked up to be, that with wealth and status came responsibilities.

'Besides, you'll find all manner of obstacles put in your way by the young man's parents,' she had said. 'If they have any standing in Society, they'll fight you tooth and nail. They'll have a bride all picked out for him, unless, of course you set your cap at someone old, but then he's like to be a widower with a ready-made family.'

Maddy had grimaced at the idea. 'No, that won't do. I want people to envy me, to look up to me, to take what I say seriously. I want to have a grand house, a carriage and servants. No one, no one at all, will dare look down on me or take me for granted ever again...'

'A tall order, Maddy. My advice is to take what is offered and enjoy it without wishing for the moon.'

Although Marianne knew about her ambition, she did not know the reason for it. She did not know the inner fury that still beset Maddy every time she thought of Henry Bulford and his uncaring parents. It had not diminished over the years. All through her early struggles, she had nursed her desire for…what was it? Revenge? No, it could not be that, for Henry Bulford had inherited the title and was married and she did not envy his top-lofty wife one bit. They had attended the same theatrical party once and he had not even recognised her. But then why would he connect the skinny, pale-faced kitchen maid he had tried to rape with the beautiful actress who had taken London by storm?

A great deal of water had flowed under London Bridge since then, some of it so dreadful she wished she could forget it, but it would not go away and only strengthened her resolve. She had risen above every kick dealt her by an unkind fate, but sometimes it had been touch and go. She had nearly starved, had begged and even stolen—and she was not proud of that—until she had found a job as a seamstress. Hours and hours of close work, living in dingy lodgings, quite literally working her fingers to the bone and all for a pittance.

Her ambition was smothered by the sheer weight of having to earn a living, but it did not die altogether and one day in 1820—she remembered the year well because it was the year the King had tried to divorce his wife and become the butt of everyone's ribaldry—she found herself delivering a theatrical costume to the Covent Garden theatre. Her employer sometimes helped out when they had a big production and this was wanted urgently. She had told Maddy to take it round there on her way home.

On this occasion, the whole company was carousing, having just pulled off a great performance at a large aristocratic mansion. The troupe was led by a colourful character called Lancelot Greatorex, who fascinated her with his strange clothes and extravagant gestures. Seeing her ill-concealed curiosity, he demanded to know if she were an actress.

'Oh, no,' she said.

'How do you know you are not?'

'Why, sir,' she had said, laughing, 'I have never been on a stage in my life.'

'That's of no account. You don't need to tread the boards to play a part, we all do it from time to time. Do you tell me you have never had a fantasy, never pretended to be other than you are?'

'I hadn't thought of it like that.'

'You speak up well. What do you do to earn a crust?'

He may have been speaking metaphorically, but to her a crust was all she did earn, and sometimes a little butter to put on it. 'I am a seamstress,' she said.

'Are you good at it?'

'Yes, sir. I did most of the stitching on the costume I have just delivered.'

'Quick, are you?'

'Yes, sir.'

'How much do you earn?'

'Six pounds a year, sir.'

He laughed. 'I can double that.'

'Oh, I do not think I can act, sir.'

'I am not asking you to. Actresses are ten a penny, but good seamstresses are like gold dust. Would you like to join my troupe as a seamstress? Having work done outside is not always convenient.'

Maddy had not hesitated. The flamboyant life among stage folk appealed to her and, somewhere in the back of her mind, her sleeping ambition revived. If she wanted to better herself, to act a part for which she had not been born, then where better to learn it?

She had become a seamstress, sewing, mending and pressing costumes and from that had progressed to becoming a dresser for Marianne Doubleday, chatting to her in her dressing room, learning, learning all the time. She was quick and eager and when they discovered she could read, they gave her the job of prompter, so that when one of the cast fell ill, who better to take her place but Maddy, who already knew the lines? And so Madeleine Charron, actress, had been born.

But was it enough? Did it fulfil her dream? Was she still burning with that desire to be a lady? A real one, not a fantasy. Could she pull it off? Was she, as Marianne suggested, wishing for the moon? She smiled at her friend. 'So you don't think I should go?'

Marianne shrugged. 'It is up to you. You do not have to commit yourself, do you? The invitation is to supper, nothing more.'

'And nothing more will be offered, I assure you.'

She had been out to supper with countless young men before and enjoyed their company, each time wondering before she went if this was the one who would fulfil her dream, but before the night was over, she had known he was not.

There were so many reasons: these sycophants did not have the title she craved; they were too young or too old; they were ugly and would give her ugly children; their conversation was a little too exuberant, or not exuberant enough. Some were fools, some gave every appearance of doing her a favour in spending money on a supper for her, some were married and expecting more than she was prepared to give. She did not intend to be anyone's light o' love.

'But do have a care, Maddy, that you are not branded a tease.'

'Have no fear, dear Marianne, you have taught me well.'

Maddy lingered over her toilette the following Monday night, spending more time than usual sitting before her mirror, removing the greasepaint from her face and brushing out her dark hair before coiling it up into a Grecian knot, before choosing a gown to wear. She prided herself on her good taste, and being a seamstress and a very good one meant that her clothes, though not numerous, were superbly made of the finest materials she could afford. It made her feel good to know that she could stand comparison with those who considered themselves her social superiors.

She slipped into a blue silk, whose fitted bodice and cross-cut skirt flowed smoothly over her curves. It had short puffed sleeves and a low neckline outlined with a cape collar which showed off her creamy shoulders and neck. She hesitated over wearing a necklace but, as most of her jewellery was paste, decided against it and fastened the odd ear drop in her ear before throwing a dark blue velvet burnoose over her shoulders and venturing out into the street.

Everyone but the night watchman had left and she half expected to find the road empty. It was her own fault if it was, she had kept him waiting and she could hardly complain if he had given up and gone home. But there was a carriage waiting. It was a glossy affair, though its colour she could not determine in the weak light from the street lamp. There was no sign of an occupant. Perhaps her admirer had simply sent the carriage to fetch her to wherever he was. She was not sure she liked that idea; it put her at a disadvantage. She stood, pulling her cloak closer round her, waiting for someone else to make the first move.

A hand came out of the door of the carriage, dangling an ear drop, the twin of the one she was wearing, and she heard a low chuckle. 'If you come over here, my dear, I will fasten the other one for you. Beautiful as you are, you look slightly lopsided.'

'Are you afraid to show your face, sir?' she demanded.

'Not at all.' The door opened wide and a man jumped down and strode over to her. Young, but not juvenile, he was about five and twenty, she judged, and fashionably dressed for evening in a black tailcoat, a purple velvet waistcoat and a white shirt, whose lace cuffs fell from beneath his coat sleeves. A diamond pin glittered in the folds of his cravat. As he doffed his tall hat and bowed to her, she saw dark curls, and then, when he straightened again, humorous brown eyes beneath a pair of winged brows. His nose was long and straight and his mouth firm. He smiled, revealing even white teeth. 'Here I am, your slave, ready to do your bidding.'

'And does my slave have a name?'

'Stanmore, Miss Charron. Duncan Stanmore, at your service.'

The name was familiar, and though she teased her brain, the when and where of it eluded her. She inclined her head in acknowledgement. 'Mr Stanmore.'

'I thought Reid's for supper,' he said. 'Does that suit?'

'And if I agree to that, I suppose I am to be rewarded with an ear drop.'

'Oh, that is yours whether you come or no,' he said lightly. 'It would not be fair to dangle that in front of you like a carrot. That is not my way.' He bowed. 'But I would deem it an honour if you would have supper with me.'

'Then supper it shall be.'

He gave a delighted laugh, which revealed the boy in him without in the least diminishing his stature, and led the way to the carriage, which she noticed, as she drew closer, had a crest upon its door. So Marianne had been right; he was not a commoner.

He handed her up into the carriage and made sure she was comfortable on the velvet seats before jumping up beside her. 'Reid's, Dobson,' he told the driver.

The hotel was noted for its cuisine and was a favourite place of stage people and theatregoers alike, so it was busy, but as soon as the waiter saw her escort, he came forward with a broad smile. 'Good evening, my lord. Your table is ready.'

Duncan smiled. 'Thank you, Bundy. I knew I could rely on you.'

Her previous experience told her to expect a private room, or, at the very least, a table tucked away in some ill-lit corner where they would not be no-

ticed and where her swain could bombard her with
compliments and ply her with wine in the hope of
his reward, but Duncan Stanmore obviously did not
know the rules of the game. They were conducted
to a small table to one side of the room, which,
though discreet, gave a good view of all the other
patrons and meant they could also be seen.

'He addressed you as ''my lord'',' she said,
when they were seated and the waiter had gone to
fetch the champagne Duncan ordered.

He smiled. 'Slip of the tongue, I expect. He
knows better than that.'

'You prefer to be incognito?'

He laughed. 'That, my dear Miss Charron, would
be impossible—in London, anyway. It is of no consequence. I do not expect you to address me formally. It would quite spoil the evening.'

He paused as the waiter returned with the wine,
which he proceeded to pour for them. 'The chef
says he has a roast of beef as succulent as you're
likely to taste anywhere,' the man said. 'And
there's turbot in a shrimp sauce and suckling pig
and ham what'll melt in your mouth, not to mention
sweetmeats and puddings—'

'Goodness, I am not that hungry,' Maddy said.
She was laughing, but underneath the laughter were
memories of a time when she had been starving and
a tiny portion of the food the waiter was offering
would have been a feast. Why could she never for-

get that? 'A little of the fish removed with the beef will be quite sufficient, thank you.'

'Then I will have the same,' Duncan said.

'Oh, please do not stint yourself because of me, my lord,' Maddy said. 'I will be quite content to watch you eat.'

'I would rather talk than eat. And you forget, I am Duncan Stanmore, not Lord anything.' He held up his wine to her. 'To a beautiful companion.' He took a mouthful, looking at her over the rim of his glass. She was beautiful, and not in the artful way of most actresses, achieved with paint and powder, a certain knowing expression and an exaggerated way of carrying themselves that commanded attention. Her loveliness was entirely natural. Her skin was flawless and her eyes, the deep blue of a woodland violet, were bright with intelligence and full of humour, though he detected just a hint of an underlying sadness about her lovely mouth. Was that why she was such a great actress?

'Thank you.'

'Tell me about yourself,' he commanded, as the food was brought and served. 'Is Charron a French name?'

'It was originally. My grandfather fled from France with his wife and son, during the Reign of Terror and never went back. My father looked upon himself as English and fought on England's side in the war against Napoleon. He was killed on some secret mission, very early on. Even my mother did not know what it was.' The lies she had told so many times tripped easily from her tongue as if she had come to believe them herself.

'I am sorry if talking of it is painful,' he said. 'I should not have asked, but I thought there was something about you that was not usual for an actress…'

'And you, I collect, must have met many.'

He laughed. 'A few, but none like you.'

'Fustian!'

'It is true. There is something about you that proclaims you a woman of breeding. Your grandfather would have been an aristocrat if he had to flee the Terror, and that accounts for it.'

She smiled. Her mother had taught her well and Marianne Doubleday had completed her education. She could play the lady to perfection. But playing the lady was not what she wanted. What did she want? Seven years before she could have given the answer to that promptly enough, but now she was not so sure. Her life was good as it was. She was adored from across the footlights, should she not be satisfied with that?

She could command a good wage, could afford to dress well, was the recipient of countless fripperies she could sell or wear, whichever she chose, and she had many friends among her fellow thespians who, contrary to popular belief, were not always at each other's throats. She could flirt with the young men who besieged the stage door after

each performance, go to supper with them and
gently send them on their way without hurting their
pride. So what had she been waiting for? This moment? This man?

'Can you tell breeding on so short an acquaintance?' she asked.

'Of course. How did someone like you come to
be an actress?'

'My mother was run down by a speeding carriage when I was nine years old,' she said. 'I had
no other relatives…'

'What about your grandparents?'

'My father's parents both died some time before.
They never got over the loss of their son, so my
mother told me. I think my mother's parents must
have died too, for she never spoke of them. I was
alone in the world.'

'Oh, you poor, dear girl.' His sympathy seemed
truly genuine and she began to have the first feeling
of unease for deceiving him.

'What happened then?'

The rest was easy. The rest was the truth, or very
nearly. She told him she had been sent to an orphanage for the children of army officers, (she had
long ago upgraded the orphanage to one specifically for officers' orphans) where she stayed until
she was old enough to work, but nothing at all
about the Bulfords. That did not bear speaking
about. 'There you have my history in a nutshell,'
she said, laughing. 'Now you must tell me yours.'

'Oh, I have nothing at all interesting to report. I was born, I went to school, I became a man...'

'And married?' She was surprised that question had not crossed her mind until now.

'No, not yet, but undoubtedly my father will have me shackled before much longer. I am his heir, you see. I have a half-brother, a bantling by the name of Freddie, who will, no doubt, carry on the family name if I do not have a son, but he is very young still. That is all there is to tell.'

It was all he wanted to tell, she decided. 'So you do not have to earn a living?'

He laughed. He had an infectious laugh and she found herself smiling back at him. 'If you mean I live a life of idleness, that is far from the truth,' he said. 'My father would not allow it. I have to work on our estate, see that it is running smoothly, look after the tenants...' He stopped, on the verge of telling her that he did have another mission in life, but decided it would introduce a sombre note to the proceedings and stopped short.

'And that is work?'

'It is harder work than you might think. But I come to London for the Season, as you see.'

'To look for a bride?'

'That is the accepted way of doing it, though I am not so sure it will work in my case. My father despairs of me, says I am too particular.'

'And are you?' She was slightly breathless, as if his answer was important to her. His name was

Stanmore, he had said. Lord Stanmore, she supposed, but she could not remember any of the girls in the troupe mentioning a Lord Stanmore and they knew the names of everyone who was anyone in town; gossip was meat and drink to them.

'Oh, I don't know. I suppose I am.' This conversation was not going at all the way he had expected it to. It was not the light, teasing banter he usually employed when talking to the little bits of muslin he chose to dally with. She had more about her than they did, much more. He had not been joking when he said she had the bearing of an aristocrat. It showed itself in the proud way she held her head, the way she used her cutlery, the way she sipped her wine, the way she spoke, without that silly simpering voice young women of the lower orders used when trying to impress him. Madeleine Charron saw no need to impress him; she considered herself his equal.

'How in particular?' she asked.

'That's just it, I do not know,' he said. 'I have never troubled to analyse it. I suppose what I mean, is that I shall recognise her when I meet her.'

She laughed. 'So you have not yet met her?'

'I think I might have.' Even as he spoke, he knew the idea was preposterous, outlandish, laughable. But it would not go away.

'When did you meet her?'

'About an hour ago.'

She stared at him for a moment, then sat back in her chair and burst out laughing. 'I have heard many a proposition, but that is a new one, it really is.'

He frowned. 'You laugh.'

'Am I meant to take you seriously?'

His mind suddenly produced an image of his illustrious father, of his stepmother and his sister, Lavinia, as he presented Madeleine Charron to them as his intended wife and knew she had been right to laugh. 'We could pretend, just for one night,' he said lightly. 'It might be fun.'

'It depends what you expect of me,' she said, and she was not laughing now. 'I am an actress, pretending is second nature to me, but if you mean what I think you mean, I am afraid you have quite misunderstood my role.'

He sat back and rocked with laughter. 'Oh, the lady is the aristocrat and no doubt about it. What rank was that grandfather of yours, a *comte*, a marquis or a duke, perhaps?'

'A *comte*,' she said. Marquises and dukes would be too easy to trace.

She was not naturally a liar and suddenly she found it all very hard going. He was too nice to deceive, too much the gentleman. She knew he would not coerce her or force himself upon her as Henry Bulford had done, but if she were determined enough, she could make him fall in love with her, make him defy his stiff-necked father to marry her. The ball was in her court. Why, then, was she so reluctant to pass it back? Why, when she had the opportunity to further her long-term goal, had she lost her courage? Only the memory of her humiliation at the hands of another aristocrat kept her from confessing her perfidy.

'And one does not lightly roast a *comte*'s daughter,' he said, unaware of her tumultuous thoughts.

'I am sorry,' she said, suddenly serious.

'Sorry? Sorry for what?'

'If you have deluded yourself that I would easily succumb…'

'If I had, you have soon put me in my place,' he said with a smile. 'Let us begin again, shall we?'

'How so?'

'Tell me about being an actress. I once acted in a play my sister put on for a charity my stepmother favours and I found it quite hard work.'

'It is. What part did you play?'

'Oberon. It was *A Midsummer Night's Dream.*'

'I know it well.'

It was easier after that. They spent the remainder of the evening talking pleasantly, laughing together, comparing their likes and dislikes and Maddy found she could forget he was one of the hated aristocracy, could forget her schemes and just be herself. He was a charming and attentive companion and she paid him the compliment of genuinely enjoying his company.

* * *

At two o'clock in the morning, they found themselves alone in the dining room and the waiters hovering to clear the table. Reluctantly they stood up to leave. 'My, how the time has flown by,' he said. 'I have never been so well entertained in my life. Thank you, sweet Madeleine.'

'It has been a pleasure,' she said, allowing him to drape her cloak about her shoulders and escort her to the door.

They had almost reached it when the proprietor came, bowing deferentially. 'I hope everything was to your satisfaction, my lord?'

'Yes, indeed,' he said. 'You may send the reckoning to Stanmore House. It will be paid promptly.'

Stanmore House. Maddy knew where that mansion was and who it belonged to. Sir Percival Ponsonby had pointed it out only the week before when he had taken her out in his carriage and regaled her with who was who among the many people they had seen in the park. Why hadn't she made the connection when Duncan Stanmore had first introduced himself?

She had been having supper with the Marquis of Risley, the Duke of Loscoe's heir. The Duke was reputed to be one of the wealthiest men in the kingdom, so it stood to reason his son wanted for nothing. He had entertained her for several hours, and not once had he hinted of his illustrious background. Why? In her experience, most young men were boastful and would not have been able to keep quiet about having a duke for a father. Was he, too, playing a part?

He put his hand beneath her elbow to escort her to his waiting carriage and helped her inside. 'Tell me where you want to go and I will see you safely there,' he said.

He was being studiously polite now, as if the contract he had made to give her supper in exchange for her company had been fulfilled and that was the end of it. She admitted to a tiny feeling of disappointment. And telling herself she was being more than inconsistent did nothing to appease her. She had made it clear he could expect nothing else and he, like the gentleman he was, had accepted that. But he might have put up more of an argument!

She told him the address of her lodgings at the bottom end of Oxford Street, which she shared with several others in the company. He passed it on to his coachman and they sat in silence as the coach rattled through the almost deserted streets. There was a constraint between them now, as if they had run out of things to say and did not know how to proceed.

It was unlike Duncan to be tongue-tied, but she had bewitched him, not only with her good looks and her curvaceous figure, but also with the way she spoke, the way she held her head, the way her expressive hands drew pictures in the air, her humour. He could see that speeding coach, could see the childlike figure weeping over a dead mother, could feel her pain. And no one to comfort her, no father, no grandparents, no one except an orphanage such as his stepmother supported. It was a wonder she had not become bitter.

Instead she had risen above it and the result was perfection. He had never been so captivated. Not that any liaison other than that of lover and *chère amie* was possible. She was not wifely material, at least not for him, and suddenly he could not bring himself to spoil that perfection by suggesting they continue the evening elsewhere.

When the coach stopped at her door, he jumped down to help her to alight. 'Thank you for a truly delightful evening,' he said, raising her hand to his lips.

Dozens of young men had done the same thing, but none had made her shiver as she was shivering now. It was not a shiver of cold, but of heat. His touch was like a lick of flame that spread from her hand, up her arm and down to the pit of her stomach and from there it found its way to her groin. She had never experienced anything like it before, but she recognised it as weakness. She shook herself angrily for being a traitor to herself. This was not the way, she berated herself, allowing herself to fall under his spell was not part of the plan. He was supposed to fall under hers!

'I nearly forgot,' he said, putting his hand in his pocket and extracting the diamond ear drop. 'You must have this to remind you of the delightful time we spent together.'

'Thank you.'

'May I put it in?'

Gently he took her earlobe and hooked the jewel into it. Then he bent and put his lips to her ear, kissed it and whispered, 'I shall always remember it.' Now he was the stage-door admirer that she was used to, paying extravagant compliments and meaning none of them.

She found herself smiling. 'You are too generous, my lord Marquis.'

'Drat it, you have seen through me,' he said, laughing and breaking the stiff atmosphere that had suddenly developed between them.

'Did you think I did not know the Marquis of Risley?'

'No, I suppose not,' he said, with a theatrical sigh. 'And I thought you loved me for myself alone.'

There was no answer to that and she did not give him one. She turned and went into the house and closed the door behind her, leaning her back on it, hearing his carriage roll away. She had had her chance and she had let it go. All those years nursing a hate, all those years working towards her goal and she had fallen at the first hurdle. What a ninny she had been!

Beautiful he had called her, aristocratic, he had said, different. Oh, she was different all right. She was a fraud, a tease, for all she had told Marianne she was not. And she had been given her just reward: supper and a pair of diamond ear drops. She supposed she should be flattered that he thought her worth that much, but then diamonds were commonplace to him and would hardly make a dint in his fortune. The pin in his cravat had been worth many times his gift to her.

She toiled wearily up to her room, to find Marianne sitting on her bed, waiting for her, clad in an undress robe in peacock colours and her hair in a nightcap. 'Well?' her friend demanded.

'Well, what?' She sank on to the bed and kicked off her shoes.

'What happened? Did you find out who he was?'

'Oh, yes, I found out.'

'And? Come on, don't keep me in suspense. I was right, he is an aristocrat, isn't he?'

'Yes. None other than the Marquis of Risley.'

'The Duke of Loscoe's heir! I am impressed. What happened?'

'He bought me supper at Reid's, entertained me with anecdotes, brought me home and left me with the other ear drop.'

'That's all? He didn't suggest a private room?'

'No. He was amiable and generous and a perfect gentleman.'

Marianne laughed. 'Oh dear, and you are disappointed.'

'Not at all.' She could not tell Marianne of her doubts. 'I had no intention of falling at his feet or even encouraging him. I need to be more subtle than that.'

'More subtle,' Marianne repeated, looking into Maddy's bright eyes. 'Oh, Maddy I do hope you have not developed a tendre for him. The Duke will never allow his son to become attached to an actress.'

'But if that actress also happens to be the grand-daughter of a French *comte*, he might condescend to overlook her faults.'

'You never told him that tale of the French *émigré*, did you?'

'Why not?'

'Oh, Maddy, you will be in a serious coil, if you persist. Tell him the truth, make a jest of it before he finds out for himself.'

'I didn't know who he was when I told it. He was pretending to be a nobody while I was doing my best pretending to be a somebody, so we were both at fault. It was only harmless fun, not to be taken seriously at all. I am sure his lordship did not do so.' And that was what rankled. He had not asked to see her again and she would not be given another opportunity to demonstrate her ascendancy over him. He had been the one to draw back, as if he had suddenly remembered who he was and what she was. An actress.

'I am glad to hear it.' Marianne stood up, prepared to leave. 'Now, I suggest you go to bed. You will be fit for nothing later today if you do not.'

When Marianne had taken her leave Madeleine undressed and climbed into bed, knowing, late as it was and tired as she was, she would not sleep. Her evening out, which had been so enjoyable in one way, had been a disaster in another. Sometimes for days, even weeks, at a time she managed to forget her past and her enmity towards the aristocracy, but tonight had brought it all back and she was feeling decidedly vulnerable.

The fact that the Marquis had appeared to believe her story of her French grandfather, and had said he had known she was a lady of good breeding, made her wonder about her unknown father. She racked her brains, trying to think of anything her mother might have said to throw some light on who he could have been, but there was nothing. She could not remember Mama even mentioning him.

Her grandfather was certainly not a French *émigré*, she had invented him, but supposing the fictional character could give her an entrée into Society? And in the dark watches of the night when anything seems possible, a plan began to form in her mind, a plan so audacious it made her shiver. But she needed the help of her friend Marianne.

'Well, do I owe you twenty-five pounds or not?' Benedict asked Duncan the following morning when he came upon him at Humbold's coffee house, blowing a cloud and amusing himself watching the people passing the window. 'A week has gone by and no news of the citadel being stormed.'

'Citadel?'

'The lovely Madeleine Charron.'

'Supper we agreed and supper it was,' Duncan said, sitting down opposite his friend and beckoning to the waiter to bring a dish of coffee to him. 'Taken at Reid's with plenty of witnesses, so pay up and look cheerful about it.'

Benedict dug in his tail pocket and produced his purse. 'And?' He carefully counted out the twenty-five sovereigns in five neat heaps. 'You are going to refine upon that, I hope.'

'Nothing to refine upon.'

'You are bamming me.'

'No. What happened and what was said between us is our private business and nothing to do with the wager.'

'She turned you down!' It was said almost triumphantly.

'Not at all.' Benedict was annoying him and he was damned if he would tell him anything. 'But, unlike you, I do not rush in where angels fear to tread. I prefer to deal gently with the fair sex. It pays in the end.'

'Ah, the assault goes on. You want another wager?' His hand hovered over the coins. 'Double or quits?'

'For what?'

'For a night in her bed.'

Duncan should have refused. He should have scooped up his winnings and told his friend that he had no intention of even trying, when he realised that Benedict would take that as weakness or a lack of self-confidence at the very least and would offer to do the deed himself. The thought of his clumsy friend going anywhere near Madeleine filled him with a kind of desperate fury. He smiled. 'Done, my friend.'

'Done to the wager or done to the deed?' Benedict queried, grinning.

'The wager, you bufflehead.'

Benedict retrieved the coins and replaced them in his purse with evident relief. 'Another se'nnight?'

'No, give me credit for more finesse than that. Make it a fortnight.'

He could have bitten his tongue out. If the object of the wager had been anyone else but the lovely Madeleine Charron, he would not have given it another thought. As it was, he was consumed with shame. She had endured so much in her short life, he had no right to play with her as if she were a toy. She deserved his respect. He flung the contents of the coffee cup down his throat and with a curt, 'I will see you later,' stood up and left the premises.

He knew he ought not to see Madeleine again, but he also knew it would be impossible to stay away. He had been ensnared. It was not a condition he was comfortable with and he set off for Bond Street, where he took out his frustration, anger and guilt on his sparring partner at Gentleman Jackson's boxing saloon, until that gentleman called out to him to stop if he didn't want to be done for murder. He apologised and decided there was nothing for it but to go home and pretend nothing had happened. He had enjoyed an evening out with a pretty actress; nothing out of the ordinary in that, nothing to lose another night's sleep over.

He would pay Benedict his fifty pounds and be done with it.

Chapter Two

Being part of a theatrical troupe, Madeleine was used to strange hours, when night became day and day was a time for sleeping and she did not see Marianne again until the following afternoon when the cast met to rehearse the new play to be put on the following week.

Although he sometimes put on burlesque or contemporary plays lampooning the government, Lancelot Greatorex was chiefly known for his revivals of Shakespeare's plays to which he gave a freshness and vitality, often bringing them right up to date with modern costumes and manners and allusions to living people or recent history. The following week Madeleine would be playing Helena in *All's Well That Ends Well*, which lent itself surprisingly well to such treatment.

In it, Helena, a physician's daughter, cures the king of a mysterious illness and as a reward is allowed to choose one of his courtiers for a husband. She chooses Bertram, Count of Rousillon, but he maintains Helena is beneath him and though he is obliged to obey the king and wed her, he goes off to the wars rather that consummate the marriage. Later, Helena tricks him into bed by making him think she is another woman for whom he has a fancy and they exchange rings. When he realises what has happened, he accepts Helena for his wife.

Maddy did not like the play; she thought the hero a weak character and the ending even weaker and she questioned whether a marriage based on such a trick could possibly be happy. Now that she was contemplating a hoax herself, the question was even more pertinent. Not that she intended to trick anyone into her bed, far from it, but she did mean to deceive Society as a whole.

'Madeleine, do pay attention,' Lancelot said mildly, after she had missed her cue for the second time. 'You have been in a brown study all afternoon. Whatever is the matter with you?'

Maddy pulled herself out of her reverie and peered down into the gloom of the orchestra pit where he was standing. She knew from past experience that his mild tone hid annoyance, and it behoved her to pull herself together. 'I am sorry, Mr Greatorex. It won't happen again.'

'To be sure it won't,' he said. 'Unless you wish to see your understudy in the role. Now, let us do that scene again.'

Madeleine looked across at Marianne who winked at her. She smiled back and began the scene again and this time it went some way to satisfying

the great actor-manager. Nothing would ever satisfy him completely, he was such a perfectionist,
but he knew just how far to go with his criticism
before he had a weeping and useless performer on
his hands. Not that anyone had ever seen Madeleine
Charron weeping, not offstage, though she could
put on a very convincing act on stage if it were
required.

After the rehearsal, Marianne joined Madeleine
in the dressing room they shared to prepare for the
evening performance of *Romeo and Juliet*. 'It is not
like you to miss your cue, Maddy,' her friend said.
'Is anything wrong?'

'No, not at all. I am a little tired.'

'I hope you did not lie awake last night, fanta-
sising about the Marquis of Risley.'

'Now, why should I do that? He is one of the
idle rich and you know what I think about them.'
Her answer was so quick and sharp, Marianne
knew she had hit upon the truth.

'Then why, in heaven's name, did you find it
necessary to deceive him?'

'It just came out. It always does, when anyone
asks me about my family.'

'But why? You are admired and respected as an
actress. Why cannot you be content with that?'

'I don't know. I suppose because I have always
wanted a family of my own, someone to belong to,
and if invention is the only way—' She stopped
speaking suddenly. Her reasons seemed so trite, so

unconvincing, and yet Marianne detected the wistfulness in her voice.

'You do have a family, my dear,' Marianne said softly. 'You have me and all the rest of the company; that is your family. Mine too, come to that.'

'Yes, I know, but I can't help wishing…'

'We all have dream wishes, Maddy, the secret is to recognise them for what they are, and to be able to distinguish the attainable from the unattainable. You have it in you to be an outstanding actress, one of the few who will be remembered long after they have left this world behind, a byword for excellence. Surely that is better than being remembered for a short time for pretending to be something you are not.'

'That is what acting is, pretending to be someone else.'

Marianne laughed. 'You do like to have the last word, don't you? I will concede you right on that, but you should not extend that into your everyday life.'

Madeleine was silent for a minute, during which they attended to their make-up, but if Marianne thought that was the end of the conversation, she was mistaken. Maddy worried at it like a dog with a bone. 'You have met the Stanmores, haven't you?' she asked, apparently casually.

'Yes, the first time was when I took part in an amateur production of *A Midsummer Night's Dream* they put on at Stanmore House to raise funds for the Duchess's charitable works. The whole family was involved, even the children.'

'And they took you for a lady?'

'Yes, but only because Sir Percival Ponsonby introduced me and vouched for me. He was the one who invented my history.'

'He evidently did not mind deceiving them?'

'It was in a good cause.'

'And they never guessed?'

'Oh, it all came out in the end, of course. We never meant to deceive them permanently.'

'And they forgave you and the Duchess still receives you. I know you are sometimes included in her soirées.'

'I go to entertain the company. It is in aid of the charity and I am pleased to do it, but the Duchess does not treat me as an equal, though we deal very well together.'

'Will you take me with you next time?'

'Maddy, don't be a ninny. How can I? I go by invitation and they are not easy to come by.'

'You could fix it. Offer them a performance that needs two players and take me to assist you.'

Marianne looked thoughtfully at her friend, wondering what was behind the request. 'Perhaps I could, but the Marquis might not like his outside pursuits intruding on his home life; he might be very angry, not only with you, but with me for encouraging you.'

'He cannot know that you know my story is not true. No one will blame you. At least it will make him notice me.'

Marianne burst into laughter. 'He has already done that and you repaid him with whiskers.'

'I know. But if he believed them, where's the harm?'

'Maddy, my love, his father will have the story checked, even if the son takes it at face value. You will be in a serious coil, if you persist.'

She had not thought of that, but then brightened. 'What can he discover? So many Frenchmen came over during the Terror, there's no keeping track of them.'

'I think you would do better to own up and apologise.'

'I will. When the opportunity arises. But the Marquis did not intimate he was going to ask me out again and I can hardly accost him in the street to tell him, can I?'

Marianne laughed. 'No, but going to his home and confronting him will not serve either. Besides, he might not be there. True, he still lives at Stanmore House but that does not mean he is tied to his stepmama's apron strings. Most young men of his age, married or not, have flown the coop long before they are his age.'

'He said his papa was anxious for him to marry.'

'No doubt he is. But you must face the truth, my love, he will not look at you for that role.'

Madeleine sighed, thinking of the play they had just been rehearsing. 'If I were really a *comte*'s granddaughter, he would.'

'If you were a *comte*'s granddaughter, my dear, you would not have led the life you have and you would not be nursing a grievance against the whole *haut monde*. And if you are thinking of exacting your revenge on Stanmore, father or son, then you are like to have your fingers burned, mark my words.'

'I am not thinking of revenge. It is the *haut monde* I wish to study. I want to see the family together; I want to see how they deal with each other, if they are loving towards each other and how they treat their servants. You have taught me a great deal and I am sure there is nothing you do not know about acting the lady, but I want to see it for myself. I want to be among them just for a little while. It will be a great help to me when I have to play the great lady.'

Marianne looked at her with her head on one side, as if cogitating whether to believe her or not. 'And you expect me to collude with you in this?'

'Yes, dear Marianne, get me an invitation to the next soirée you go to, please, just this once. I won't ask you ever again.'

She was not sure why she wanted this so much. It was not as if she hoped to promote herself in the eyes of the Marquis, let alone his family, but if she could make the story of the French *comte* convincing enough, the fact that she was accepted at Stanmore House might gain her entry to a few more social occasions and maybe she could establish herself in Society without having to delude some susceptible nobleman into marrying her. And perhaps, in time, she might meet someone who could know the truth about her and still love her.

Her imagination soared; she could see herself fêted and showered with invitations and being accepted. Yes, that was what she wanted most, to be accepted. She wanted to be seen at Stanmore House in order to set the ball rolling. 'Please,' she begged. 'If you cannot ask her ladyship yourself, ask the help of Sir Percy. I believe he is a frequent visitor to Stanmore House. The Duchess will perhaps listen to a suggestion from him.'

Sir Percy was one of the few men who did not ask sexual favours for his patronage. Marianne said it was because he was in love with the Duchess of Loscoe and had been ever since she first came out, but she had married the Earl of Corringham and, after he died, the Duke of Loscoe. Having been rejected, Sir Percy had taken refuge in pretending to be an outmoded fop. He was far from that, as Madeleine appreciated, and if anyone could help her, he could.

'She might, but I doubt he will agree to hoax the Duke and Duchess.'

'It is not exactly a hoax, is it? And he will do it if you ask it of him, he is very fond of you, he told me so when we were out in his carriage last week.'

Marianne chuckled. 'Did he now?'

'So, will you ask him?'

'Perhaps, if the opportunity arises next time I see him, but I make no promises.' She adjusted her powdered wig, stood up in a flurry of silk-covered hoops and took a last look at herself in the mirror. 'Come now, put it from your mind and concentrate on the play. I can hear Lancelot calling everyone to their places.'

Madeleine's performance as Juliet that night excelled anything she had done before and the applause at the end meant she had to take several curtain calls before they would allow her to go. Her dressing room was awash with flowers and she examined each bouquet carefully to see who had sent them, but none that she could see had come from the Marquis of Risley. It was evident he was not going to further their acquaintance; she would not give him the *carte blanche* he wanted and so he had lost interest. But she would not admit to being disappointed, not even to herself.

Duncan was sipping tea in the withdrawing room of Stanmore House, having dined at home with the Duke and Duchess and their guests, his sister Lavinia and her husband, the Earl of Corringham and the Earl's sister, Augusta, and her husband Sir Richard Harnham.

'Duncan, you really must put in an appearance at Almack's at least once this Season,' Lavinia said.

'Why?' he demanded. He loved his sister dearly, but ever since she had married James six years before and borne two lively children, she seemed to think she could bully him into doing anything. He gave a quirky smile; she had always tried to bully him, even when they were children; it was nothing new. 'Why should I dress myself up in breeches and stockings and stand about like a liveried footman just for the dubious pleasure of dancing with some plain chit who thinks she can trap me into marriage?'

'How can you be so cynical, Duncan? There are any number of very acceptable girls coming out this Season. How do you know that one won't turn out to be exactly what you are looking for?'

'I doubt it. They will either be missish and just out of the schoolroom, with silly giggles and no conversation, or spinsters at their last prayers who have been residing on the shelf for years and yet each Season they dust themselves off and launch themselves at every eligible man foolish enough to go near them.'

The Duke and the Duchess, their stepmother, had been listening to this exchange between brother and sister with amused tolerance, but now the Duchess smiled. 'Duncan, don't you want to marry?'

'Not particularly, Mama, certainly not enough to jump into it simply because a young lady is considered suitable. Suitable for what? I find myself asking.'

'Why, to be a marchioness,' Lavinia said.

'But it is no certainty that someone who might make a good marchioness will make a good wife. I want to have feelings for the woman I marry, feelings that last a lifetime. I am not prepared to shackle myself to a breeding machine with whom I have nothing in common. There is more to marriage than that.'

'In other words, you want to love and be loved,' Frances said softly.

He did not think his stepmother's comment needed an answer. She understood him and had often in the past interceded for him with the Duke and he loved her for it, but if she was ranging herself alongside Lavinia in this quest to find him a wife, he was going to disappoint her.

'Somewhere out there, in the ranks of the nobility, there is someone who will answer for both,' Lavinia persisted. 'You must give Society a chance.'

He smiled at his sister. 'You were fortunate that your choice of husband was also suitable from the point of view of the *haut monde*, Lavinia dear, no compromise was asked of you. It does not happen often.'

'Thank you very much,' James put in drily.

'You know what I mean.'

'All I am saying is that you should attend those functions where you might meet suitable young ladies,' Lavinia went on. 'But if you do not go out and about, how can you possibly make a choice?'

'I do go out and about, I am not a recluse.'

'Oh, yes, you go about with your dandified friends and hover about stage doors dangling after actresses, but you won't find a wife there, now will you?'

'Vinny!' her husband admonished her. 'It is not for you to comment upon how your brother spends his evenings.' He paused, curious. 'How do you know so much anyway?'

'Benedict told his sister and she told me.'

'What did he tell her?' Duncan asked, suddenly interested.

'Oh, nothing of import, except that you were rivalling each other to take a certain actress out to supper. Felicity said there was a wager on it.'

Duncan muttered darkly under his breath. Trust Willoughby to empty the bag. If the object of the wager had been anyone but the delectable Miss Charron he would have answered teasingly, but there was something about their meeting the evening before that did not warrant that; it was the confidences they had shared, the private moments when they had not been flirting with each other, when he had been privileged to see the real Madeleine Charron hidden behind the actress. It was something he wanted to keep to himself; now that Benedict had made light of it, he was angry.

And disturbed. If that second wager were to become common knowledge, he would be in a coil, not only with Madeleine herself, but with his father, who would never countenance a lady being used in that way, actress or not.

'Benedict Willoughby should keep his tongue between his teeth,' he said.

'Did you win it?' James asked.

Duncan felt trapped. He could not be impolite to his brother-in-law, but he was aware that he was being forced into a corner. 'Yes, a light supper, no more, and it has nothing to do with whether or not I go to Almack's.'

'Then you will come,' Lavinia said, delighted her ploy had worked.

'I suppose I will have no peace until I agree.'

'Then we shall go on Wednesday week. It is a special occasion to mark the anniversary of Waterloo. I believe Wellington will be there.'

'Oh, then I am safe; the ladies will be all over him and will ignore me.'

'Duncan, I despair of you,' Lavinia said.

But Duncan was not listening; he was employed in puzzling his brain into devising a way of making Benedict stay mum about their second wager without losing face.

The Duchess smiled. 'Duncan, what are you doing tomorrow?'

'Nothing I cannot postpone, if you need me, Mama,' he said cheerfully.

'Will you come to the orphanage with me? I have a pile of clothing I have collected and I need a strong arm to carry the baskets.'

It was typical of the Duchess to take them herself; she liked to be personally involved and the fact that the orphanage was not in the most salubrious part of town did not deter her. But she had promised the Duke she would never go unescorted, and as he was rarely free to go with her due to government business, she would ask Duncan or James or sometimes Sir Percy.

The mention of the orphanage reminded Duncan of Madeleine and the story she had told him, a story that had tugged at his tender heart. He really must stop thinking about her; it clouded his judgement. 'Of course, Stepmama, I am at your service. What time do we leave?'

'Ten o'clock—that is, if you can rouse yourself from your bed in time.'

'I will be ready and, just to show you my good intent, I will not go out again tonight, but retire early.' He was only teasing; he was quite used to staying up until the early hours, dawn sometimes, and he could still rise bright and early.

He was as good as his word and presented himself in the breakfast parlour in good time to eat a hearty breakfast and oversee the loading of two large laundry baskets full of donated clothes into the boot of the carriage before handing his step-mother in, settling himself beside her and instructing the coachman to take them to Maiden Lane.

'You are thoughtful,' remarked the Duchess when they had been going for a few minutes and he had not spoken. 'You do not mind coming with me? I have not kept you from more pleasurable pursuits?'

'No, not at all,' he said abstractedly.

'Then you are troubled about something else.'

'No, Mama, not a thing,' he said, falsely bright. They were crossing the square in front of St Paul's and he had just spotted Madeleine Charron walking arm in arm with Marianne Doubleday towards the market.

Having spent a wakeful night trying to decide what to do about that disgraceful wager, he was unprepared for seeing her again so soon. The sight of her, laughing with her companion as if she did not have a care in the world, set his heart racing. If she knew what was going on in his mind, she would not be laughing. She would be angry.

His head was full of her and his loins were stirring with desire, even now, in this busy square. He had made a wager of which he was thoroughly ashamed and yet the fulfilling of it would give him a great deal of pleasure. One-half of him goaded him, telling him the pleasure would not all be his, he knew how to give pleasure too and he could be very generous to those who pleased him and what else could an actress expect? The other half of him knew that such thoughts were reprehensible and dishonourable and he ought to have more respect for her than that. Why, he would not treat the lowliest servant in that cavalier fashion.

The ladies had stopped and were looking towards the carriage and it was then that the Duchess saw them. 'Oh, there is Miss Doubleday. I need to speak to her.' And before Duncan could make any sort of comment, she instructed the coachman to pull up.

The carriage drew to a stop beside the actresses and Duncan had perforce to jump down and open the door for his stepmother to alight.

Marianne took a step towards them and curtsied. 'Your Grace, good morning.'

'Good morning, Miss Doubleday,' the Duchess said. 'I hope I find you well.'

'Oh, exceedingly well, my lady.' She smiled, almost mischievously. 'My lady, may I present my friend and colleague, Miss Madeleine Charron.'

Frances turned towards Madeleine, while Duncan stood silently behind her wondering what was coming next. 'I am pleased to meet you, Miss Charron, though I would have known you anywhere. You are become quite famous and rightly so. I saw your performance in *Romeo and Juliet* and it moved me almost to tears.'

'Thank you, my lady.' Madeleine made a curtsy, though she always maintained she would never bow the knee to anyone just because they were aristocrats, but she did not want to embarrass Marianne, nor alienate the Marquis. And her ladyship was not behaving like a top-lofty aristocrat at all, getting down from her carriage to speak to them.

Her ladyship indicated Duncan with a movement of her gloved hand. 'This is my stepson, the Marquis of Risley, a keen theatre-lover.'

Duncan held his breath, half-expecting Madeleine to say they were already acquainted, but she simply smiled coolly at him and inclined her lovely head. It was not a bow, simply an acknowledgement. 'My lord.' When she looked up again, he saw the merriment in her violet eyes and found himself smiling back at her.

'Miss Charron,' he said, doffing his hat. 'I am honoured.'

If the Duchess noticed the conspiratorial look that passed between them, she ignored it and instead turned back to Marianne. 'Miss Doubleday, I am glad we are met, I wanted to have a word with you about a little musical evening I am planning. If you are free of engagements, I should be very grateful if you would perform for us.'

'I will deem it an honour, my lady. But it would depend on the day. A Thursday would be best. We have no evening performances on Thursdays.'

'Yes, I know. I will bear that in mind and send you a note.'

'Then I shall look forward to hearing from you, Your Grace.'

'I leave the choice of offering to you,' the Duchess added. 'I am sure you will think of something suitable.'

'I will give it some thought, my lady.' She jumped as she felt Madeleine's fingers digging into her back. 'Perhaps a dialogue, my lady, that is, if you would allow Miss Charron to accompany me.'

'An excellent idea.' She looked at Madeleine and smiled. 'Do please come, Miss Charron. It is all very informal and having both of you at once will be a great draw. Don't you think so, Duncan?'

'Oh, without doubt,' he said promptly, aware that Miss Charron was looking at him with a strange light of mischief in her eyes, as if she were bamming him. She was up to something and he hoped she was not going to put him to the blush in front of his family and the top-lofty friends his stepmother invited to her soirées. But she could not possibly know whether he would be present or not. He seldom attended his stepmother's routs; they were more often than not exceedingly boring and he usually had to be coerced into putting in an appearance.

'Then it will be my pleasure, my lady,' Madeleine said.

Having made their adieus, the Duchess and Duncan returned to the carriage and were carried away, leaving the two actresses staring after them.

'Well,' Madeleine said, letting out her breath, which she suddenly realised she had been holding. 'I never thought it would be so easy.'

'And I am not so sure I shouldn't make your excuses and go alone,' her friend said. 'I am afraid you will stir up a hornet's nest.'

'No, I will not. I will be the embodiment of decorum, you will be proud of me.'

'How can I be proud of you, when I know what a deceiver you are?'

'One tiny fib, that's all I told, and it harms no one. Besides, I told you I would confess, if I ever find myself talking to the Marquis privately again.'

'Oh, there is no doubt you will, I saw the way he looked at you. And you smiling back at him, like the temptress you are.'

'I am not!'

'Oh, my dear, I sometimes think you do not know when you are on stage and when you are off it.'

'"All the world's a stage and all the men and women merely players",' Maddy quoted, remembering Lancelot Greatorex's words the day she had first met him. *You don't need to tread the boards to play a part. We all do it from time to time. Do you tell me you have never had a fantasy, never pretended to be other than you are?* Oh, she had certainly done that.

'That may be true,' Marianne said. 'But we can only play the role for which we have been cast...'

'You played the lady,' Madeleine interrupted her. 'You went to Stanmore House and deceived the whole company, so why can't I?'

'The reasons for doing it were very different. I was enrolled to help catch a blackguard who meant to harm Lady Lavinia.'

'You never told me that.' Madeleine was glad to divert the conversation away from her own motives; if Marianne continued to question her about them, she would be hard put to answer truthfully because she did not know what they were herself. Was she still nursing a grievance against the whole nobility? And how could making a fool of the Marquis of Risley assuage that?

Was it simply that she wanted to see what it was like to be a lady of consequence? Or was she so ashamed of her past that she had to invent one nearer to her liking? But that must mean she was ashamed of her darling mother who, poor as she was and without a title, had been a gentlewoman in the truest sense of the word. Such a thing was inconceivable; she was proud of her mother. But oh, how she wished Mama had told her something of her father. But he was a shadowy figure, a wraith, with no substance.

Perhaps it was envy that the Marquis of Risley could trace his forebears back generation after generation while she did not know who she was. Her name wasn't even Charron, it was Cartwright. But could she even be sure of that? Her mother might have fabricated that too, just as she had invented the French *émigré*. And having brought him into existence, she was stuck with him.

Marianne smiled. 'Maddy dear, you have gone into another of your daydreams. If you do not keep your wits about you, one of these days you will be run down by a coach.'

Her words pitched Madeleine back fifteen years. She was standing outside a haberdashery shop and her mother, who had just come from the shop, was pulling on her gloves and saying something about getting home. She heard again the clatter of horses' hooves, the sound of carriage wheels, the yells as the driver tried to pull the horses up. She saw his contorted face as the carriage careered out of control and then her mother wasn't beside her any more. She was lying in the road, white and still, and a small trickle of blood was coming from under her head and growing wider. Maddy could still hear her own screams.

'Maddy! Maddy! Whatever is the matter?' Marianne's voice came to her, loud and insistent. 'You are white as a sheet.'

Madeleine gave a huge shudder and looked about her. She was back in 1827, in front of the colonnaded arcade of Covent Garden. The traffic flowed past her; there was no one lying in the street and her friend was tugging on her arm.

'I was thinking of my mother.'

'Oh, Madeleine. The Lord smite me for the fool I am. I forgot. I am sorry. Will you forgive me?'

'There is nothing to forgive.' She smiled at her friend and took her arm. 'Come, we had better be going.'

But the memory remained at the back of her mind, as if she needed a reminder of why she was what she was and why she had to break free from the constrictions of the past. And it had been her mother who had invented the name of Charron, so it was her mother who was guiding her now. It made her feel better.

'You did not tell me you were arranging a musical soirée,' Duncan said, as he and the Duchess continued to their destination.

'Is there any reason why I should have? I have them regularly and you have never shown the slightest interest in them before.'

'Yes, I have. I attended the last one.'

'Only under extreme duress and you only stayed fifteen minutes.'

'Perhaps I had another engagement.'

'Oh, undoubtedly. At White's or Boodles, I shouldn't wonder.'

'Mama, you make me sound like a regular gamester, and you know I rarely gamble.'

Frances smiled, remembering how he had played truant from school and gone to a gaming hell when he was only fifteen. The Duke had rung a peal over him and extracted a promise not to visit such places again. Oh, she knew he went to the gentlemen's clubs, but he had matured enough not to gamble more than a few guineas, which he could easily afford to lose. 'So, I collect, you wish to come to my next gathering. Could it, perhaps, have something to do with the delightful Miss Charron?'

He looked startled. 'Now, why do you say that?'

'Because I know you very well and I know you cannot resist a pretty face.' She paused. 'Was she the one you and Benedict were wrangling over?'

'We were not wrangling. He challenged me to take her out to supper without telling her who I was, that was all. I wish now I had not.'

'Why?'

'It seemed an ungentlemanly thing to do.'

'And so it was.'

'She told me her history and I felt so ashamed. She comes from a good family, Mama, her grandfather was a French *comte* who fled the Terror. Her father was killed in the late war and her mother was run down by a carriage when she was nine years old. She has been forced into acting by a need to earn her own living.'

'If it is true, then it is very sad.' She paused. 'But do be careful, Duncan, you do not raise hopes in her that can never be fulfilled.'

He laughed a little harshly. 'Oh, Mama, you are as bad as Lavinia. I took her out to supper and escorted her home afterwards. Nothing untoward happened, I promise you. I am not a rake.'

'Oh, my dear boy, I know that.'

The coach drew up outside the orphanage in Maiden Lane and he was saved any more embarrassing revelations. His stepmother was very astute and he could no more have tried to deceive her than fly to the moon.

Duncan helped the coachman carry the baskets of clothes into the orphanage, where they were gratefully received by the ladies who looked after the orphans. Duncan, who had accompanied his stepmother on other occasions, had never before paid much attention to the inmates, nor the conditions in which they lived. The house was clean, the children clothed and fed and that was as far as his observation had taken him, but now, thinking of Madeleine Charron's story, he looked with new eyes.

While the Duchess talked to Mrs Thomas, the woman who ran the place, he wandered round the house, looking in all the rooms: the dining room with its long table and benches; the dormitories with their rows of beds, which reminded him of his boarding school; the room converted into a tiny chapel; the kitchen where some of the little inmates toiled at preparing the meals for the others. Was this how Madeleine had lived?

She had said the orphanage she lived in had been for the children of officers, so perhaps it was a little more comfortable. But what was comfort when you were all alone in the world? How could comfort make up for the loss of a dear mother? His mother had died when he had been twelve years old and he had found that hard to take, but he still had a father and a sister and, for the last ten years, a step-mother he had come to love dearly. What must it be like to be all alone in the world and the prey of any jackass of a dandy who fancied he could buy your favours? He suddenly felt very protective towards Miss Madeleine Charron.

London audiences were usually appreciative, if somewhat noisy, but on the first night of *All's Well That Ends Well* some of them seemed to be in a mood to find fault. They did not wait for the other actors to speak their lines to Madeleine, but called out witticisms and then laughed loudly at their cleverness, earning sharp rebukes from those who wanted to see the play in peace. Marianne found it extremely hard to ignore them and to carry on with the performance and she was glad when the curtain came down on the last act.

'They did not like the play either,' she said to Marianne when they returned to their dressing room. 'It makes me wonder why Mr Greatorex chose it.'

'Fustian! Most of the audience loved it,' Marianne said. 'It was only that rake Willoughby, who fancies himself a pink of the *ton*, causing trouble.

Didn't you see him? He was with a crowd of young rakehells, all foxed out of their minds and intent on making themselves unpleasant. The rest of the audience was trying to silence them.'

'And made them worse. They think that wealth and position give them the right to do as they please, that they can be brash and inconsiderate and spoil other people's enjoyment and no one will say a word against them. They think they can get away with murder.' She could not help thinking about her mother's death at such times. It had been such a one who had run her down.

'I was surprised to see Stanmore with them.'

'Was he?' She tried to sound indifferent, but mention of the Marquis set her pulses racing.

'Yes, I caught sight of him sitting next to Willoughby as I was waiting for my entrance, so you see he is no different from the rest.'

'I did not say he was.'

It was hard to admit it, but she was bitterly disappointed. He had seemed a pleasant and attentive supper companion, who had talked to her as an equal, which had made her think that perhaps he was different from others of his breed. But he was not. She had been a fool to confide in him, telling him things about her past she had never told anyone except Marianne. Now, she supposed, he had regaled his drunken friends with the story and they had decided to have a little fun with her. She felt mortified and furiously angry and was certainly in no mood to accept the huge bunch of red roses the Marquis sent to the dressing room with a note to say he would be waiting for her when she came out.

'You may take them back,' she told the messenger who brought them. 'Tell his lordship I have no need of his bribes and I shall be dining with friends.'

'Well, I am surprised at you,' Marianne said, when the man had gone, then laughed. 'Now, I suppose, you are going to play hard to get.'

'I always was hard to get,' Maddy snapped, thinking suddenly of Henry Bulford, now Lord Bulford, of course. Marianne was right; they were all alike. So be it. Far from confessing her deception to the Marquis, she would play the nobleman's granddaughter for all she was worth. Someone would pay for her humiliation, not only tonight's but all she had ever suffered.

'Oh, my dear child, they were loud and uncouth and very annoying, but you must not take it to heart. After all, you have endured worse than a little calling out and hissing in the past and risen above it like the great actress you are, so don't let tonight's nonsense make you bitter.'

Madeleine smiled suddenly. 'Always my inner voice, dear Marianne, the one that keeps me from my excesses, be they of rage, resentment or the dismals. What would I do without you?'

'I am sure you would manage, my dear. Now, I am off to dine with Sir Percy. What will you do?'

'I think I will go straight home. I am excessively fatigued and it may be why my performance was not at its best tonight.'

'Fustian! It was as good as it always is. Take no notice of a handful of drunken rabble-rousers.'

'The Marquis of Risley, among them.' She paused. 'There is no need to ask Sir Percy about going to the Duchess's, seeing we have managed it without his help. The fewer people who know my intentions the better.'

'You still mean to go through with it, then?'

'Yes, more than ever.'

Marianne finished dressing just as Sir Percy arrived to take her to supper. He was dressed in an outrageous coat of puce satin with a high stand collar and huge pocket flaps in a darker pink velvet. His waistcoat was a striped green marcella and his trousers were cream coloured and strapped under his red-heeled shoes, left over from a time when he was young and red heels were the height of fashion. He knew perfectly well that everyone laughed at his dress and some of the young bucks laid bets on what colour he would be wearing next, and it amused him to amuse them.

He executed a flourishing leg to both ladies. 'Delectable, my dear Marianne,' he said, surveying her from head to toe. 'Does Miss Charron come too?'

'Oh, no, dear sir,' Madeleine said, laughing. 'The role of chaperon does not suit me. I am for home and bed.'

'Do you say so?' he queried, lifting a dark eyebrow. 'Now, I thought I saw Risley's coach outside. It must have been there for one of the others.'

'I expect it was.'

'Come along, my dear.' He addressed Marianne. 'I am as hungry as a hunter.'

They disappeared in a flurry of rainbow colours, leaving Madeleine to complete her *toilette* alone, dressing in a green round gown with leg o'mutton sleeves and a sleeveless pelisse of light wool and topping her dark curls with a small green bonnet, decorated with a sweeping feather. She took her time, hoping that the Marquis would give up and go home, but when she ventured out into the street, the carriage was still there. Straightening her shoulders and lifting her head, she walked past it.

'Madeleine!' Her name was spoken softly but urgently. 'Madeleine, wait!'

She swung round, but could see nothing but his dark shape in the shadow of the building. 'I have nothing to say to you, sir.'

'Why not? Have I offended you?'

'I will let your conscience be the judge of that, sir. *If* you have one, that is. I bid you goodnight.'

He reached out and put his hand on her arm to detain her. 'Let me escort you home, then you may tell me how I have displeased you.'

She shook him off. 'I do not need to ride in a carriage for that, my lord. It is easily told. You mocked the play. You brought your drunken friends to make fun of me. You threw orange peel on to the stage and cut off my speeches before they could be properly delivered. I am used to being derided, Lord Risley, but I had thought you were more sensible of my talent. You certainly made a great pretence of appreciating it last week, but that was before I refused to become your paramour, wasn't it? Was this your vengeance?'

'Vengeance? Good God! Surely you do not believe I am as contemptible as that?'

She ignored his denial. 'And now I suppose those…those…rakeshames are privy to everything I told you in confidence.'

'No, never! I was with those fellows, but I did not know what they would do and I certainly took no part in their bad behaviour. Please believe me. I would not for the world have you hurt.'

'Hurt, my lord,' she said haughtily. 'I am beyond hurting. I am angry that other people's enjoyment of the play was spoiled by a handful of idle ne'er-do-wells.'

'So am I, believe me. Please allow me to take you home. You cannot walk through the streets alone at this time of night. Anything could happen.'

She smiled slowly in the darkness. 'You are concerned for my safety?'

'Naturally I am.'

'And you would walk with me?'

'If you prefer that to riding in my carriage, then I will be honoured to do so.'

'Then send your carriage home. It is not fair on the horses to keep them waiting so long.'

He turned and instructed his coachman to take the equipage home, then offered her his arm. She laid her fingers upon it and together they strolled off in the direction of Oxford Street. He would have to walk home from there, but she did not care. It served him right.

Chapter Three

Neither spoke for several minutes, both deep in thoughts they could not share. Though she was still very angry with him, Madeleine was obliged to admit, if only to herself, that she was glad of his company. She could easily have asked the stage door-keeper to fetch her a cab, but instead she had elected to walk home, a decision she regretted almost as soon as she had made it, but her pride prevented her from retracting. To reach Oxford Street from Covent Garden on foot meant going through a most insalubrious area of town, where footpads and other criminals abounded and a lone woman was fair game. Furious with her escort she might be, but she was glad of his protection.

Duncan was fully aware that his fellow carousers had assumed he had left them to take Miss Charron home in pursuit of the wager, which he wished with all his heart he had never made. Tomorrow they would demand chapter and verse in order to be convinced that he had succeeded in climbing into the actress's bed. He sighed heavily; he would have to admit failure and put up with the ribaldry that was bound to follow. He would never live it down. And he prayed most heartily that Miss Charron herself never got to hear of it. How, in heaven's name, could he explain it to her and still keep her good-will?

Judging by the peal she had rung over him a few minutes before, he had lost it already and he cursed himself for agreeing to dine with Benedict and his friends and accompanying them to the theatre afterwards. Once they began hectoring the performers, he had tried to restrain them, but they were all so drunk, they took no notice and, to his eternal shame, he had given up.

'Miss Charron,' he said at last, 'I most humbly beg your pardon if I have offended you—'

'It is not me alone you offended, my lord,' she said in her haughtiest voice, 'but all the other performers and the audience too who could not hear the play for the noise you and your friends were making. You call yourselves gentlemen! I have seen more gentlemanly behaviour in street urchins.'

'You are right, but in my own defence I can only say I did not know my friends would behave in such a fashion; they had taken a drop too much.'

'A drop!' She spoke scornfully, walking swiftly, head high, so that her words were carried to him over her shoulder. 'A barrel would be more accurate. And that is no excuse, though I am aware everyone thinks it is. Now, I beg you to say no more about it, for talking about it is making me angrier by the minute.'

'If you will not hear my apology, then I will remain silent.'

'Please do.'

They resumed their silent contemplation as they walked, more quickly now. The streets had been busy around the theatre, which was lit by street lamps, but now they were in an unlit area, where the houses were crowded together and what little moonlight there was could hardly penetrate. Every now and again a door opened to reveal the noisy interior of a low tavern, as people came out to wend their way drunkenly homeward. There were puddles in the road and unpleasant smells whose source could not be determined. There was a scurrying of mice around a pile of rubbish and a cat screeched as someone threw something at it from a bedroom window.

Madeleine shuddered, realising she had become soft. Not so many years before, she would have walked through here and thought nothing of it. No one would have accosted her; she was a child of poverty, just as they were, and had nothing to steal. What a long way she had come. But not far enough, nowhere near far enough. She smiled suddenly.

'My lord, I am sorry.' She laid a hand on his arm and the slight contact heightened her awareness of him as a man—a tall, muscular, handsome and very virile man. 'That was unkind in me when you have taken the trouble to see me safe home. Talk if you wish to, I shall listen.'

The sudden change in her tone of voice took him by surprise. The virago had gone and been replaced by a woman who appeared to care that she had berated him unjustly. And the hand on his sleeve was as warm as the smile she turned towards him. He could see her face clearly by the light coming from the window of a house they were passing. The rest of her—her clothes, her hat, her small feet in patent leather shoes—were in shadow, but the face, framed by the soft outline of the feather in her bonnet, was clear, the eyes bright and the lips slightly parted.

She was beautiful and desirable and if she were not who she was and if he were not who he was, he could easily fall in love with her, properly in love, not as a man loves his mistress, which would be acceptable in Society so long as he kept her in the background, but as a man loves the woman he would like for his wife. The unthinkable thought shook him to the core and he took a moment to compose himself before he spoke again.

'I am not a great talker,' he said, reaching across himself to put his other hand upon hers. He did not know why he did it; it only served to heighten his already excited senses. 'But I would like us to be friends and if I have in any way endangered that by my insensitive behaviour, then I am truly penitent. I will insist on Mr Willoughby offering you an apology.'

She laughed lightly. 'Oh, I do not think that will be necessary, my lord. An apology not heartily meant is not worth the effort of making and I doubt he even realises he has anything to apologise for. Pray, let us forget it.'

'I will,' he said, 'if you will stop addressing me by my title. I prefer Duncan, or if you cannot manage that, then Stanmore. Sometimes, you know, a title can be a dreadful encumbrance.'

'You don't say so.'

'Indeed, I do. It can have a very restricting influence on a fellow.'

'You mean because everyone knows you and you cannot get into the least scrape without the whole world knowing of it?'

He grinned in the darkness; she was right about that. 'Something of the sort. But it also means some people, those whose opinion I value, are uncomfortable with me, afraid to speak their minds.'

'Can you wonder at it? You are all-powerful, or at least your father, the Duke of Loscoe, is; earning your disapprobation could easily ruin a man. Or a woman, come to that,' she added softly.

'I collect you have no such constraints.'

'Should I have?'

'No, certainly not. That is what I like about you. You say what you think and if it means giving me a jobation, then you do not hold back, do you?'

She laughed. 'No, you must take me as I am. I have never been in a position to learn the niceties of Polite Society but, from my limited observation, I have come to the conclusion that a great deal of what goes on is empty sham. One must do this. One must on no account do that. The hierarchy of status must be maintained at all costs…'

'Everyone in Society is not like that,' he said softly. 'My own parents are as liberal as anyone can be.'

'Yes, the Duchess was very amiable when she spoke to me last week, but that does not mean she would accept me in her circle of friends.'

'I do not see why not. You are the granddaughter of a count.'

She did not like to be reminded of that untruth, but she was not yet ready to confess her fault, for all she had promised Marianne she would. 'A French count, that is not the same as an English one, is it?'

He smiled. 'Perhaps not, but Mama would make no distinction.'

'I imagine the Duke would.'

'Not necessarily. Oh, undoubtedly he can be top-lofty, it was especially true when my sister and I were children, but the present Duchess has tamed him, you know. You will see, when you come to the house for the soirée, how very agreeable he can be.'

'Will he be there?' She had not thought much about facing the Duke before and she began to tremble at her own temerity. It was easy to boast to Marianne of what she meant to do, but putting it into practice was proving harder than she had imagined; the Marquis of Risley was turning out to be much too good-natured and caring for her peace of mind. If she were not vigilant, she might even find herself liking him too much. And that would never do. 'I had thought it would only be ladies.'

'No, there is usually a sprinkling of gentlemen my stepmother has coerced into donating funds to her charity.'

'And does that include you?'

'I would not miss it for the world,' he said. 'The delectable Miss Charron gracing the Stanmore drawing room, that is something to be seen. Mama was right, you will draw the *haut monde* like a magnet.'

'Fustian!'

'Oh, indeed yes. The evening will make a great deal of money for the orphanage.'

'Orphanage,' she echoed in a small voice, watching her feet, unable to look up at him in case he saw her agitation in her face.

'Yes, did you not know? Mama has been involved in providing homes for soldiers' orphans ever since the war. Why, when they opened the one in Maiden Lane, she rolled up her sleeves and helped to scrub it out.'

Madeleine breathed easily again. The orphanage she had attended had been in Monmouth Street, not Maiden Lane. 'Then, I hope you are right and she does well from it. I shall do my best to help.'

'Of course,' he said, suddenly remembering. 'I had forgot you have lived in an orphanage yourself.'

'I do not dwell on it. It is in the past.' She did not want to be questioned about it; it made her feel even more guilty and uncomfortable.

'I understand.' He squeezed her hand gently. 'It must be particularly painful for you, being of gentle birth as you are. But perhaps one day, you may find you have a family after all.'

She gave a short laugh that grated in her own ears. 'I think not, sir, or they would have come forward when Mama died. I am resigned to being without. I have my work and my friends…'

'I hope I may count myself one of them,' he said softly.

'Oh, that you may,' she said, laughing to try to lighten the atmosphere which had become tense. 'So long as you behave.'

'For the reward of being your friend, I will be a model of good behaviour,' he said, matching his mood to hers. 'I will only throw orange peel if you are not on the stage.'

'You will not throw it at all.' She paused. 'Why did you come to the theatre tonight? I would have thought a play about a nobleman being duped into accepting for his wife the physician's daughter he had disdained is surely a little too hard for you to stomach.'

'He deserved it for behaving so ungallantly towards her.'

His vehemence made her laugh. 'It is only a play, my lord, and Helena was forced upon him. I am sure you would not allow yourself to be hoaxed in that way.'

He grinned. 'If she were as beautiful as you, I would be giving thanks for my good luck.'

It was simple flattery, she knew that, a flirtatious dallying with words, meant to heighten their awareness of each other, as if she needed anything to do that. She was already strung like a bow and almost ready to break. 'My lord, you do not have to empty the butter boat over me, you know. I am quite vain enough as it is. I play the parts I am given to the best of my ability and if my acting serves to make the audience think, then I am doubly rewarded.'

'It certainly made me think,' he said. 'I find something new to admire every time I see you.'

'More flummery.'

'It is true, my dear. I find myself speechless with admiration.'

'And that I do not believe. For one who says he is not a great talker, you are not short of words.'

'And, I collect, you bade me be silent,' he said ruefully.

They were so busy with the cut and thrust of a dialogue that hid more than it revealed, they had not noticed their surroundings, which were dismal in the extreme and best ignored, but now they were turning into Oxford Street and almost at their destination. Madeleine began to feel sorry that she had made him walk so far out of his way and would be alone on the return journey, a prey to any scamp who caught sight of his fine clothes. But if he thought she was going to invite him to stay the night with her, he would have to think again. She did not intend to succumb that easily; she did not intend to succumb at all.

Deep in thought, she did not notice the man dart out of a side alley until he grabbed hold of her, pulling her round in front of him, using her to shield his own body, and brandishing a wicked-looking knife. 'Now, sir, unless you want me to spoil the lady's good looks, you will hand over your valuables,' he said, addressing Duncan.

He was a big man and very powerful. She could smell the drink on his breath and the odour of his unwashed body and it made her feel sick, but the knife was perilously close to her face and she dare not struggle. 'Let me go,' she begged. 'Please let me go.'

'I will, as soon as lover-boy has coughed up his gewgaws.'

But Duncan did not seem in any hurry to remove the diamond pin from his cravat or the fob from his waistcoat; he faced the man squarely and stood his ground. 'I think not,' he said mildly. 'I am rather attached to them.'

Madeleine gasped, hardly able to believe he would sacrifice her to keep his jewels.

She opened her mouth to scream, but the robber anticipated her and clamped a hand over her mouth, while the other still held the knife to her throat. 'I mean it, sir, your valuables, if you please. '

'Don't be a damned fool, man,' Duncan said evenly, stepping towards him. 'It's not worth it, you know.'

'You keep your distance, this knife is sharp as a razor.' He took a step backwards, pulling Madeleine with him. Her hat came off and rolled in the dirt. 'Come on,' he said. 'I ain't got all night.'

Duncan began slowly—too slowly for Madeleine, who was fighting for breath—to undo the pin and then the fob, but he did not hand them over, but weighed them in the palm of his hand. 'Do you need these so badly?' he asked calmly.

'Course I do. D'you think I'd hold you up if I weren't driv to it? Now, 'and 'em over. And yer blunt too.'

'You may have them with my compliments if you release the lady at once. Unharmed.'

'Do you take me for a fool? She goes free when I've got 'em safe in me 'ands.'

'Then how are you going to possess yourself of them?' He dangled the jewellery in front of the man. 'You have only two hands and at the moment both seem full.'

The man took his hand from Madeleine's mouth and reached out to take the spoils and in that instant Duncan grabbed his wrist and twisted his arm, making him release his prisoner. Madeleine threw herself to the ground. She heard the man grunt in pain as Duncan brought his arm up behind his back and forced him to drop the knife.

'Are you hurt?' Duncan asked her, dropping the jewels into his waistcoat pocket, in order to have two hands to hold on to the captive, who was struggling ineffectually in a surprisingly strong grip.

'No,' she said, scrambling to her feet, but she was shaking so much she had to lean against a house wall for support.

'I meant no 'arm to the lady,' the would-be robber said, almost defiantly. 'But there ain't no other way, I've got no work and me childer are starvin'…'

'And they will starve even more if you are in prison, you fool,' Duncan said.

'Don't hand me in, sir, I beg you.'

'No, I do not think that will put bread in the mouths of your children, will it? I think you would do better to find work.'

'You think I ain't tried?'

'Then I suggest you try again. Go to Bow Street first thing in the morning, the house next to the magistrate and say Stanmore sent you. They will help you.' He paused. 'And I suppose if I am not to have your hungry children on my conscience tonight, you had better have this.' He released the man in order to extract a few coins from his purse. 'But buy food with it, do you hear?' The man stood, as if uncertain whether or not to believe his luck. Duncan smiled. 'Go on, man, before I change my mind.'

He scuttled away and Duncan turned to Madeleine who was still leaning against the wall, knowing that if she pushed herself away from it, her shaking knees would not support her. 'Oh, my love, I am sorry,' he said, taking her in his arms. 'I would not for the world have had that happen to you. Are you all right? No bruises or anything?'

'I shall know that tomorrow,' she said shakily, trying to laugh. 'But my goodness, how brave you were to stand up to him like that.'

'He was more afraid than I was.' He stooped to pick up her hat, but it was crumpled and muddy and she could not wear it. 'Now we must get you home. I am sorry there are no cabs in this vicinity and I dare not leave you to fetch one. Do you think you can walk?'

'Oh, yes. I am a little shaky, but unharmed.'

'I do not think we should loiter. Come, let me help you.'

They walked on, but now his arm was about her and though she recovered quickly, she liked the feel of it there, the warmth and security of his tall presence and the knowledge, spreading through her like liquid fire, that he had called her his love, and in a voice so full of tender concern, she could not doubt his sincerity. But she would not spoil the moment by trying to analyse how she felt about that.

'You could have been hurt, even killed, and it was all my fault,' she said. 'I should never have suggested going home on foot. And now you have a long walk back and he may be lying in wait for you.'

'Oh, I do not think so. I have met such fellows before, they are not true criminals, but driven by desperation.'

'And this house in Bow Street?'

'Oh, a place that finds work for such fellows. I heard of it quite by chance.' A statement that was not exactly true, since he had founded it and paid for its upkeep.

'But for my silly pride you would have had your carriage.'

'And then, the journey would only have been of a few minutes' duration and we would not have had time to become friends again. You would still be angry with me.'

'Perhaps.' She laughed shakily. 'And now you have every right to be angry with me.'

'Not at all, my dear Madeleine. I believe I understand you.'

'Do you?' she asked softly, thinking that if he did, it was more than she did. Sometimes she thought she knew what drove her, sometimes she was a mass of indecisiveness.

'Yes. Your art is important to you, it is your expression of your true self and anyone who makes light of that is a reprehensible shagbag and deserves your wrath. You are proud, yes, and you have a right to be, though sometimes that pride works against you. Now, have I got it right?'

He was far too perspicacious for her comfort. What else had he deduced about her? She laughed to cover her chagrin. 'Oh, yes, exactly. I wish I could read your character so readily.'

'Oh, I am easy to read, my dear. I am the spoiled son of a nobleman who falls into a tantrum when he cannot have his own way, but can be a pleasant companion when he has it, which can be said of almost anyone of my ilk.'

'I do not believe that. Others of your ilk, as you put it, would not have been so lenient with that man just now. They would have called out the watch and had him taken to gaol, even supposing they could overcome him as you did, which I ask leave to doubt.'

'You think I should have turned him in?'

'I don't know,' she said doubtfully, not at all sure that the man might not be lurking somewhere to pounce again. 'If you are right, he deserves our pity.'

'Pity is not enough,' he said softly.

She looked at him sharply, surprised by the hint of regret in his voice, as if he had somehow failed the man who tried to rob him. 'I have not met many aristocrats,' she said. 'but those I have met have certainly not betrayed such sentiments. I think you may be different.'

He laughed and pulled her close against his side. 'Oh, I do hope so, my dear Madeleine, I do hope so.' They had arrived outside the door of her lodging and now he stopped and turned her to face him, though he still kept his arms about her. 'You will be all right now?'

'Yes, thank you.'

'It was fortunate I was with you tonight. You could have been attacked, left for dead, stripped of your clothes and…' He could not put that particular fear into words, but she knew what he meant.

'I collect it was your valuables he was after. I have none.'

'If I had not been there, it might have been different. I want you to make me a promise, my dear. I want your word you will not attempt to walk home alone again. Go with Miss Doubleday or take a cab, or send for me. I will come, you know.' He was looking down at her with such an expression of tender concern it turned her heart over and, try as she might, she could not harden it. This was not how she had meant it to be. Not this softness.

'I know,' she said. 'I will remember. But it is you I am concerned about. I do not like to think of you walking home alone. Won't you come in? My landlady might be persuaded to find you a bed.'

He wondered briefly if she were offering him her bed. If he had been the man his friends thought him to be, he would have jumped at the offer and won his wager. He would be fooling himself if he said he was not tempted, but the special bond they had established was so fragile, it would not survive if he availed himself of her invitation, especially as he longed to do more than take her in his arms. He might make a fool of himself. 'Best not,' he said, returning her crumpled hat to her. 'I might forget I am a gentleman.' He bent and put his lips to her forehead. 'Good night, sweet Madeleine. Sleep well.' And then he was gone, striding away down the street and not looking back.

Madeleine turned slowly to go indoors. She was confused and angry with herself. How could she go on with the masquerade? How could she deceive him so? How could she go to the Duchess's soirée and pretend to be someone she was not? He was nothing like Henry Bulford, nothing at all. He was brave as a lion, cool in a crisis, and he respected her, even if it was only for her talent as an actress. Would he respect her when he knew that she had deliberately deceived him? Marianne had been right; she had got herself into a dreadful coil.

He would come to the theatre again; she knew it as surely as she knew she would be there herself. She would have to turn him away, pretend to have another engagement, let him know that she looked on tonight's episode as nothing more than an adventure they had shared and that it meant nothing to her. Nothing at all.

She went upstairs to her room, flung the battered hat and her pelisse on the bed and kicked off her shoes, then she walked across to the window. The street was dark and empty. He had gone from sight, if not from her mind. She prayed he would arrive home safely.

Duncan was not especially concerned for his safety. He had met many such fellows as the one who had accosted him tonight and they were only men, just as he was a man, but much less fortunate. As soon as they realised he was not their enemy, they usually became amenable. Even so, he took the precaution of walking down Oxford Street instead of going back the way he had come. By the time he reached the junction with Bond Street, he would find a cab.

The night was still comparatively young; he could go to his club, but, knowing Benedict Willoughby and his cronies would be there, waiting for him, wanting to know what had happened, he decided against it. He could not tell them the truth: that he had developed a genuine *tendre* for Madeleine Charron and could not take advantage of her, that he wished with all his heart that he could somehow transform her into someone his father would accept. They would laugh him to scorn. Nor could he lie. He could not pretend he had shared Madeleine's bed and take Willoughby's money. That was even more unthinkable.

He would go home. Tomorrow morning, very early, he would blow away the cobwebs by going for a gallop in Hyde Park and then he would go to Gentleman Jackson's boxing establishment and go a few rounds with whoever happened to be there. After that, dressed in an anonymous-looking drab coat and a low-crowned hat, he would visit the house in Bow Street to see if the man had turned up there. They usually did. After that, if there was time, he would visit Newgate prison. It would take his mind off Miss Madeleine Charron and give him something else to think about.

His interest in prisons and prisoners had begun three years before when he had gone with a lawyer friend who was defending a fellow accused of stealing two loaves of bread and a quantity of tea from a house on Piccadilly. He and the friend were going to the races later in the day and, as he had nothing better to do, he had gone with him to Newgate. The visit had changed his life.

He had known, of course, that being imprisoned was not a pleasant experience; it was not meant to be a bed of roses, but a punishment for crime; he had not, until then, given it much thought. If a man picked his pocket, that man must go to gaol. But he had been appalled at what he saw. It was difficult to believe that the filthy ragged inmates with matted beards and tangled hair were human beings and not some strange animals, caged because they were dangerous. Nor, until his friend had enlightened him, had he realised how many offences had been punishable by death—over two hundred, so he had said.

'Besides murder, treason, piracy and arson,' he had told him, 'you could be hanged for highway robbery, housebreaking, shoplifting, rick-burning and poaching, and a host of other seemingly slight offences, like sending a begging letter signed with a pseudonym or impersonating a Chelsea Pensioner, and hundreds more, equally curious. Of course, Peel is full of reforming zeal and has managed to reduce the huge number of crimes for which hanging is the prescribed punishment, but that has done little to reduce crime and only serves to make the prisons more crowded than ever.'

'Mrs Fry has been pioneering for prison reform for some time, has she not?'

'True, and she has achieved much for the women and children, but the men still spend their days in idleness, gambling and drinking…'

'Drinking?'

'Yes, cheap gin is readily available from the wardsmen if you have money to pay for it. You can hardly blame them for wanting to drown their misery.'

It was not until he had met and talked with some of the prisoners that he discovered that most of them were not murderers, nor even deeply felonious, but petty thieves and minor delinquents, often forced to steal in order to provide for their families, and he had come to the conclusion that it was not the people who needed to reform so much as the system that made them what they were.

He had taken his seat in the House of Lords in 1820, when everyone entitled to sit there had been obliged to attend that travesty of a trial aimed at disgracing the Queen and allowing the King to divorce her, but he had not been much interested in politics and did not attend the House afterwards. Following that visit to Newgate, he had resumed his seat and become a vociferous advocate of treating convicted people as human beings whatever they had done. But it did him little good; he was said to be too enthusiastic and would have the country go so far down the road to leniency as to invite anarchy. Why, if he had his way, so these greybeards said, men would come to welcome prison as an alternative to going out and earning an honest living.

He had taken the criticism with a shrug of his shoulders and continued his campaign in private, leaving his father and Robert Peel, the Home Secretary, to make the public speeches. Instead he did what he could, taking clothes and food in to the prisoners and, in some cases, paying for a lawyer, or using his name and consequence to obtain employment for them when they were released. It was why he had set up the house in Bow Street. Just as the orphanage was his stepmother's charity, the prisoners and their families had become his.

It was not something he boasted of. In fact, his contemporaries in the *haut monde* would be astonished and horrified if they knew about it. He doubted if any of them, and that included Benedict Willoughby, would have sympathised. They would say he had taken leave of his senses. And so he told no one, doing good by stealth. Except that now Madeleine Charron had an inkling of it.

There he was, thinking about her again. Why could he not contemplate anything—his social engagements, his charitable work, what coat or cravat he should wear, whether to dine at his club or at home, whether to go to Almack's or not—without thinking of her, putting her into the context of his life? He turned from Oxford Street into Bond Street. An empty cab rattled past, but he made no attempt to hail it. He had not yet concluded the inner debate that raged within him and he needed more time.

Madeleine Charron was an actress, a very fine actress, but not socially acceptable. His father, his stepmother, his sister and her husband, not to mention all their friends, would never countenance a marriage. He stopped suddenly. Marriage. When had that thought entered his head? It had not been a conscious one and it must be banished at once. He set off again with renewed purpose. He needed a stiff drink. A very stiff drink.

He paused outside White's, but, knowing Benedict would probably be there, he continued on his way to Stanmore House. One day, some time off yet, for he loved his father, it would become his. His wife would be its mistress, his son the heir to everything: the London house, the Risley estate in Derbyshire, the hunting box in Leicestershire, the Scottish castle where his Uncle John lived, almost a recluse, not to mention shipping interests worldwide. He was not even sure how much there was. The future Duchess of Loscoe would have to be a very special person and must be chosen with care.

What had he said to his stepmother, the present Duchess, only two days ago? *I want to have feelings for the woman I marry, feelings that last a lifetime.* Which was more important, his feelings or the future of the Loscoe inheritance? It was not a matter of pleasing himself, because so many other people depended on a healthy estate: tenants, workers, servants, employees. He was not free to have feelings.

He clattered up to the door and, despite the late hour, it was opened by a footman. There was always someone on duty, night and day; he did not even have to open a door for himself. He thanked the man, remembering to call him by his name, and continued up the grand staircase to his room on the second floor. He was met by his valet, slightly disheveled, it was true, as if he had been woken from sleep, but none the less ready to serve him.

'Davison, I told you not to wait up for me.'

'I know, my lord, but it is a chilly night, for all it is June, and I thought you might like a hot drink.'

How could he be churlish when faced with such devotion? The idea of the stiff drink was abandoned in favour of hot chocolate. 'Thank you, yes, please. And then go to bed. I am perfectly capable of undressing myself. You can tidy up in the morning.'

'Yes, my lord.' Davison busied himself with a small spirit stove on a table in the corner of the large room, put there for occasions like this when his master came in late and they did not want to disturb the downstairs servants by asking for a hot drink to be made. 'What shall I put out for you?'

'I'm going riding very early. I'll dress myself.'

'My lord, I would die of mortification if anyone was to see the way you tie a cravat.'

'I thought I was rather good at it.' He surveyed himself in the mirror. The struggle with the would-be robber had left him in a sorry state. The sleeve of his coat was torn and dirty, his cravat was a crumpled mess and his carefully arranged curls were tumbling over his brow. Davison must have noticed but, like the good servant he was, had made no comment.

'Why should you be good at it, my lord, when it is the province of your valet to tie your cravat?'

He placed a dish of hot chocolate on the table beside his master. 'Though I see I did not do a very good job this evening and I beg your pardon for it.'

Duncan laughed aloud. 'Oh, do not be so roundabout, man. You can see I have been in a scrape and you are dying of curiosity.'

'My lord?'

'I will satisfy it, but only if you swear not to say a word to anyone.'

'My lord, I have never betrayed your confidence in me and never will.'

'I know that, Davison, I know that. Tonight I was set upon.'

'Set upon, my lord? You mean you were robbed?'

'Oh, no, I was not robbed, for I turned the tables on my attacker, but it has left me as you see.' He took his diamond pin and fob from his waistcoat pocket and handed them to the valet to put away safely.

'My lord, are you hurt?'

'Not at all.' He laughed suddenly. 'Oh, do not look so concerned, I have not spent hours and hours at Jackson's without learning how to look after myself.'

'Where was your carriage, my lord?'

'Oh, I sent it home, I fancied a walk.' He flung off the offending cravat and began to undo his waistcoat.

'I think, my lord, that you take too many risks.' The words were spoken deferentially, but Duncan could see that his servant was worried about him.

'Life would be very dull if we did not draw a bow at a venture now and again, but you know, I always calculate the risk, so do not worry.'

'Very well, my lord.' The jewellery safely disposed of, Davison went to the wardrobe and fetched out Duncan's riding coat and a pair of fine tan breeches and laid them across a chair ready for the morning. A white lawn shirt, a fresh cravat and wool hose were fetched from the drawer of his dressing chest and put with them. 'Is there anything else?'

'No, get yourself to bed, man.'

The valet retreated and Duncan was left to drink his chocolate and finish undressing alone. It had been a memorable evening but one he was not in a hurry to repeat. He had told Davison he always calculated the risk and if he had been only speaking of overcoming a footpad, there might be some truth in it, but what of the greater risk of spending too much time in Miss Madeleine Charron's company? She had charmed him, bewitched him, so that he was unable to think sensibly.

She set his mind in a whirl of admiration, protectiveness and desire, which went round and round, looping in and out of his consciousness like the intricate lace he used to watch his old nurse making when he was a small boy. Her flying fingers had threaded the bobbins in and out, over and under, and the result was a cobweb design it was impossible to pull out. His life, hitherto uneventful, was beginning to knot itself up like that.

His father wished him to marry. He knew he should marry. He wanted to love the woman he married. He wanted her to love him. But Madeleine Charron? Where had that idea come from? She was an actress, totally unsuitable. But she was also the granddaughter of a nobleman. Did that make her acceptable in Society? Was she to be forever condemned to its fringe? And in and out of the web went that dreadful wager Benedict had imposed upon him and the sure knowledge that if the lady ever heard of it, he would be damned forever in her eyes. And back went the bobbin again. Did it matter? He could not marry her.

Fully undressed now, he stood before the mirror and surveyed himself. He was in the prime of his life; his legs were long, his thighs muscular, his arms strong and his face not at all bad, if you discounted a nose that was a little too long and a chin that could jut dangerously when provoked. He knew he was attractive to women; it was not only his fortune that drew them to him. He might as well take his pleasure where he could, before he was irrevocably hitched to the marriage cart.

He could seduce Madeleine Charron; he did not doubt she had succumbed before. And even as the thought came to him, he dismissed it. Miss

Madeleine Charron was not *chère amie* material, not a demi-rep to be kept in the background. She was meant to shine, to be seen and admired and preferably on his arm. The spider's web had trapped him like a fly and the more he struggled, the tighter it became. He reached out and grabbed his nightshirt, pulling it over his head, shrouding himself in fine cotton, as if covering himself would return him to his normal good sense.

'I will not see her again,' he said, as he turned out the lamp and climbed into bed. 'I will put temptation out of the way.'

The audience behaved itself the following night, there were no rowdy scenes and no orange peel on the stage. Madeleine was, as usual, besieged by admirers at the stage door, but the Marquis of Risley was not among them. She went to supper with Marianne and several of the others of the cast and a bevy of young bloods vying with each other for her favours, much to the amusement of Marianne, who, being of middle years, was quite content to sit beside Sir Percy and laugh at them.

She did not need the Marquis of Risley, Maddy told herself. He had been having a little fun with her, whiling away a dull evening or two, taking risks by venturing into the sordid slums where his sort never went, just for devilment and to boast of it to his friends afterwards—that encounter with the ruffian would add a piquancy to the telling. No doubt he would tell them he had saved her life, that she had been terrified and allowed him to put his arms about her to calm her.

But she could not convince herself that he would do that. He had seemed to care, not only for her but what became of the robber. He had called her his love, had refrained from taking advantage of her. Why? Because he was a gentleman? But her experience of gentlemen did not incline her to that view. Did he not find her attractive? Was he having a little sport with her? Or had he sensed in her the hidden aversion in which she held all aristocrats and knew she was playing with him, as one might play a fish caught on the end of a line. He would not come again if he thought that. Why was she such a mass of contradictions?

'Maddy, you are dreaming again,' Marianne murmured, while the noise of the party eddied around them.

She pulled herself together with an effort. 'Sorry, I was thinking.'

'I never did hold with too much thinking,' Sir Percy said, with a smile. 'Brings on premature wrinkles, don't you know.'

She laughed. 'You are no doubt right, Sir Percy. I will endeavour to empty my mind of all but work.'

'And pleasure, my dear,' he said reaching out and laying a hand upon hers. 'One as beautiful as you must not devote yourself only to work. Enjoy life.'

'Oh, I do.' She paused. 'Sir Percy, you know the Duchess of Loscoe very well, do you not?'

'Indeed, yes. I have known her since she had her come-out, though I will not be so ungentlemanly as to tell you how many years ago that was. Why do you ask?'

'We have both been invited to the Duchess's soirée on Thursday,' Marianne put in quickly before Madeleine could answer him. 'We have been asked to perform for her guests and have been wondering what to do. Do you have any ideas?'

'I am sure whatever you choose will be a great success,' he said.

'Will you be there, Sir Percy?' Madeleine asked.

'Wouldn't miss it for all the tea in china, m'dear.'

'I am told the Duke might put in an appearance,' she went on. 'And the Marquis of Risley.'

'I shouldn't count on it,' he said. 'The Duke is a very busy man; as for young Stanmore, he has his own pursuits. Has to find himself a wife, don't you know. He'll be off doing the rounds of the balls and routs, taking his pick of this Season's hopefuls.'

'Oh.' Why was she disappointed? What else did she expect? 'And I collect they must be ladies equal in station to his lordship.'

'Not necessarily; there would not be enough to choose from if he insisted on that, but she would have to be of a good family known to the Duke. *Noblesse oblige* and all that, you know.'

Marianne was looking at her and shaking her head imperceptibly. She smiled. 'I have often wondered what it must be like to have a come-out. I think that perhaps it is not all enjoyment, being paraded like a horse at Tattersall's, hoping someone will like you enough to make an offer.'

'Suppose it is, dear girl, but it works the other way too. The young eligibles are being looked over as well, you know. They must come up to the mark.' He smiled. 'But the Marquis of Risley can afford to be choosy. I think perhaps he is, for he has been putting off becoming leg-shackled for the last three Seasons to my certain knowledge.'

The young men were becoming a little disguised and making noisy jokes, to which Marianne always had a ready answer, but Maddy, though she smiled, was still in the dilemma that had beset her the first time she had spoken to Duncan Stanmore and paid little attention. Now the date of the soirée had been confirmed and was only a few days away, she was shaking at the prospect. Could she go through with it, could she go on pretending?

The Marquis of Risley was not the only fish in the sea, she told herself sternly. She would go to the soirée at Stanmore House and she would somehow contrive to have a little conversation with the

Duchess, tell her about her French grandfather in the presence of other people and from that another invitation would come and then another. All she needed was for everyone to accept that she was of noble birth, fallen on hard times through no fault of her own.

'Sir Percy, I think Madeleine is tired out,' Marianne said. 'I think I will take her home.'

He rose at once. 'My carriage is at your disposal, my dear. We will leave the young gentlemen carousing, shall we?'

They bade the others goodnight, amid loud exclamations that the evening had hardly begun, then Sir Percy escorted the ladies to his carriage. 'Soon have you home,' he said, helping them both up the steps and following behind. He was a kind man who did not ask questions, though Madeleine was fairly sure he missed very little. Whether he had heard the story of the French *comte* she did not know, but he would certainly know if the granddaughter of such a one would be acceptable in Society. One thing she was sure of: a nobody would not stand a chance.

Was she a nobody? she asked herself as she climbed into bed an hour later. The Marquis had said there was something about her that proclaimed her a woman of breeding. Could it possibly be true? Could her father have been something more than a humble soldier? But if he was, why had her mother never told her of it? Perhaps the gossips had been right and her mama had never been married.

She shook the dreadful thought from her; her mama would never have allowed anything like that to happen. But supposing Mama had been subjected to the same sort of assault she had suffered from Henry Bulford and been unable to throw her attacker off. It did not bear thinking of. If that were true, then all the noble grandfathers in the world would not help her. Perhaps, if she tried to find out about her early childhood, who she was, where her father and mother had come from, she might feel better about herself. She might learn contentment. But where to begin, she had no idea.

Chapter Four

Almack's Assembly Rooms were already crowded and noisy when the Stanmore party arrived, a little late as etiquette demanded. The sound of chattering voices died away as everyone realised who the late-comers were and a concerted sigh went up from all the young single ladies at the sight of the Marquis of Risley; and from some not so young, who were undoubtedly at their last prayers.

He was superbly dressed in a dark blue evening coat, white breeches and stockings and a richly embroidered waistcoat. A fob lay across his broad chest, a diamond pin glittered in a cravat that Davison had taken hours to launder and tie for him and a quizzing glass dangled on a cord about his neck. He was twenty-five, rich and handsome and the heir to the Duke of Loscoe, so they had every justification for sighing. And hoping.

Most of them were pretty in a vacuous kind of way, and no doubt their credentials were perfectly acceptable or they would never have been given vouchers to attend. Almack's balls were by invitation only and those not easily come by.

'Well,' Lavinia whispered, 'you certainly made an entrance. Every single one of them is gaping, even those already spoken for. You may take your pick.'

He did not want to take his pick, he did not want any of them; he wanted the vivacious Miss Madeleine Charron who could knock every one of these into a cocked hat. But he had come to please the Duchess and Lavinia and so he smiled round the room, as the music started again. Mamas were prodding daughters and whispering in their ears, no doubt telling them how best to attract his attention. It happened every time he attended such a function and he would be glad when he was safely married and the interest died away.

There was only one way to go on and that was to plough straight in. 'Present me to one of them,' hc asked the Duchess.

As she led him across the floor, he was aware that all eyes were following their progress, wondering who would be selected. He did not care. They might speculate all they liked, he would not choose any one over another. He would keep them guessing until such time as Madeleine Charron was accepted as one of their number and came to this very room. Then they would see how superior she was in every way.

The Duchess was making for a group consisting of a plump, red-faced man of about seven and twenty, a tall, imperious-looking woman whose quizzing glass never left her eye and a young lady. 'The man is Lord Bulford, recently come into his baronetcy,' she explained in an undertone as they walked. 'The tall lady is his wife and the other is his sister.'

The man bowed to the Duchess as they approached. 'Your Grace.'

'Lord Bulford, I do not think you are acquainted with my stepson, the Marquis of Risley,' the Duchess said.

The two men bowed.

Frances smiled. 'Lady Bulford, may I present, the Marquis of Risley.'

Her ladyship inclined her head in acknowledgement. 'My lord, we are indeed pleased to make your acquaintance. May I present my sister-in-law, Miss Annabel Bulford.'

'My lord.' Annabel dropped so deep a curtsy Duncan began to wonder if she would be able to rise again and put out his hand to raise her up. She blushed furiously as she took it. 'May I have the honour of this dance?' he asked, still holding her hand.

A nudge from her sister-in-law helped her to smile her agreement and they took to the floor.

She was stiff as a board and half afraid of him. He smiled to put her at her ease. 'I wonder I have not seen you about before, Miss Bulford,' he said. 'Perhaps this is your first Season?'

'Yes, it is.' She spoke a little breathlessly, but her voice was not unpleasant. 'I am to have my come-out ball later in the Season.'

'Ah, that accounts for my not having met you before. I should certainly have remembered it.'

'You would?'

'Naturally I would have noticed you.' She was pretty in a colourless sort of way, the sort of prettiness that Society approved of. She had a small oval-shaped face, with a pale complexion that made her pale eyes seem extra large, and fair ringlets, caught in a comb just above each ear. Her figure was just on the plump side of slender and she danced very well. She was smiling at his compliment.

'I have always known of you,' she said.

'Oh dear, that sounds ominous.'

'No, no, I did not mean anything bad. You have always been put forward as a splendid example of this country's nobility.'

He laughed lightly. 'I cannot think who would say such a thing, unless it be my stepmama or sister. Only they could be so blind to my many faults.'

'Oh, no, it was not either of them. It was my brother Henry.'

'I do not think I have had the pleasure of making his acquaintance before tonight.'

'He has been on an extended Grand Tour. He came back a year ago when Papa died. He married Dorothy last summer.'

'Then how can he be in a position to pronounce upon my virtues?'

She seemed very flustered. 'Mama said it too.'

'Then I am indebted to her ladyship.'

'Since Papa died, we have been retired to the country, but my sister and I are come to stay with my brother for the Season.'

'Then the Season cannot fail to be a success.'

She coloured at the compliment. 'My lord, would it be considered presumptuous of me to invite you to attend my ball? I should very much like you to be there. I know Dorothy is going to invite the Duke and Duchess of Loscoe and the Earl and Countess of Corringham.'

'I should be delighted,' he said. The music was coming to an end and he made her a flourishing leg and received a deep curtsy in reply. Then he offered his arm and paraded her round the room once, along with the other dancers before taking her back to her brother and sister-in-law.

She was pink and glowing and Lady Bulford's face was a picture of triumph. He must be careful, he told himself, not to favour one before another or the tabbies would have the wedding bells ringing before the word 'offer' was ever uttered. He bowed to both ladies and strolled away to ask someone else to stand up with him.

By the time the evening drew to a close, he had danced with every young lady who could be considered even halfway eligible, and some who were not, and he was exhausted. It was not the dancing which had worn him out—he could dance all night if the mood took him and he had a beautiful partner—it was talking to them, watching his every word lest he give any the idea that he was considering them for his marchioness.

Some were coy, some were arch and some playfully flirtatious, which he had no difficulty in dealing with. The troublesome ones were those who were so completely overawed they had nothing to say at all. They had obviously been schooled by their mamas on no account to say this and to refrain from saying that, and always to remember to address him by his title, with the result that they dare not open their mouths. He had been especially kind to those.

From the point of view of the ladies who organised these weekly balls and according to the mamas whose daughters he had noticed, it was a great success, but as a palliative for his own troubled emotions, it failed. All the time he had been dancing, he had been imagining Madeleine in his arms, moving gracefully to the music, her animated face looking into his, laughing with him. It was easy to smile and pay compliments to his partners with that vision before him.

'Well, that was not so bad, was it?' Lavinia said, as they left.

'It was mortifying. I felt like some prize bull.'

'Oh, Duncan, how can you say so? You are a very handsome man and you have prospects...'

'Oh, I am aware of the prospects,' he said, as the coaches in which they had arrived were brought to the door. 'I could see the gleam in every mama's eyes as she totted up what I must be worth. I do not want to be married for my prospects.'

'Then it is up to you to find the one for whom prospects are not the main attraction, brother dear.'

Had he already found such a one? he asked himself after he had said goodnight to his sister and her husband and they had been borne away in the Corringham carriage. Did Madeleine Charron care for his prospects? Was she the same as the others, drawing a bow at a venture in the hope that the arrow would find its mark? No, he did not believe it of her. She was too independent, too proud, too much the mistress of her own life, to sacrifice any of that for riches and a title. And the last time they had met, she had made it clear that she despised aristocrats. Did she feel let down by her father? She seemed to know so little about him.

'This Season's young debutantes are more than usually bright,' Frances said, when they had settled themselves into the coach.

'Are they?' he said without thinking. 'Have I been inspected by them all or are there more to come?'

'No doubt there are others who were not considered up to a voucher tonight, but most of the truly acceptable ones were there. Did you see any you especially liked?'

'No, though if I were forced to choose, I suppose Miss Annabel Bulford has more about her than most, though that is not to say I am thinking of making an offer.'

'Good heavens, no! It is much too soon.'

'But I did agree to attend her come-out ball.'

'You did? That will be quite a feather in her cap, Duncan. If you do not want her to think she has been picked out for special attention, you will have to go to all the others.'

He groaned. 'What, all of them?'

'I am afraid so. At least those who are possibles.'

'Mama, I cannot believe you, above all people, are being so cold-blooded about this.'

'Oh, my dear boy, I am not. But Vinny was right, you know, if you do not go out and about and meet people, how are you ever to find the one to whom you can truly give your heart? It is all I wish for you.'

He smiled to himself in the darkness of the carriage. His heart was already irrevocably given and soon he hoped to announce it to the world, but until then he would play Society's game. In the meantime, he must persuade Madeleine to open her heart to him, for he was rapidly coming to the conclusion he could not live without her.

'I see your admirer was in his box again tonight,' one of the girls in the troupe told Madeleine as they stood on the stage after the last curtain had closed at the end of the week.

'My admirer?' Maddy queried, pretending ignorance, though she had seen the Marquis of Risley in his box and been aware of his presence throughout the performance. It was almost enough to make her stumble over her lines, but whatever she was or whoever she was, she was a professional performer and was soon in control of herself again.

'The man in the Loscoe box. You must have seen him.'

'And what does that signify except that the gentleman likes coming to the theatre?'

'He also likes you, that much is clear. He did not take his eyes off you all evening, even when you were not speaking.'

'And you should have been paying attention to what you were doing, Lucy, not allowing your eye to rove all round the audience. You can be sure Mr Greatorex will have noticed it.'

'I have nothing to do except stand about,' the girl said. 'And you can hardly miss anyone in the boxes near the stage, can you? And him so fine and handsome.' She sighed. 'I wish I had young gentlemen swooning after me. It must be grand to be given flowers and presents and taken out to supper...'

'When you have learned your craft well enough to be noticed by the management and the public, then perhaps you will have admirers too, but if you spend too much time looking about you and dreaming, that will not happen, believe me.' She did not know why she was so sharp with the poor girl; she had done her share of dreaming, but she was coming to realise that was all it was, dreaming. The reality, contrary to what everyone said, was here, on this stage. The world outside was the fantasy, the granddaughter of the French *comte* was fantasy, the hope of a future in Society was fantasy. She had come to that conclusion in the dark watches of the night, after that supper with Sir Percy.

'No need to fly into the boughs,' Lucy said. 'I only said your admirer was in the audience.'

She smiled and patted the girl's arm. 'I'm sorry, Lucy. I am a little jumpy tonight.'

Everyone was leaving the stage to go to dressing rooms and Madeleine followed more slowly, knowing there would be a message from the Marquis waiting for her and not knowing how to deal with it. If he was still in pursuit of her, he could only have one thing on his mind and that, as far she was concerned, was not going to happen. Oh, she knew perfectly well that other actresses, far more renowned than she was, became mistresses to gentle-

men of the *ton*. It seemed to be perfectly acceptable
in the half-world of the demi-rep, but it was not for
her. Henry Bulford had done more than try to rape
her, he had given her a determination never to be
used by any man for sexual gratification. And that
included Duncan Stanmore.

The trouble was that she liked him; she more
than liked him and it would be so easy to fall in
love with him, so easy to let things take their
course, but it could only lead to disappointment and
sorrow when he took a wife, a wife from the same
background as himself, a wife who knew exactly
who she was and what her antecedents were. Better
to stop now, stop thinking about him, stop yearning
for him.

She entered her dressing room, to find it filled
with flowers and Marianne stripped to her shift and
taking off her make-up. 'From you know who,' she
said, smiling. 'And, there's a package on the table.'

Madeleine picked up the small box Marianne had
indicated and opened it. It contained a brooch,
beautifully crafted in silver filigree studded with
tiny diamonds in the shape of a small bird with an
emerald for its eye. It was so lovely it took her
breath away. But costly presents like that could
only have one meaning. 'Oh, no. Marianne, this has
gone too far.'

'How can you say so? Is it not all part of your
scheme? Am I not supposed to support you in it,

even though I warned you it would all end in tears?'

'And you were right. I do not want him for a lover and I cannot have him for a husband and it is breaking my heart.'

'Oh, my love.' Marianne came and put her arms about her and drew her close. 'Tell me you have not fallen in love with him.'

'I think perhaps I have.'

'You foolish, foolish girl. Now you will just have to fall out of love again.'

'How can I?'

'You must harden your heart. Remember you have a loathing for all aristocrats and keep that in the forefront of your mind.'

'I have been thinking that was very wicked of me. Some noblemen must be good and kind, they cannot all be bad.'

Marianne smiled. 'Then this episode has not been a total disaster. You have learned tolerance and that is a good thing. Now put the Marquis from your mind and hurry up and change. Lancelot will be waiting.'

Lancelot Greatorex was always throwing parties: first night, end of the week, end of a run, last night, a new backer—all warranted celebration and to-night was for the most successful first week he had had in years. Madeleine did not feel like going, but she knew it was expected of her, and it would mean she could turn the Marquis of Risley away with a clear conscious if not a whole heart. What she had not expected when she and Marianne arrived at the nearby assembly rooms was to find that Lancelot had invited others besides the cast to the celebrations and Duncan Stanmore was among them.

He came over to her at once, tall and straight in his dark blue evening coat, and bowed before her. 'Miss Charron.'

'My lord.' She curtsied, keeping her eyes downcast. He was wearing narrow pantaloons, she noticed, with a strap under his shoes, which shone with a valet's care.

'Are you well?'

Was she well? She was trembling as though she had a fever and her legs felt weak, but lovesickness could not be admitted. She lifted her head to face him squarely. He was smiling at her in a way that set her pulses racing faster than ever. His eyes were holding her gaze quite openly, almost as if they were speaking to her, wordless questions, wordless answers. And yet she must answer him. 'Quite well, my lord. And you? Did you suffer any ill effects from your encounter with the footpad?' She was surprised how calmly the words were uttered.

'None at all. Did you?'

'A slight bruise on my side from falling against the wall, nothing of consequence. Do you know if he went to the house in Bow Street?'

'Yes, and was found work at a nearby hostelry, so I believe.'

So he had taken the trouble to check that the man had followed his instructions. 'I think you must have a very trusting nature, my lord.'

'I have almost always found that if you trust people, they are usually trustworthy,' he said.

Her breath caught in her throat and made it difficult to breathe, let alone speak, but she could not stop herself from asking, 'And if they are not?'

'Why then, I do not trust them again. It is as simple as that.'

She fell silent, having no response to that. She had deceived him and he would not forgive her and she was afraid if she pursued the subject he would want to know why she asked and then he would see the guilt written on her face.

'Enough of him,' he said cheerfully. 'I came to congratulate you on your performance tonight. It was, as always, outstanding.'

'You have seen the same play twice now. I wonder you are not bored with it.'

'How could I be bored when you are on stage?' He paused. 'Did you receive the flowers and my little gift?'

'My lord, it is not a little gift.' She found herself whispering in case they were overheard, but Marianne had melted away and there was no one close at hand. Everyone else was crowding round Lancelot Greatorex, who was being exceptionally expansive tonight and holding his listeners in thrall. Madeleine was in a different kind of thrall, like a fly caught in a spider's web and the worst of it was, she had flown into it willingly. 'It is a very costly gift and I cannot accept it.'

'Why not?'

'My lord, do you need to ask?'

'Yes, I do. And will you stop this ''my lord'' nonsense. I am Duncan Stanmore, a perfectly ordinary man.'

'But you are not a perfectly ordinary man, and pretending does not make you one, any more than pretending will make a lady of me.'

'Pretending?'

'That's what you said, wasn't it? That first night when we had supper together. ''Let's pretend, just for tonight, it might be fun.'' '

'Did I?'

'You have forgotten? Or are you only *pretending* to forget?'

'No, I remember. I remember everything.' He took her arm and drew her towards the door. 'Come, we will find somewhere private to talk. I need to find out what all this nonsense is about.'

'There is nothing to talk about,' she said, resisting him, but, short of creating a scene, she could not make him let go of her. He had her arm firmly in his grip and was leading her down the stairs and out of the door to his carriage.

'Get in,' he commanded. 'We will go for a drive.'

'Lord Risley, are you abducting me?' she asked, as he instructed his coachman and climbed in beside her.

'No, but how else am I to find out why you have changed so suddenly?'

'Changed?' she echoed. They were so close in the confines of the coach, she could feel his thigh against her skirts, his breath on her cheek, his hand reaching for hers. And when she risked a glance towards him, she could see, by the intermittent street lights, that he was looking steadily at her, a slightly mocking smile on his face and one of his fine brows lifted quizzically.

'Oh, yes. You are different tonight, cold, as if you have withdrawn yourself from me, as if I had done something wrong, something to anger you. I thought you had forgiven me for allowing that disgraceful display my friends subjected you to.'

'I have.'

'Then this must be some new transgression. Tell me, what have I done?'

'Nothing, my lord.'

'Then why can you not accept my gift?'

'Because it comes too dear.'

'I am the best judge of the price of what I buy.' He spoke sharply, impatient with her for questioning the value of his gift. It had been costly, but he had not wanted to insult her by offering tawdry gewgaws.

'I did not mean that. I meant...' She groped for words. 'I meant too dear for me.' She took a deep breath. 'I, too, would have a price to pay.'

'Oh, I see.' He was silent for a long time. The carriage rolled on through the streets of London, going she knew not where, just as she had no idea how to extricate herself from the bumblebath she was in. When he spoke again, his voice was soft. 'I did not mean to offend you, simply to show you how highly I regard you. I exact no price.'

'Why not? Every other man I have met expects his reward.'

He smiled suddenly. 'And if rumour be true, you have sent them all away disappointed. Why should I expect to be treated differently?'

'But you do, don't you? You think that because you are a marquis and rich enough to afford expensive presents, I will succumb. But I tell you this, my lord, I cannot be bought.'

He let go of her hand and leaned back against the padded seat, utterly deflated by her logic. Was he trying to buy her? For what? To win a shameful wager? He had told himself over and over again to let her go, to stop seeing her, but when Greatorex had invited him to the party tonight, he could not resist accepting, simply to see her again. And having accepted, it was an easy step to buying flowers and a trinket to please her.

'Buy you? Why should I want to buy you? I assure you, if I have need of feminine company I do not need to buy it.'

'Nor do I need to sell myself.'

They were both angry now; he because she had made a stab at his pride, she because, without the shield of anger, she had no defence against him. The tension in the carriage was almost tangible.

'I am sorry,' he said at last. 'I seem to have made a dreadful mull of everything.'

'It is not your fault,' she said. 'You were bred to expect everything to fall into your lap and because for most of the time it does, you are non-plussed when it does not. I am an actress, actresses are fair game; they live for the adoration of their public and if some of that adoration becomes very personal, then who are they to complain? Presents can be useful, if only for the money they fetch, seeing that most of our kind earn very little. I turn your own question back at you, my lord. Why should I expect to be treated differently?'

'Because you are different. You are a lady and should not be an actress at all.'

'But I am one. And you cannot change that.'

'I would if I could. Madeleine…' He leaned towards her and took her hand again. 'I find myself at a stand. If you could only cease to be an actress—'

'But I cannot,' she put in before he could go on. She knew perfectly well what he meant and did not want to hear it. 'How am I to live if I do not work? And do not suggest you will take care of me, or I shall feel obliged to slap your aristocratic face.'

He laughed. 'You said that with such venom, my dear, I am left wondering what has happened to you in the past to warrant it.'

'Nothing.'

'It must have been an aristocrat. Could it have been me?'

'No, my lord. You have always treated me with courtesy, but that does not mean—' She stopped. She could not tell him about Henry Bulford, who had given her a loathing of wealthy young men from what was termed the *haut monde*. She knew there must be exceptions to the general rule that they were filled with self-importance and rode roughshod over anyone they considered beneath them, but she was not yet prepared to concede it.

'Go on,' he said quietly.

She was floundering. 'My lord, I pray you cease to quiz me. It is unfair, since I cannot escape.'

'Cannot escape?'

'I am in your carriage and it is going at a fair pace. I think I might break my neck if I tried to jump out.'

'True,' he said, a slight smile softening the line of his mouth. 'I have taken an unfair advantage. Shall I bid the coachman stop and we can continue this discourse on the pavement?' He turned from her to peer out of the window. 'Though I am not exactly sure where we are and I would not want to risk another adventure like the one we had the other night.'

'You are teasing me.'

'No more than you tease me.'

'I do not,' she protested.

'Oh, yes, you do, my sweet Madeleine. Every word you utter, every flutter of your eyelashes, every quirk of your delicious mouth, teases me. One minute you are sweet and amiable and the next a virago, and I cannot for the life of me understand why.'

She laughed, but it did not sound like a laugh at all, but a cry of anguish. 'Because I am me, my lord. Actresses are known to be temperamental, are they not? They are not constrained like Society ladies always to be cool and distant. They fly into rages and raptures with equal vigour. You must take me as I am.'

'Would that I could,' he said softly.

It was all too much for her. If they continued travelling together in the darkened carriage much longer, her self-control would snap completely and she would fall in a boneless heap on the floor, begging him to love her. 'If you will not stop the coach,' she said, putting on her haughtiest voice, 'please direct your coachman to drive me home. It is too late to return to the party.'

'Very well, if you insist.' He wrapped on the roof. 'Dobson, the lower end of Oxford Street.'

He leaned back in his seat again. Madeleine sat stiffly beside him. They had nothing to say to each other. The silence was oppressive, relieved only by the sound of the horses' hooves and the rumble of the carriage wheels.

When the coach drew up at her door, he jumped out to help her down. She allowed her hand to rest in his for a few moments while she thanked him formally for his escort.

'It was my privilege and pleasure,' he said, still holding her hand. 'And I am sorry.'

'What for?' She was genuinely puzzled.

'Sorry that I have disappointed you. But will you keep the brooch? It was bought with you in mind and I wish you to have it. There is no price to pay. There never was.' He raised the back of her hand to his lips. 'Goodnight, Miss Charron.' And with that he turned on his heel and went back to his carriage.

She stood watching him being carried away, her vision blurred by tears. So much for hardening her heart and making herself fall out of love. She had played with fire and she had been burnt and it was no more than she deserved. She could have told him the truth, there had been opportunity in plenty, but it had suddenly occurred to her, when he mentioned her fictitious grandfather, that if he could not love her as she was, whoever she was, then she did not want him to love her as a count's granddaughter. Love that had conditions was not love at all.

She went into the house and groped her way up the stairs to her room, glad that she had left Marianne at the party. She could not bear anyone to see how she had been humbled.

He loved her. There was no doubt in his mind now, but what to do about it, he did not know. How could he go to his father and tell him that he was to have an actress for a daughter-in-law, that the Loscoe inheritance would go to the offspring of a theatrical performer? The fact that her grandfather had been a French nobleman would hardly count with the Duke, unless she could prove it and was accepted in Society. But how could he go to Madeleine and say, 'Prove it.' He could imagine her reaction. He smiled grimly in the darkness of the coach carrying him homeward. She would slap his aristocratic face.

He went to his club, which he realised, as soon as he entered, was a mistake. Benedict Willoughby and three of his cronies were there, playing cards.

'Ah, the lover returns,' Benedict said, waving a cigar at him. 'We have not seen you in a se'ennight, Stanmore. Are we to infer you have been busy earning your fifty golden boys?'

The others chortled, making Duncan realise the wager had become public knowledge. It infuriated him. 'I have been busy,' he said coldly.

'Oh, yes, we know that. What we want to know is to what purpose? Have you had the lady in your bed yet?'

Duncan clenched his fists, but held himself in check with an effort. 'The bet is off,' he said.

'Off?' Benedict echoed. 'Oh, no, you cannot get out of it that easily. If you have not got the bottom for it, then say so and pay up.'

'Oh, I say, Ben, that's going it too brown,' said one of the others. 'There's another se'ennight to go. Give the man a chance.'

'I do not want a chance,' Duncan said coldly. 'Your disgraceful behaviour at the theatre the other night was the outside of enough. It was despicable. And I do not like being tarred with the same brush.'

'Oh ho, so she was angry, was she?' Benedict laughed.

'Exceedingly. And I do not blame her.'

'And so you are using that as an excuse for giving up on a wager. It is not done, you know, not in proper circles. A wager is a wager. It is like a debt of honour.'

'I would rather pay you than insult the lady a second time. I'll send a banker's draft round in the morning.'

'Insult? Insult? How can it be an insult? You are a man, aren't you, and she is only an actress, after all.'

The only way he could stop himself from hitting the man was to turn on his heel and march out, though he knew perfectly well that his defection would be all round town in twenty-four hours and he would be the butt of a thousand jokes. He prayed Madeleine would not hear of it.

'Duncan, me boy, where are you off to in such a hurry that you cannot acknowledge an old friend?'

Duncan suddenly realised that he had angrily pushed past Sir Percival Ponsonby in his hurry to escape. He stopped. 'Sorry, Sir Percy. I was thinking—'

'Furious thoughts, by the look of you. You have a face like thunder.' Hearing the sound of raucous laughter, he looked into the room past Duncan's shoulder. 'Willoughby and his crowd, is it? It ain't like you to let them get the better of you.'

'Ordinarily they would not, but it is a delicate matter.'

'Ah,' he said, smiling. 'There is a lady in the case. And would I be right in supposing the lady in question is the beautiful Miss Madeleine Charron?'

Duncan looked startled. 'You have heard.'

'I saw you leave the party with her.' He put his arm on Duncan's shoulder. 'Come, m'boy, let us go and find somewhere more amenable and you can tell me all about it.'

Duncan allowed himself to be drawn away from the club and across the street to Boodle's, where Sir Percy was also a member. Having found a couple of comfortable armchairs in the corner of the reception room and ordered two bumpers of brandy, he sat back and observed his young friend over steepled fingers. 'You have got yourself into a coil, am I right?'

'Yes, and thoroughly ashamed I am. I suppose I should have realised Willoughby could not keep his tongue between his teeth. And if Madeleine were to find out...'

'Find out what?'

'That Ben offered odds I could not get her to bed. I have repudiated the whole sordid business but that does not stop him noising it abroad.'

'I cannot see what the problem is. Tell her the truth, she will understand, especially if you have refused to accept it.'

'But I did to begin with and now...'

Percy smiled. 'And now you have developed a real *tendre* for the lady?'

'Yes.' He paused. 'My father wishes me to marry and...'

'Marry then. It does not stop you taking a *fille de joie* and if Miss Charron is agreeable—'

'She is not,' he put in quickly. 'And I do not wish it.'

'My dear fellow, you surely do not mean you wish to marry her?'

'I think perhaps I do.'

'The Duke will never countenance it, you know that.'

'Madeleine is a lady, you have only to look at her to see that. Her grandfather was a French aristocrat. Her father, his son, died in England's cause in the late wars. She should be perfectly acceptable.'

'If such were the case, it might make a difference, but she would still be an actress. She has not lived like a lady.'

'She has not been in a position to, that is not to say she could not. She has had to use what talents she has to make a living.'

'And prodigious talents they are. She is a fine actress, but think of this: if she can make you believe fantasy when she is on stage, who is to say she could not make you believe anything she liked off it?'

'She would not lie. It is not in her nature.'

Sir Percy smiled. His young friend was certainly in the throes of a great emotion and belittling it would only hurt him. 'Perhaps she is not lying,' he said softly. 'Perhaps she believes what she says to be true because someone in the past has told her so, but that does not make it fact.'

'I suppose not,' Duncan said dubiously.

'I believe your best course would be to try and find out the real truth. Do it before you make a cake of yourself.'

'I have already done that,' Duncan said wryly. 'She despises me for being an aristocrat and if she ever hears about that shameful wager, she will despise me even more. I am tempted to renounce my inheritance and run away with her.'

'My dear boy, you must do nothing of the sort. The scandal would only serve to make everyone miserable, your father and the Duchess, your sister and little stepbrother, who all love you dearly. And there are others apart from your family to consider. You have wider responsibilities you cannot shirk.'

'I know.'

'And you would not be happy, you know. What you had done would always prey on your mind and would come between you and your wife. It is better to put honour and duty first. I am sure you do not need me to tell you this.'

'No. I have been over and over it in my mind and told myself again and again I must give her up.'

'Does she know what is in your mind?'

'No, I have not spoken of it.'

'Then, I pray you, do not.'

'But if it is true that she is of noble birth?'

'If it is true.' He paused, watching his young friend, aware that he was on the brink of indiscretion, if not something worse. 'Would you like to find out?'

'Is that possible? Could you?'

'Not me, but perhaps Major Greenaway can.'

Major Donald Greenaway had, since he had been retired on half-pay at the end of the war, supplemented his income by what he called investigation.

He looked for lost relatives, tracked down criminals, recovered stolen goods, and he had connections everywhere, high and low. He had helped the Duke in the past and was a good friend of the Stanmore family and Sir Percy.

'Then ask him, Sir Percy. Arrange for me to see him and then I can tell him as much as I know, though it is very little.'

'Very well. But promise me one thing. Promise me you will do nothing foolish in the meantime.' He smiled encouragingly and beckoned to the waiter to refill their glasses. 'We will drink to success, eh?'

The brandy was drunk and they prepared to leave. Duncan was feeling a little more cheerful now he thought there might be a happy outcome after all. Oh, he knew he still had to convince Madeleine, but when she realised how earnest he was and that he meant nothing short of marriage, she would come round. She had to.

'One other thing,' Sir Percy said, as they parted in the street. 'Try not to be too downpin at home; it will only distress her ladyship. Try and please her.'

Duncan laughed, suddenly light-hearted. 'You know, I do believe you are doing this entirely to protect the Duchess.'

Sir Percy smiled. 'Naturally I am. What else did you expect? Now run along, I will let you know when I have spoken to Major Greenaway.'

He had been dismissed like a schoolboy, but he did not care. There was something to be done and he would throw himself wholeheartedly into the investigation. He would not let himself consider what he would do if it proved fruitless. He would also attend his stepmother's soirée and stay the whole time, not only to please her, but in order to see and speak to Madeleine again.

Two days later, he was riding alone in Hyde Park when he saw Sir Percy and Major Greenaway coming towards him. He smiled to himself when he saw them. The Major had been involved in so many secret assignments that he had developed a disinclination to hold important conversations indoors and nearly always chose the open air for consulting with clients and informers.

He and Sir Percy were riding slowly, apparently deep in conversation, but then Sir Percy appeared suddenly to see Duncan. 'Risley, good day to you,' he said.

'Sir Percy. Major Greenaway.'

'Lord Risley.' The Major acknowledged him with a slight inclination of his head.

All three drew rein and then dismounted to stand in the shade of an oak tree, while their horses cropped the grass. 'Devilish hot today,' Sir Percy said, loosening his cravat. 'I'd as lief be indoors in the cool with a cold drink at my elbow.'

'You may leave us if you wish,' Duncan said.

'No, I want to hear what's said. Interested, don't you know?'

'Has Sir Percy told you anything of the matter?' Duncan asked the Major.

'He has said the lady's name is Madeleine Charron, that she claims to have a French count for a grandfather and that her father was killed in the service of the crown in the last war.'

'That's it in a nutshell.'

'Then let us see if we can crack it open. The *comte*'s name was presumably Charron?'

'I assume so. She has never said anything to the contrary.'

'And her father was an officer?'

'Yes.'

'Regiment and rank?'

'I have no idea.'

'Where was she born? Who was her mother? Where were they living when her mother died?'

'I don't know that either. She told me she was put into an orphanage for officers' children when her mother was killed. She was nine years old at the time.'

'And how old is she now?'

Duncan shrugged. 'Three and twenty, perhaps four and twenty. I never asked.'

'It's not much to go on, is it?' He was looking at Duncan quizzically, as if he could not quite believe what he was being asked to do.

'I suppose not.'

'Perhaps you could endeavour to find out more from the lady herself and let me know.'

'I'll try, but I do not want to alert her to what I am doing.'

'Why not? Does she not wish to know her own history?'

'She will think it an impertinence.'

'Perhaps Marianne can throw some light on the subject,' Sir Percy said.

'Ah, the redoubtable Miss Doubleday,' Donald said, smiling at the memory. 'I collect she was the one who pretended to be Lady Rattenshaw and brought that rakehell Wincote to book. A formidable lady. If you think she can help, then ask her.'

'But she must not breathe a word to Madeleine,' Duncan said. 'I will tell her myself when we have something to report.'

'And do you think she will thank you?' Sir Percy asked.

'If it means she can take her place in Society where she belongs, then of course she will,' he said, unaware of the lack of conviction in his voice.

They drew a little apart and remounted. He bade the two men goodbye and turned his horse to gallop across the grass away from the formal ride. He had had little exercise just recently and he needed to feel the wind on his face. Riding was an exercise he enjoyed above all other and he wondered if Madeleine rode. Somehow he doubted it, but when she had taken her place in Society he would enjoy teaching her. In the meantime he could look forward to seeing her again at his stepmother's soirée. He would see how she managed in the company of the Duchess's friends. He had no doubt she would acquit herself commendably.

Chapter Five

The long line of vehicles waiting to deposit their occupants at the door of Stanmore House was enough to make Madeleine want to turn tail and run. She had never felt so nervous in her life. It was all very well for Marianne to tell her it was no different from giving a performance on stage and she had done that thousands of times but she could not quite believe her.

For a start, she would not be separated from the audience by footlights, so that she could not see them properly; she would be almost face to face with them, her costume, her every gesture scrutinised and commented on. Secondly, and that concerned her most, Duncan Stanmore would be in the audience, in his own home, on his own territory, so to speak, and that gave him a tremendous advantage.

'It is what you wanted, isn't it?' Marianne demanded, as their cab waited in line with all the others. 'You asked to come, prodded me in the back and as good as forced me to have you included in the invitation. You wanted to study the *haut monde*, to see if you could act the lady and now's your chance. When the performance is over, we shall be invited to mingle with the guests. The Duchess is like that, very gracious.'

'And if she asks about my family?'

'Oh, well, that is up to you,' Marianne said. 'You have your story off by heart, haven't you? Or you could tell the truth for once.'

Madeleine did not answer. What answer could she give? She knew her friend was right. A play lasted a few weeks, no more, but she had contemplated playing the part of a *comte*'s granddaughter for the rest of her life. If she had not fallen in love with the Marquis of Risley, it would have been easy; she could have stuck with her plan to use him as an entry to Society, a way of meeting others of the *ton*, to be accepted as one of their number. Now she was not interested in any others. He believed she came from a good family, a pretence it would be impossible to keep up for any length of time.

The truth would come out and then whatever good opinion he might have had of her would be blown away on the storm of his anger. But she was angry too, angry to think that it was so important to him that she should be well born. The granddaughter of a French nobleman might be acceptable but little Miss Charron, a lowly dressmaker's daughter, meant nothing at all to him. He was as bad as Count Roussillon in *All's Well That Ends Well*, too full of his own importance.

'Hoist on my own petard,' she murmured, as they drew up at the door.

There was no time for Marianne to comment, which was as well, for Maddy knew her friend would probably have something pithy to say to the effect that she had warned her. They stepped from the cab and followed the long line of other guests up to the front door. On giving their names, the footman beckoned another servant and directed him to conduct them to an anteroom on the first floor where they could prepare for their performance.

They could hear music playing and the sound of conversation and laughter coming from a room nearby, and every now and again the stentorian voice of a footman announcing newcomers; judging by his booming voice, most of them came from the ranks of the titled. It did nothing to calm Madeleine's nerves.

Madeleine was delving in the hamper that contained their costumes and props when the Duchess arrived. She smiled with genuine warmth. 'Oh, good, your things have arrived.'

Madeleine hurriedly straightened up and curtsied. 'Your Grace.'

Marianne, who was standing in her drawers and chemise, tried to follow suit but she looked so incongruous the Duchess laughed. 'Oh, do not mind me, Miss Doubleday. I only came to ask if there is anything else you need? I have had a plain back-cloth set up as you requested.'

'Thank you. I think we have all we need.'

'Word has gone out that you are going to per-form for us,' the Duchess went on. 'I do not think we could squeeze another body in if we tried. And so many gentlemen! That is good, for they will be generous and the orphanage will benefit. There will be a little music first, to set the mood, and then I will announce you. Is there anything special I should say?'

'No, my lady, except to name the play and the scene.' She scrabbled about for her reticule, which she had put down among the costumes. 'I have it written down here for you.' She found the piece of paper and handed it to the Duchess. 'It is from *The Rivals.*'

'There will be refreshments after the entertain-ment,' the Duchess said. 'I shall be delighted if you would join my guests. I am sure everyone will wish to ask questions about your work. I hope you will not find such enquiries too impertinent.'

'Not at all, your Grace.' It was Marianne who answered because Madeleine was suddenly con-fronted with the reality of what she had done and what she might yet do. It was happening. What she had hoped for, what she had planned, was actually happening and she was filled with foreboding.

'I will leave you to finish your preparations,' the Duchess said.

'Come on, Maddy,' Marianne said, as soon as their hostess had gone. 'Stop dreaming and start dressing, or we shall not be ready. I can hear the orchestra beginning the music.'

Madeleine pulled herself together and dressed in the heavy hooped brocade court dress of fifty years before, made up her face with a great deal of powder and rouge, added a couple of heart-shaped patches and donned the mountainous white powdered wig that was so heavy she was almost bowed down by it. She was growing more and more nervous but when a footman finally came to fetch them she took a deep breath and followed Marianne into the ballroom, which had been set out with chairs like a small theatre. They were received by a round of applause, which was stopped by a drum roll. The Duchess rose from her seat on the front row to introduce Marianne as Mrs Malaprop and Madeleine as Lydia Languish in a scene from Sheridan's famous play.

Once she was into her part, Madeleine's nerves disappeared and she forgot her audience. This was what she did best, this was her life and work and whatever had been going on in her head a few minutes before was banished. It was the same for Marianne, they were a perfect foil for each other and the enthusiastic applause at the end bore witness to that.

'There, it was easy, wasn't it?' Marianne said as they returned to the anteroom to change out of costume and into ordinary evening dress.

'Yes, but the words were already written and I had rehearsed them, what comes next is what terrifies me.'

'What comes next is entirely up to you.'

'You think I should deny the French *comte*?'

'Yes, I do.' She paused in the act of stripping off her costume. 'Maddy, it is much better for you to be noted for your acting than for a hoax that will undoubtedly go wrong and ruin your reputation into the bargain. Now, if you are going to join the guests, do hurry and dress.'

They helped each other into their gowns. Madeleine had chosen a pale azure gauze over a light green silk underskirt. It had a low round neckline and short puffed sleeves, padded to make them stand out, and a wide dark green sash, tied at the back in an enormous bow. Its skirt stopped short of her ankles, showing white clocked stockings and green satin pumps. White elbow-length kid gloves covered her arms. She wore no necklace, but put Duncan's eardrops in her ears. She brushed out her hair and pulled it on top of her head, securing it with combs, so that curls cascaded about her ears.

'Lovely,' Marianne said, looking her over. 'What about me?'

Madeleine looked at her friend with her head on one side. Marianne was in rose pink and white striped satin with a matching feather head-dress. She had a necklace of rubies, which Sir Percy had given her years before. 'Regal,' Maddy said.

They left the anteroom arm in arm and made their way back to the ballroom. The rows of chairs had been placed at the side of the room and the guests were milling about, talking animatedly. Duncan, in an evening suit of dark blue superfine, saw them enter and hurried over to them.

'Miss Doubleday, Miss Charron.' He bowed and they curtsied.

'My lord,' they said in unison.

'Do come and meet everyone.'

With one on each side of him, he led them forward and before she knew where she was, Madeleine was standing before the Duke and Duchess and Marianne had disappeared. 'Sir,' Duncan said, addressing his father. 'Mama has already met Miss Charron, but may I present her to you.'

Madeleine could see where Duncan's good looks came from; the Duke was a very handsome man. He was tall and upright; his almost black hair had a few streaks of silver at the temples and his dark eyes were full of humour, as if he found life very pleasant. But then why would he not, considering his wealth and position?

'Miss Charron.' He inclined his head towards her.

'Your Grace.' She found herself dropping into a full curtsy, something she had sworn never to do, but somehow she could not help herself. He seemed to command that courtesy without being in the least stiff-rumped.

'I congratulate you on your performance,' he went on, as she straightened and faced him. 'I have seen you act often in the theatre, of course, but never so close.'

'Thank you, your Grace, you are very kind.'

'It must be difficult being right on top of your audience like that,' the Duchess said. 'Not like being on the stage at all.'

'It was rather daunting,' she admitted. 'But once I am into a part, I find myself so absorbed I am hardly aware of people watching me.' She smiled suddenly. 'Though in the theatre if people start to hiss or throw things on the stage, I am soon made aware of them.'

'That was not likely to happen tonight.'

'No, your Grace, your guests are all gentlemen and ladies.' She looked pointedly at Duncan as she spoke.

He laughed. 'Mama, Miss Charron is referring to Willoughby and Scott-Smythe, who barracked and threw orange peel on to the stage the other night.'

'How very uncivil,' Frances said. 'I wonder they dare call themselves gentlemen.' She paused, turning to her husband. 'Miss Charron is of French extraction, Marcus, the granddaughter of a *comte*. Her family were forced to flee the Terror and made their home in England.'

'Is that so?' The Duke looked at Madeleine carefully as if considering the veracity of the statement,
making her squirm inwardly. She wished the polished floor would open up and swallow her. Any
minute now she would be exposed and she dreaded
Duncan's reaction. It would not only be the end of
her hopes for a life in Society, it would be the end
of her career as an actress.

'I have no way of verifying the truth of it, your
Grace,' she said, weighing her words carefully.
'My grandfather died soon after I was born, I never
met him.'

'And your father?'

'I do not remember him either. He was in the
army and was killed in the war. My earliest recollection is of living with my mother in London.'

'Miss Charron became an actress after her
mother was killed in a street accident,' Duncan put
in. Madeleine was unsure whether he had forgotten
about the orphanage or whether he had deliberately
left out that part of her story, but she decided not
to remind him.

'Have you no other relatives?' the Duchess
asked. 'No uncles or aunts to whom you might have
applied?'

Madeleine looked at the Duchess, wondering if
her ladyship was probing deliberately, but her expression was kind; there was no malice behind it.
How could she go on lying in the face of that? She
was tired of the pretence, but if she retracted what

she had said, she would be damning herself as a liar. 'None that I know of, my lady. Certainly none came forward when my mother died. Sometimes I wonder if the whole story might be a myth and best left in mystery.'

She heard Duncan draw in his breath beside her, but he did not speak. Oh, if only she could run away!

'You are probably right,' the Duchess went on. 'The past often clouds the present and it is better to concentrate on what is happening here and now.'

'Yes, but if Miss Charron should wish to marry, it would surely have some bearing on her choice of husband,' Duncan put in.

Both the Duke and Duchess looked sharply at him, then the Duchess smiled. 'I suppose it would depend on the man she chose. For my part, I think the person we are now is more important than where we have come from. I have met scoundrels in the ranks of the nobility as well as among the lower orders.'

Oh, bless you, dear Duchess, Madeleine thought, but do you really know what you are saying? 'I have no immediate plans to marry,' she said quietly.

'For my part I am glad to hear it,' said the Duke, smiling. 'Then we shall not lose one of our most consummate actresses to domesticity just yet.' He paused. 'Duncan, I can see a whole congregation of young men waiting to meet Miss Charron. We must not keep her all to ourselves.' He bowed to her. 'I hope you enjoy the rest of the evening.'

'Thank you, my lord.' Another curtsy and the interview was at an end.

'There, that wasn't so bad, was it?' Duncan said as he led her towards a throng of young men, all eager to make her acquaintance.

'No,' she said, though she was still quaking with the enormity of her duplicity. She had not exactly lied, but she had not denied the story either and it was clear that both the Duke and Duchess were inclined to believe it.

Somehow she managed to put it to one side and smile as she was introduced to several young men of Duncan's acquaintance, men who would not normally attend one of the Duchess's soirées, but who had been unable to resist coming to meet her. At least that was what Duncan whispered to her. She put on her brightest smile.

Soon she was being besieged by questions about how she came to be an actress and the parts she had played, all of which were easy to answer. And then Benedict Willoughby sent her heart into her shoes again when he suddenly asked, 'Is it true, your grandpapa was a French aristo?'

She took a deep breath. 'It was the story I was told when I was a little girl. I have no way of proving it.'

'You were born and raised in England though?'

'Yes, naturally I was.'

'Oh, where?' queried another.

Madeleine was stumped. She searched her mind for a place which was not too well known, nor too isolated, knowing whatever she said someone was sure to have visited it or knew everyone of consequence who lived there. It was easier to tell the truth and so she repeated what she had told the Duke, that she did not remember her grandfather and had been brought up by her mother in London.

'And your father?' someone else asked. It was clear the story of her past was intriguing them.

'He died in the war.'

'On whose side, I wonder?' Benedict murmured.

'On ours, you ninny,' Duncan put in, before she could answer. 'But I do not think we should quiz Miss Charron about her family, it must be painful for her. Do speak of other things. Do you not agree her performance tonight was excellent?'

There was murmur of agreement and the conversation turned to how she approached each role and how she learned her lines and she began to relax. She was in the middle of explaining something of the routine of the theatre when she became aware that other people had joined the group.

'Stanmore, good evening,' said a voice that sent her whirling back through the years and took her breath away. She stopped speaking, unable to go on, unable to move, caught like a terrified rabbit in a trap.

'Miss Charron, may I present Lord Bulford,' Duncan said.

Slowly she forced herself to turn and face Henry and inclined her head, no more. She would have refused to address him by his title, even if her voice had not been snatched from her.

'Delighted to meet you,' he said, his eyes roaming over her, but she realised quite suddenly that his appraisal was that of a man for a pretty woman; he had not recognised her.

'You are too kind,' she murmured, concealing her shaking hands in the folds of her skirt and preventing him from taking one of them. The last thing she wanted was for him to touch her.

'May I present my wife, Lady Bulford.' She was taller than he was, and gaunt, with a long nose and very dark eyes. They seemed to burn into Madeleine, though, as far as she was aware, they had never met before. Did Lady Bulford know about her husband's proclivity towards young servant girls? she wondered, as she acknowledged the woman without speaking.

'And this is my sister, Miss Annabel Bulford,' Henry went on. 'She saw you in *Romeo and Juliet* and has been anxious to meet you ever since.'

'Really?' was the only word Madeleine managed to utter. She knew perfectly well who the girl was. When Annabel was small she had often run away from her governess and come to the kitchen, begging sweetmeats. Being the younger of the two girls she had been thoroughly spoiled, but there was no malice in her.

'Oh, yes,' the girl said breathlessly. 'I was enthralled by it. It was as if I were part of the play, as if I knew you well...'

'Oh, that is all part of the illusion,' Madeleine said quickly. 'I am flattered.'

Lady Bulford tugged on her husband's arm. 'My lord, I think we should move on, we cannot spend all our time talking to *performers*. It will be commented upon.'

As they drifted away, Madeleine heard Henry say, 'My dear, don't you think that was a trifle rude?'

'Not at all. She is only a common actress, for goodness' sake. I cannot think what Fanny Stanmore is thinking of, allowing her to mix with her guests.'

'She is the granddaughter of a *comte*, Dorothy.'

'Only a French one and what is that to the point? She is still an actress...'

Annabel, who had not left with them, had heard her sister-in-law. 'Oh dear, I am so sorry,' she said. She was standing so close to Duncan, she might have been glued to his side.

'There is nothing to apologise for,' Madeleine said, glad that Annabel Bulford had not recognised her. 'You are not at fault.'

'You shall be my friend,' Annabel said. 'The Duchess accepts you and that is good enough for me. May I call on you?'

Madeleine thought about the simple lodgings in Oxford Street and tried to imagine the young lady drawing up in her carriage and found herself smiling. 'Perhaps one day,' she said. 'But you see, actresses keep very strange hours; they sleep most of the day and work all evening. But you are welcome to come backstage next time you come to the theatre.'

'I should like that above everything,' she said. 'But I know Henry would not allow it.' She smiled at Duncan. 'Perhaps his lordship could contrive it?'

He bowed his assent and they continued a desultory conversation, animated on Annabel's part, polite on Duncan's and almost monosyllabic on Madeleine's. She caught sight of Marianne looking at her and tried to convey, with her eyes alone, that she needed rescuing, but Marianne simply smiled and carried on her conversation with Sir Percy and the Duchess.

Duncan wished Miss Bulford would go and find someone else to talk to. He badly wanted to speak to Madeleine on her own. He had told Major Greenaway that he would try and find out more about her family, but she had already endured the questioning of his father and his friends and he was reluctant to pursue the subject. But why had she suddenly said the story of the *comte* might be a myth? What was she afraid of?

He considered excusing himself, but he could not drag himself away from Madeleine in case she let slip something of importance and he missed it. Instead he took both the ladies into the dining room for refreshments, after which they returned to the ballroom to promenade the room, subjected to an indifferent pianist and a terrible screeching soprano. He endured Annabel's chatter, answered politely, and smiled at others who came to bid him good evening and make the acquaintance of Miss Charron. He was perfectly aware that they viewed her as an oddity, a supposed gentlewoman turned actress, whom they would never have acknowledged but for the fact that she had spent ten minutes talking to the Duke and Duchess.

He was relieved when everyone started drifting away and Henry Bulford came to claim his sister and take her home. Once the goodbyes had been said, he turned to Madeleine. 'May I escort you home?'

'No, thank you, my lord. I came with Miss Doubleday and shall go home with her. The Duchess has arranged for her carriage to take us.'

'Very well, I will see you safely to it.'

She laid her hand upon his arm and together they left the ballroom. The Duke and Duchess stood together at the door, saying goodbye to the last of their guests and Madeleine went to curtsy to them.

'Thank you for asking me, your Grace,' she said, addressing the Duchess.

'Not at all, Miss Charron. It is I who should thank you. I think we have made more money than ever before and that will be a great help to the orphans. There are so many of them, you know, and we need to acquire more premises.'

'I am very glad if I have helped.' Uttering a prayer of thanksgiving that she had come through the evening relatively unscathed, she walked beside Duncan out to the street, where the Loscoe carriage stood waiting with Marianne already seated in it.

'You are not expected to work on Sunday, are you?' Duncan asked, as he handed Madeleine up.

She smiled. 'No, even actresses have a rest day.'

'Then will you come for a carriage ride in the Park with me on Sunday afternoon?'

She should have said no, she knew it, even if she had not seen Marianne's warning look, but she just could not resist. To ride out in daylight with the Marquis of Risley would be a great feather in her cap. After all, it was what she had been working towards most of her life, wasn't it? And perhaps she would be able to pluck up the courage to tell him the truth.

'I shall be delighted,' she said.

He kissed the back of her hand. 'I shall call for you at two o'clock if that is convenient.'

'Quite convenient.'

He released her hand and shut the door. 'Until then.'

'You are playing with fire, you know that, don't you?' Marianne said, as the coach carried them away.

'I know.'

'Sir Percy thinks you would be wise to try and found out about your true parentage.'

'Why?'

'I suppose he thought the devil you know…'

'But I do know. I am the daughter of a common soldier and a lowly seamstress, and if the tattlers at my mother's funeral are to be believed, not even born in wedlock. Without the French *comte*, I am nothing.'

'You are one of the finest actresses to be seen on the stage for the last thirty years. Remember that.'

Why was she so confused? Until she had met the Marquis of Risley, she had been reasonably content. Her ambition to be a somebody rather than a nobody had smouldered in the background of her life, there, but not there. She hardly thought about it, but if she did, it was in relation to her success as an actress. Duncan Stanmore had fanned it back into life, made a fire of it, and conversely it was Duncan Stanmore who had made her see herself as she really was: envious, revengeful, a fantasiser, a liar.

But it was so difficult to let go of the lies that had sustained her for so long. They had breathed life into her when she almost died of starvation. They had made her into an actress, able to play many parts. In the end she had almost come to believe them herself and they had restored her pride in herself. Without them who was she? Was Sir Percy right? Ought she to delve into her past before that dreadful night when Henry Bulford had changed her life? Was she afraid of the truth?

But even if she did, where should she start? The orphanage seemed the obvious place. She hardly expected anyone who had known her still to be there, but they might have kept records. If the home was specifically for soldiers' children, wouldn't they have required evidence that she qualified?

She did not sleep that night, so it was not difficult to rise early the next morning and set off for Monmouth Street. It was over twelve years since she had left the orphanage and her memory of the place was flawed by strange memories, memories of misery so deep, so overwhelming, she had not been aware of her surroundings, nor even of who it was who had taken her there. A rough hand on her arm and a voice that was not unkind, but was certainly nothing like her mother's, had told her she would be looked after and not to be afraid.

It was the interior she remembered, simply because she had spent three years there, long enough for the layout and the fabric of the place to imprint itself into her very soul. She could see it clearly: the long narrow dormitory made from two rooms knocked into one, where she had cried herself to sleep night after night; the dining room where they had gruel for breakfast, a wholesome but uninspired dinner in the middle of the day and bread and dripping for tea; the kitchen where she had done her share of the chores. They were not starved, nor even treated with deliberate cruelty, but the real love was lacking, the affection that could have made it into a home. Even so, compared with Number 7 Bedford Row, it had been a haven.

But where was it? She found Monmouth Street easily enough; it was a street lined with second-hand shops and pawn shops, but she could not see anything that reminded her of the orphanage. She stopped to ask an old hag, who sat on a doorstep smoking a clay pipe.

'Oh, that be gone,' the old woman said, squinting up at her over the bowl of the pipe.

'Gone? You mean pulled down?'

'That I do. Years ago. Six or seven, I reckon.'

Madeleine was stumped. 'What happened to all the children?'

'I heard tell they went to a new place...'

'Where?'

'Now, my memory ain't what it was...' She looked slyly up at her questioner from small black eyes.

Madeleine scrabbled in her reticule and took out a small handful of coins, which she dropped into the woman's lap. 'Perhaps this will refresh your memory.'

'Oh, aye, I do remember now. They moved to Maiden Lane, lock, stock and barrel. It were just after that poor woman got murdered…'

But Madeleine was not listening, she was hurrying away to Maiden Lane, wondering if she was on a wild goose chase. It was unlikely, after seven years, that any of the women who had run the place would still be there and surely no records would have been kept that long? But having set out with the intention of making enquiries, she decided she might as well continue.

She was not prepared for the sight that met her when she finally arrived. It was not only a huge house, it was newly painted, with gleaming windows and a polished knocker on the door. Beside it was a brass plate which simply said Corringham Academy. But what stopped her in her tracks was the carriage standing at the door. She had ridden in that carriage only a few hours previously. It belonged to the Duchess of Loscoe.

This was the Duchess's orphanage, this was where her charitable money was spent. She had been told it was in Maiden Lane, but at the time had felt only relief that it was not Monmouth Street. Now, she was in a most dreadful coil. She could not go in, could not even be seen lurking in the vicinity, could not go on with her enquiries. And the orphanage had been her only hope. She turned and hurried away.

In the next two days, she changed her mind about going for the carriage ride with the Marquis a dozen times. She felt ashamed to face him. And yet nothing had changed. Her story had not been disproved and probably never could be, so why should she not go? Why should she not milk her connection with the Stanmore family, for all it was worth? Because it was dishonest, she told herself, because, sooner or later, someone or something would trip her up and she would damn herself. Most of all because she had fallen in love with Duncan Stanmore.

When his carriage arrived outside her lodgings promptly at one o'clock on Sunday, she was in her room, half dressed, still undecided. 'Tell him I'm not coming,' she said, when Marianne came to tell her he was waiting for her. 'Tell him I am unwell.'

'I will not. That's the coward's way out. You cannot put off telling him the truth by refusing to see him; he will know something is wrong and if I know him he will not give up until he has wormed it out of you. You might as well go with him and get it over with.'

Reluctantly Madeleine agreed and, while Marianne went downstairs to tell Duncan she was on her way, she finished dressing in a green taffeta carriage dress with cape-style sloping shoulders and full sleeves. She perched a high crowned hat on her curls, slipped her feet into kid shoes and, taking a huge breath to calm herself, went down to meet her fate.

He was standing in the hallway and looked up as she slowly descended the stairs. Every time he saw her, she seemed more lovely. Her clothes were not gaudy or spectacular, but she had a way of wearing them that made her stand out from the crowd, though her figure was slight. Regal was a word that came to his mind. But she was very pale and he wondered if she had slept. He smiled and, as she reached the bottom step, held out his hand. 'Miss Charron.'

'My lord.' She took his hand and looked down into his face and was almost lost in the depth of his brown eyes. She could not look away and for what seemed an age, his eyes held hers, turning her insides to palpitating jelly. It was as if he could read her mind and knew the confusion that beset her, fear and pride jumbled up into a knot that was almost a physical pain in her chest. She forced herself to take the last step and the moment was broken.

'I am sorry I kept you waiting,' she said, forcing a smile.

'It is of no consequence. I was so eager for our outing, I arrived early,' he said gallantly. 'Shall we go?'

He led her out to his curricle. There was no room in the small open carriage for more than two and she realised he was going to drive them himself. It was both intimate and very public. Is that what he intended? He handed her up and jumped up lightly beside her and picked up the reins.

It was a hot day, the sky an almost unbroken blue, and everywhere people were out, enjoying the sunshine, young bloods, families, children, beggars and other more unsavoury characters. Oxford Street was almost as crowded as on a weekday, and the park, when they entered it, was full of vehicles of every kind, as well as riders and pedestrians. He was concentrating on tooling the carriage and had little to say, for which Madeleine gave thanks, though she knew it could not last.

This, she realised, was what she had been scheming for, this ride where she could be seen sitting beside the most eligible bachelor in the land, smiling and bowing this way and that to acquaintances. She was in no doubt that it was his presence beside her which made people bow acknowledgement from their own carriages, or wave in greeting. But instead of enjoying it, she was numb with misery.

'You are silent,' he said, expertly avoiding a phaeton coming in the opposite direction. 'What are you thinking of?'

She smiled. 'I was thinking how well you handle the ribbons. Several times I have thought there would be a coming together, but you managed to avoid it without the least trouble.'

'Are you afraid?'

'In your company, my lord, how could I be?'

He grinned. 'Thank you, my lady.'

She was startled. 'Why did you call me that? I am not a lady.'

'Of course you are.' He did not go on because they had come abreast of Lord Bulford with his wife and both his sisters in an open carriage and he was obliged to draw up.

'Good afternoon, Stanmore,' Bulford said. Then to Madeleine, 'Miss Charron.'

She smiled thinly but did not speak, as if afraid her voice would give her away.

'Miss Charron, how nice to see you again,' Annabel said, then to her sister, 'Hortense, may I present Miss Madeleine Charron?'

'Miss Charron,' Hortense murmured, looking Madeleine up and down, making her squirm inwardly. Hortense was older than Annabel by four years. She had not often come to the kitchen when Madeleine worked at her home, but she remembered one occasion when Hortense had summoned her to her bedchamber to complain that her washing water was cold. Maddy had had the temerity to say that it had been hot when it had been brought up and if it had been left standing, it was bound to cool down. Hortense had yelled at her, threatening to sack her, but as she had no power to do so, Madeleine had survived until the encounter with Henry.

Now, afraid she might be recognised, she was inclined to shrink back in her seat, but her pride came to the fore and she sat up and looked straight at the woman, almost defying her. 'Miss Bulford, how do you do?' she said amiably.

'I feel we have met before,' Hortense said.

'That's just what I said,' Annabel said. 'But I think it can only be that I have seen her on the stage.'

'On the stage?' The expression on the woman's face was comical. It was a mixture of surprise, scorn and disgust. 'You are a play actor?'

Madeleine heard Duncan chuckle beside her and his low voice, which held a note of warning, said, 'Miss Charron is an actress and a very fine one, but that does not mean she is not a lady.'

'Henry, tell the coachman to drive on at once,' the lady said. 'We are blocking the carriageway.'

They were gone in a moment and Madeleine turned to see Duncan laughing. 'It is not funny, my lord.'

'Oh, but it is. Miss Bulford was so stiff-rumped, it was good to see her taken down.'

'I think perhaps you should not be seen out with me.'

'Why ever not?'

'I am making you a laughing stock.'

'Oh, no, my dear, I am to be envied. There isn't a young buck in town that would not willingly change places with me now.'

'Is that why you asked me to come, so that you might boast of it to your friends?'

He had almost forgotten that wager with Benedict and her question had come so close to what might, two weeks before, have been the truth, that he did not immediately answer. Guilt and shame flooded over him. Benedict had not believed his half-hearted attempt to cancel the wager and he should have sought him out to admit his failure and pay him. But that would mean Benedict himself would make the attempt. He could not let that happen.

'No,' he said. 'What I mean is that it was not my intention. Madeleine, shall we walk in the shade of the trees? It is easier to talk when I do not have to concentrate on driving.' He did not wait for her to answer, but drove on a little farther where there was space to pull up without blocking the carriage-way. He jumped down, threw the reins over the rails and turned to help her down.

They had been walking for several yards before he spoke. 'Madeleine, this cannot go on.'

'What cannot go on, my lord? The ride? The Marquis of Risley taking an actress in his carriage?'

'You do not have to be an actress.'

'No, but that is what I am. It is how I earn my living.'

'I could change that.'

'Why do you want to change it?' She turned to look up at him, trying to read his motives in his eyes, but he was staring into the distance as if trying to see into the future. 'If you are ashamed to be seen with me, why did you ask me out?'

'Because I want to be with you every hour of every day and—'

'I will not become your paramour, Lord Risley. I do not know why it is that everyone thinks that all actresses are harlots.'

'Madeleine, how can you accuse me of that?'

'That's what you have in mind, is it not? That is what the flowers and the presents have been all about, to get into my bed. Deny it if you can.'

'I do deny it.' She was so near the truth and yet he had to convince her that his intentions had changed. 'My feelings for you go deeper than that, far deeper.'

She was so startled, she almost stumbled and he put out a hand to steady her. Pulling herself together, she forced a cracked laugh. 'The intention is the same.'

'No.'

'You are content with friendship? If so, you have overpaid me.' She was taunting him, she knew it, and soon she would make him very angry, and yet she could not help herself. She needed something to hold on to, something to keep her sane, and if tormenting herself and him was the only way, then she would endure it, welcome it even.

They had stopped walking and he pulled her roughly round to face him. 'It is not friendship I need and you know it. I am not the kind of man for wanton dalliance. When I say I am in love then I mean it.'

She could hardly breathe. 'How can you say that? You know nothing about me. My past is open to conjecture, my present is unacceptable to Polite Society.'

He recognised the truth of that; Hortense Bulford had demonstrated it plainly enough. 'What about the French *comte*?'

'You think he is important?'

'To me, no, but to a Society based on rank and position, he is.' He paused, watching her face. She was pale and her violet eyes had darkened with anger. And yet there was a great sadness mirrored there too. He was at a loss to know how to make her understand. 'Madeleine, if we could only give him some substance, bring him to life, as it were, it would make all the difference. You could take your rightful place in Society.'

'My rightful place is exactly where it is,' she said furiously. 'In the theatre, as an actress. If you cannot accept that, then I am sorry.'

'Why are you so stubborn? Are you afraid of what you might uncover?'

'There is nothing to uncover. Do you think I have not tried?'

'I could try. I know people—'

'Don't you dare! I will not be investigated like a thief and a liar.'

'That isn't what I meant, and you know it. I only want to help.'

'I do not need your help, my lord. I am grateful for your interest but there is nothing to be gained by it.' She took a huge breath and forced herself to continue, to close the door for ever on what could never be, to shut him out of her life. 'I thought I would enjoy being accepted by Society, it is the only reason I went to Stanmore House, the only reason I agreed to come out with you today, to be seen riding in your carriage, to be noticed. It was fun while it lasted, but it is over now. I know it can never be more than pretence.'

'You have been using me?' he demanded. A dark flush stained his cheek and his eyes blazed.

She knew she had gone too far, but she could not retract. 'Yes,' she said. 'It brings more people into the theatre and I have an arrangement with the management—'

'You scheming little hussy! And here was I prepared to sacrifice everything for you, my inheritance, my family, even my good name. What a fool I have been!'

'Yes, my lord,' she said quietly. 'We have both been fools.'

Taken aback by the sadness in her voice, he seized her face between his hands and forced her to look at him. She stared at him, opening her eyes wide to prevent them filling with tears. Neither spoke. Suddenly he lowered his head to kiss her. It was an angry bruising kiss meant to hurt. She struggled ineffectually and then gave up. She deserved his wrath and if being kissed by him was her punishment, then she accepted it gladly.

He was the one to break away. She had not resisted, had not tried to push him away. She was not even angry. She was nothing more than a barque of frailty, after all, paying in kisses for an hour or two of a gentleman's company. He was disgusted with himself for playing her game and yet her lips had tasted sweet and fresh, stirring a desire in his loins he could not control. He was suddenly reminded of the wager that had started it all, a wager still unpaid. 'So, you are not averse to a little dalliance, after all,' he said bitterly. 'I should have known an actress as accomplished as you are would have subtler ways of trapping a man than a common whore.'

His answer was a sudden and violent slap to his face that rocked his head back. Then she marched back to the curricle and, without waiting for him to help her up, clambered into her seat and sat waiting for him to take her home.

He followed more slowly, jumped up beside her and turned the carriage round. He would not go

back along the crowded carriageway, where everyone would see her stony looks and the red mark on
his face and would draw their own conclusions. He
left the park by the Serpentine and out of the
Lancaster Gate on to the Bayswater Road. Neither
spoke.

They were nearly at her lodgings when he said,
'That was unforgivable of me. I am deeply sorry.'

'And I am sorry I could not be what you wanted
me to be, my lord.'

He pulled the curricle up at her door and jumped
down to hand her out. 'Madeleine…'

'My lord, there is nothing more to say.' She
broke away from him and ran into the house, slam-
ming the door behind her. And only then did she
allow herself the comfort of tears, hot scalding tears
that ran down her face unchecked, tears for lost
dreams, for a life that could never be.

Chapter Six

It was only her professionalism that kept Madeleine going in the days that followed. She played the part of Helena, scheming to get the Count of Roussillon in her bed and so make him love her, while all the time her heart was breaking for love of the Marquis of Risley. She knew perfectly well she had deliberately goaded him into saying the things he had because she could not accept the truth, that he might love her for herself alone. Had he really been prepared to give up his standing in Society for a woman who was nothing but a sham, a liar? She could not let him do that. Better to make him dislike her. Better to hold him in aversion. But she could not.

She found herself looking for him in the audience every night, but he did not come. She listened to the gossip among the girls who surrounded her, hoping to hear him mentioned; she read the Society columns of the newspapers, looking for his name. It was there, of course; the doings of London's most eligible bachelor were always news. He had escorted Miss Annabel Bulford to the come-out ball of Miss Elizabeth Tremayne and stood up with both ladies twice; he had attended the opening of an art exhibition in the company of his stepmother, herself a noted painter; he had been an honoured guest at the wedding of Miss Martha Hartwood to the Earl of Bentley. His racehorse had won at Newmarket but the odds were so short it was hardly worth putting a wager on it.

He had gone back to his life before he met her, doing the things he had always done, secure among family and friends, wealthy and confident. On the surface she had done the same, returned to her life in the theatre: on stage every evening; rehearsing and sleeping most of the morning; going to suppers and routs after the performances. Some of the invitations came from the edges of the *haut monde* who had heard the story of the *comte* and had decided she was acceptable in Society. She should have been triumphant, but, unable to keep up the pretence, she rarely went.

She was loved in a theatrical kind of way by her fellow thespians, but that was little comfort. It could all float away on a breeze and what would she be left with? One day she would grow old and raddled, living on the memories of her long-lost fame. Alone.

'Maddy, are you coming or no?' Marianne's voice broke in on her reverie and she found herself sitting half dressed in front of the mirror in her dressing room, with a hair brush in her hand. She could not remember how it had got there. The run of *All's Well That Ends Well* had come to an end at last and she was heartily thankful. Next week, it would be *Love's Labour's Lost*, a tale of courtship and masquerade in which no one was who they seemed to be, which she found ironic. Shakespeare had a wonderful way of holding up a mirror to life, she decided, even if it was distorted.

She smiled. 'Yes, I'm coming. You go on. I'll follow.'

'Very well, but do not be long.'

Marianne hurried off to join the party to celebrate the successful conclusion of the run, leaving Madeleine to finish dressing. The end of the Season was not far off, when the *haut monde* would be leaving London for their country estates and those left in the capital—those who had no country estates, those whose business kept them in town, the vast army of artisans, servants, shopkeepers, for whom the *ton* had little relevance except as a source of income—would settle down to a more humdrum existence and there would not be so many people coming to the theatre.

Lancelot might declare a holiday or take a few of the company on tour to provincial theatres. She had been on tour with him before; though she enjoyed it in some ways, it was hard work and they never stayed in one place more than a week. But now she might welcome a few weeks away from

London, anywhere would do, so long as she did not have to think about the Marquis of Risley.

Sighing, she put on an evening gown of turquoise gros de Naples. With its gigot sleeves and a crossover bodice fastened at the centre front of the low décolletage with a satin rose, it was the height of fashion. Its skirt had a deep border of puckered crepe in the same colour. When she made it, she had been dreaming of being taken out by the Marquis of Risley and imagining his compliments on how she looked. Foolish, foolish girl! Impatient with herself, she slipped on her shoes, picked up her reticule and made for the door.

The theatre was deserted; she must have been longer than she intended and everyone had gone. Luckily it was only a short step to the rooms that had been hired for the party and she did not bother to call a cab. The theatre watchman let her out of the stage door and into the lane.

'Well, my beauty, you took your time.'

She whirled round to find herself facing Benedict Willoughby. 'Oh, you startled me, Mr Willoughby.'

'Did I? Then I beg your pardon.'

'What are you doing here? The performance finished well over an hour ago.'

'Waiting for you, my dear. And I must say, you look superb. That colour makes you look like a nymph rising out of the sea.'

She ignored his flattery. 'Why were you waiting for me?'

'To take you to supper.'

'I am already engaged for supper, sir.'

'With whom? Not Stanmore, I know, for he has already reported his failure to make headway with you.'

'He talks to you of me?' she demanded furiously. How could he? How could he make their meetings a subject for tattle? But then he had no high opinion of her and young gentlemen must have their fun! She had been a fool even to think it could be any different.

'Why should he not?' he said. 'You are the talk of the village, or didn't you know? Is she or isn't she what she seems? Is she nobility or a flycatcher? Demure as a whore at a christening or a clever bit of muslin, luring us poor men into her trap?'

'You are talking nonsense. Let me pass.'

'When you say you will come to supper with me. Stanmore has had his chance, now it is my turn.'

'Your *turn*?'

'Yes, it's only fair, after all. I can see why you fell out with him, he is not half the fun he used to be. He has become very morose. I think it is because his papa is urging him to get himself shackled and no man likes that, not before he has had time to live a little…' He paused and looked sideways at her, smiling. 'Enough of Stanmore, what about supper?'

'I told you, not tonight, Mr Willoughby. My friends are waiting for me.'

'Come with me instead. They will not miss you. We could have a grand time. I am not ungenerous.' He laughed a little. 'Besides, I have just come into fifty pounds and who better to spend it on than a beautiful woman?'

'No, thank you, sir,' she said disdainfully. 'Please let me pass.'

'Good heavens! I never met anyone so top lofty. Is that what comes of having an *aristo* for a *grand-père*? Surely you did not think that a mere *comte* would signify with the Duke, did you? He will not have you for a daughter-in-law, never in a million years, even if Stanmore himself wished it, which I doubt. His intentions were strictly dishonourable, don't you know?'

She shut her ears to what he was saying; she did not want to hear it. 'Mr Willoughby, I asked you to let me pass.'

'Very well, but you must pay the forfeit of a kiss and promise to let me take you to supper another night.'

'Certainly not.' She went to push past him and he put his arms round her and held her in a fierce bear hug which took her breath away. All at once she was back in Bedford Row, struggling with Henry Bulford. She would not allow this man to succeed where Henry had failed. She wriggled desperately to free herself, cursing him in language that was certainly not ladylike. It only served to amuse him.

'Now we have the truth of it, the *sans culotte* shows her true form. I always said you were too good to be real. Now, I will show you how a doxy should be dealt with. Stanmore was too soft with you.'

He leaned over her, smelling of wine and spirits, and then suddenly she saw a fist appear from nowhere and smash into his face. He let go of her so suddenly she nearly fell over with him as he toppled to the ground. A hand, the same hand that had made the fist, steadied her.

'Are you hurt, Miss Charron?' The voice was Duncan's, but the tone was measured, cold almost, as if he were talking to a stranger.

'No, I have come to no harm, thanks to your timely intervention.' She matched his coolness with her own, determined he should not know how much of an effort that was.

He looked down at his prostrate friend. 'Get up, Ben, you are not hurt.'

Willoughby scrambled to his feet, wiping the blood from his nose with his lace handkerchief. 'There was no call for that, Stanmore. Fair's fair. I was only doing what you tried and failed to do.'

Duncan's jaw was rigid with trying to control the impulse to let fly at him. 'Go home, before I land another facer.'

'You know I am no pugilist.' His voice had a nasal twang due to the fact that he was holding his nose. 'But no man knocks me down with impunity.

Be sure you are at home when my representatives call on you.'

'Don't be ridiculous, man. I am not going to fight you.'

'Then you will be known for the coward you are.'

'Oh, for goodness' sake, will you both stop it,' Madeleine said. 'You are behaving like spoiled brats. I am not a toy to be argued over.'

'I beg your pardon,' Duncan said, bowing to her. 'I was passing and saw a lady in distress and came to help. I would have done it for anyone.'

That had put her in her place, she decided, and smiled crookedly. 'Then I thank you.' She heard Benedict Willoughby grunt, but ignored him. He ambled away, still holding his nose, and she turned to go in the opposite direction.

Duncan caught her arm. 'No, Madeleine, you do not go alone. Remember your promise?'

She wrenched herself away. 'I am only going across the street to join my friends. I do not need an escort, particularly yours.'

'If you do not want my company, I will follow at a distance until I see you safely indoors.'

'If you think… God, do you men never give up?'

'Give up? No, my dear Madeleine, I cannot give up. Not yet.'

'I will burn in hell before I let you make a whore out of me, Lord Risley. Be on your way and leave me alone.'

He winced at her words. 'I will. After I have seen you safely to your destination.'

'And how can my safety matter to you? I am little more than a common whore. They were your own words, were they not?'

'That is not what I meant, I was angry. I am deeply sorry. Can you not forgive me?'

'It is of no consequence whether I do or no. I am merely a subject of tattle, an object of fun and ridicule, if Mr Willoughby is to be believed.'

'What has he been saying?'

'Ask him. He is your friend. I have nothing more to say to you.' They had crossed the road and were approaching the assembly rooms where the theatre party was in full swing, judging by the noise and laughter coming from inside. He stopped to open the door for her.

'The reason I wanted to speak to you tonight, besides asking your pardon,' he said, 'is that Miss Annabel Bulford is holding me to my promise to bring her backstage to see you and I wanted to be sure you would still welcome her.'

She had forgotten that invitation and wished he had. The last thing she wanted was to entertain someone who had everything she did not: a family, a secure place in Society, acceptance as *wifely* material. She doubted if the girl even had a genuine interest in the theatre, but coming backstage and talking to theatre people was the height of daring which she could boast of to her friends. *The*

Marquis of Risley took me. How intimate that sounded. But she could not withdraw the invitation, it would look too much like sour grapes.

'I have no quarrel with Miss Bulford, my lord,' she said, keeping her voice level. 'And I am not so lacking in manners that I would let my loathing of you affect other people. Bring her to the first night of *Love's Labour's Lost.* Tell her I look forward to meeting her again.' And with that she went in at the door and shut it behind her, leaving him standing on the pavement.

He turned to go, cursing himself for his stupidity, Madeleine for her stubbornness and Benedict most of all. What had the fool said to Madeleine? Whatever it was, it was enough to drive the wedge between them even deeper. If there had been the smallest chance that she would forgive him, she would never do so now. He had lost her. He crossed the square to where Dobson waited with the carriage and went home, where he proceeded to get very drunk in the privacy of his own room. It did not help.

The next afternoon he sent in his card at Bedford Row where Lady Bulford was at home, entertaining her cronies of the *beau monde.* It was known that her ladyship, tired of having to act as chaperon to her sisters-in-law, years after they should have been running households of their own, was anxious to fire them off. Hortense at twenty-five was already at her last prayers, but Annabel, four years younger, and much the prettier of the two, had every hope of making a good match.

Duncan knew perfectly well he was her ladyship's main prey, which until a couple of weeks before he had found amusing, but since that evening at Almack's and Miss Tremayne's ball when he had danced twice with Annabel and taken her into supper, it had developed into a serious campaign. Why, oh why, had Madeleine made everything doubly difficult by inviting her backstage? The girl kept talking of it, not only to him but to everyone she spoke to, so he had no choice but to comply. It was not difficult to imagine what the world would make of that.

Miss Annabel Bulford was acceptable in every way. She had breeding, good looks and a pretty way with her. She was not particularly intelligent, but there were plenty who would say that was an advantage; her conversation was not sparkling but certainly not contentious; she was healthy and would bear strong children and if she did not know how to run a household, she would soon learn. She would be compliant and undemanding.

He almost grinned to himself while he waited to be announced; Society had a way of weighing up the pros and cons of the suitability of a prospective wife as if they were buying a breed mare at Tattersall's. But it was not amusing when he was the one they were endeavouring to draw into their trap.

The room, when he entered it, was already crowded with several single young ladies and their mamas and an equal number of eligible young men. He crossed the room to where his hostess sat, with the Misses Bulford on either side.

'Lady Bulford, your obedient.' He executed a flourishing leg. 'Miss Bulford, Miss Annabel.'

'Good afternoon, Marquis.' Her ladyship was visibly preening herself, her face pink with pride. 'How good of you to honour us with your company.'

'Not at all. Are you well?'

He should not have asked that question for she launched into an account of her various illnesses, chief of which seemed to be megrim from constantly worrying about her dear sisters, whom she wished to see happily settled. She drew breath at last and he was able to ask if the ladies would care to accompany him to the first night of *Love's Labour's Lost*.

'Is that the new play Miss Charron is acting in?' Annabel asked.

'It is indeed,' he said.

'Well, I do not care to go,' Lady Bulford said. 'I am not fond of the theatre, but I suppose Hortense and Annabel may chaperon each other, if they wish to go.'

'Oh, I should like that above everything,' Annabel said breathlessly. 'Do say you will come too, Hortense.'

'Please do, Miss Bulford,' Duncan added. 'I will call for you in my carriage at seven thirty.'

'Very well,' Hortense said stiffly, as if she were doing him a great favour. In Duncan's opinion it was no wonder she had not found a match.

He stayed the customary fifteen minutes, making meaningless conversation with others of the company, and then took his leave, glad to escape. Annabel he could tolerate; he liked her. If it had not been for Madeleine Charron, who haunted his every waking moment and much of his sleep, he might have considered her for a wife. But Lady Bulford and Hortense were so stiff-necked they made his hackles rise. They could not see past his title and wealth to the man behind it. He supposed in their eyes, and probably Bulford's too, that's all he represented, a title and money.

He said as much to Lavinia when she called the following afternoon. The Duchess, who had not been expecting her, was out visiting the orphanage. 'Stay and have tea with me,' he said, ringing the bell for a servant. 'Mama will probably be home by the time we have finished.'

They adjourned to the morning room, smaller and more intimate than the withdrawing room, which was situated at the back of the house and looked out on to a terrace and a well-tended garden. The teatray was brought and the maidservant sent away.

'What are you doing at home all alone in the middle of the afternoon?' Lavinia asked, pouring tea for them both.

'Enjoying the peace and quiet,' he said.

'Oh?' She raised one well-defined brow, so like his own they could only be brother and sister. 'Why do you need peace and quiet? Have you been in a scrap?'

'Not exactly.' He paused. 'Lady Bulford is working very hard to push me into the arms of Miss Annabel Bulford and Benedict Willoughby has called me out.'

'Benedict!' She laughed. 'You are bamming me.'

'No, I am not. He sent Harry Scott-Smythe and Johnny Tremayne round this morning.'

'But you must have quarrelled with him quite badly for him to go to such lengths. Whatever was it all about?'

'I tapped his claret for insulting a lady.'

'What lady? Surely not Miss Annabel?'

He smiled wryly. 'No, Miss Charron.'

'The actress?'

'She may be an actress, but she is also a lady and I could not stand by and watch him force his attentions on her.'

Lavinia shuddered. Once, many years ago, when she was sixteen, Benedict Willoughby had tried the

same trick on her and she had been rescued by
Frances and James. 'He always was uncouth. But
surely you did not accept the challenge?'

'No, I sent them away, told them to tell their
principal I did not have a quarrel with him that
could not be resolved over a glass of brandy at
White's. Goodness knows what he will make of
that.'

'If it gets noised abroad, there will be a terrible
scandal.'

'I can't help that. I could not stand by and let it
happen, could I? In any case, I think Ben will be
too ashamed to say anything and you are the only
other person who knows.'

'And Miss Charron, of course.'

'And Madeleine. But she will not say anything.
She is angry with us both.'

'Madeleine? You use her given name?'

'Why not? It is how I think of her.'

She looked closely at him. 'Oh, Duncan, do not
tell me you have developed a *tendre* for her.'

'What if I have?'

'I suppose it is not so unusual for a young man
to take a fancy to an actress; they are usually very
beautiful and exciting and make good mistresses. If
you are discreet—'

'Good God, Vinny, do you think I am as bad
as Willoughby? I am deadly serious. I want to
marry her.'

'Oh, Duncan.' She looked pityingly at him. 'What are you going to do?'

'I don't know.'

'I suppose if she is really the granddaughter of a French *comte*, she might be acceptable, especially if she gives up the stage and begins to live in a more genteel fashion. You would have to talk to Papa about it.'

'He will ring a peal over me. I do not know if I am ready for that.'

'He will understand. He once fell in love with someone his parents considered unsuitable and he let her go and married Mama instead and you know they were never happy together.'

'I never knew that.' For a moment his thoughts were diverted from Madeleine. His parents had never been loving towards each other and for most of the time had lived apart, but he had been a child, not old enough to realise it was anything out of the ordinary. When the family had so many homes, it was not surprising that husband and wife were not always in the same one. 'Who was she?'

Lavinia laughed. 'Why, Stepmama, of course. It was before she married James's father, the Earl of Corringham. She was not highly born enough for Papa's parents and they forbade the match. It was not until they were both widowed that they were able to be together.'

'Why did I never hear of it?'

'You were away at school most of the time. I learned of it when Papa brought me to London for the first time and took me to Corringham House to have painting lessons.'

'You think that will make him more sympathetic to my problems?'

'I don't see why not. Talk to him. Better still, talk to Stepmama. She will know how to approach him. But I would keep quiet about Mr Willoughby's challenge, if I were you.'

He did not need to be told that. But what was the point of saying anything at all to his parents when Madeleine herself was so cold towards him? Somehow he must make up their quarrel and tell her how he felt about her, that he would move heaven and earth to marry her and if that meant falling out with his father, then so be it. It reminded him that the next time he saw her, he would be escorting Annabel Bulford.

'Vinny, you could do me a very great favour,' he said.

'I will if I can, you know that, but if you want me to speak to Papa on your behalf, I do not think that would be a good idea.'

'No, I am perfectly capable of speaking for myself. I am engaged to take the Misses Bulford to the first night of *Love's Labour's Lost* and I wish you and James would come too and make a party of it. I do not want everyone to think that I am taking Miss Annabel exclusively.'

'I should think not, considering what you have just told me. Why did you ask her in the first place?'

'I was backed into a corner. Annabel was being enthusiastic about the play and Madeleine herself asked her to go backstage after the performance and she is holding me to taking her.'

'Oh, dear, what a coil you have got yourself into, brother dear. I hope for everyone's sake you can find your way out of it.'

'So, will you come?'

'I'll speak to James. If he has no prior engagement, I am sure he will oblige. Don't worry, I will say nothing of what you have told me. I would like to see the play myself.'

'Thank you, Vinny. We will have supper at Reid's afterwards.'

'Not with Miss Charron, I hope.'

He grinned lopsidedly. 'No, I do not think that would be a wise move.'

The last dress rehearsal for *Love's Labour's Lost*, which Lancelot had decided to put in a contemporary setting, maintaining that Shakespeare was always up to date, had taken place early in the morning, leaving the cast free to spend the afternoon in whatever way they chose to prepare themselves for the first night. Some went to bed, others sat about talking, playing whist for farthings or muttering their lines. Marianne and Madeleine decided to accept Sir Percy's offer of a carriage ride in the park.

It was a beautiful day, with hardly a cloud and the ladies, in sprigged muslin gowns with small puffed sleeves, sheltered under frilled silk parasols as they rode side by side for all the world like the elegant women of the *ton* who used a ride in the park to see and be seen, to look around to see who was favouring whom and keep up with the gossip. That they belonged to the grey world of the *demi-monde* was not immediately apparent. Sir Percival Ponsonby was known as an eccentric, but his antecedents were impeccable and he was well liked. They would not be snubbed while they were with him, even though he was wearing an outrageous green and white striped coat and a purple waistcoat.

'It seems the news of your illustrious *grandpère* has spread, Miss Charron,' he said, as everyone acknowledged them. 'You are being courted. How many invitations have you had?'

She laughed. 'Too many to count. But I know it is only empty curiosity and so I do not go.'

'It is the mystery that surrounds you,' he said. 'They love a mystery and refusing to go only deepens it.'

'Yes, Marianne told me you thought I should make a push to solve it. I did try but achieved nothing.'

'Pity, that.'

'Oh, it is of no consequence, Sir Percy. I have lived all my life until now without knowing. I can continue in ignorance.'

'But, my dear, surely you wish to make a good marriage?'

'If you mean by good, one that is based on love, then, yes, of course I would like that, but not one dependent on whether my grandfather was a nobleman or not. I would as lief remain single.'

He smiled and reached across to pat her hand. 'I understand, my dear, but you know it is the way of the world. A man can be ostracised for making a marriage that Society considers in any way unusual and that does not only mean being given the cut direct. It can affect his standing in the community so that instead of being respected, he is derided and then he cannot govern his land and his people properly. His associates do not trust him in business matters, his servants are disrespectful, particularly to his wife, and that is passed on to everyone about them. It is downhill all the way.'

She gave a cracked laugh. 'I am not contemplating marrying into the top one hundred, Sir Percy.'

'No?' he queried, lifting his black-lined eyebrows almost into the curly black wig he wore.

'Maddy has fallen out with the *haut monde*,' Marianne put in, with a sympathetic smile towards her friend.

'What, all of them?'

'Not you, Sir Percy,' Madeleine hastened to assure him. 'But the others. They have only one thing on their minds and vie with each other on how they achieve it. Do you know Mr Willoughby and the Marquis of Risley were arguing about whose *turn* it was? Do you wonder I gave them both the right about?'

'How very uncivil of them,' he murmured. 'I would not have believed that of Stanmore.'

'It was Mr Willoughby who said it. Du— His lordship knocked him down.'

He laughed. 'Did he? I should have liked to have seen it.'

'It is not a laughing matter, Sir Percy. Mr Willoughby challenged the Marquis to a duel.'

'The devil he did!'

'I was mortified. Lord Risley said he would not fight him, but I do not think Mr Willoughby will let it rest and I am afraid his lordship's sense of honour will force him to accept. I am so worried they will harm each other. I am not worth it, Sir Percy. I would rather die myself...'

'Oh, no need for that, m'dear,' he said cheerfully. 'Young men are always challenging each other. They will shake hands and make up, you'll see.'

'Can you make them do that, Sir Percy?' Marianne asked. 'Can you intervene?'

'You may be sure I will speak to them.'

'Thank you.'

They had come to the end of the North Ride and the carriage was turned to take them back to the Cumberland Gate, where they set off towards Oxford Street.

'Will you be in your box tonight, Sir Percy?' Marianne asked, as they neared home.

'Of course. I would not dream of missing the start of a new play. Would you both do me the honour of dining with me afterwards?'

'Thank you,' they said together.

At least that would save her from the young blades who besieged the stage door wanting to take her out, Madeleine thought. It was only curiosity; she had been right about that. But it was not only the young dandies that filled her with apprehension, it was the prospect of meeting Duncan Stanmore with Miss Annabel Bulford.

The knot inside her was tighter than ever by the time the curtain rose on the first scene. She stood in the wings, her heart beating so loudly she wondered that those sitting in the front row did not hear it. Luckily as the Princess of France, she did not appear until the beginning of the second act and by that time the audience had settled down and so had her nerves. The play absorbed her to the exclusion of everything else and by the time the final curtain went down, she had almost forgotten the ordeal ahead of her.

The applause was enthusiastic; several of the audience stood up to cheer and call her name. She took several curtain calls before she was allowed to leave the stage and return to her dressing room. Sir Percy was already there, lounging in a chair while Marianne undressed behind a screen. Madeleine joined her to take off her costume and slip into a dressing robe of blue quilted satin, before emerging and sitting before the mirror to clean off the stage paint. She had hardly had time to brush out her hair before a page ushered in the Marquis of Risley, the Earl and Countess of Corringham, and the Misses Bulford.

She rose but did not curtsy. This was her world, a world where she was queen and she could observe protocol or not as she pleased. And at the moment it did not please her. 'Good evening, my lords,' she said. 'Ladies. As you see, I have not quite finished my toilette.'

Duncan was lost in admiration, not only of her coolness but her beauty. With her dark hair flowing loose over her shoulders and her face clean and shining from the cream she had used to remove the paint, she looked adorable. If the room had not been packed to suffocation with people, he would have taken her in his arms, talked softly to her as one would to a frightened kitten and convinced her of his sincerity. He wished everyone, his sister and brother-in-law, Sir Percy and Miss Doubleday, and especially the Bulford women anywhere but where they were, standing round gaping.

It was Annabel who broke the silence. 'My goodness, you do not have much room in here, do you? However do you manage?'

'Oh, we are quite used to it,' Madeleine said.

'And are these your costumes? There are so many. I wonder you have time to change them between scenes.'

'We do have a dresser to help us,' Marianne said laconically. 'And when there are only two sharing, there is room enough. Changing costumes, like learning lines by heart, is all part of the job.'

'It must be very exciting,' Annabel went on, ignoring her sister who was looking round disdainfully. 'Miss Charron, I must congratulate you on your performance tonight. I was quite mesmerised by it all and was sad when it all came to an end.' She turned to the others. 'Marquis, do you not agree?'

'Oh, wholeheartedly,' he said, looking directly at Madeleine.

'Do you never forget yourself and find you are acting a part when you are off stage?' Hortense asked.

Duncan held his breath as Madeleine looked hard at her questioner. And then she laughed lightly. 'Hardly ever, Miss Bulford, hardly ever.'

'And do you always play the lead? Do you never play the nurse or a servant?'

Madeleine laughed again, almost recklessly, making Duncan wonder why. 'I have done in the past, Miss Bulford. Oh, yes, I know how to play the servant as well as the princess. After all, are we not all women when we take off our clothes?'

Sir Percy chuckled aloud at this and Hortense turned to glare at him. 'Disgraceful,' she said, though she did not make it clear just what it was she found so deplorable. 'Annabel, have you seen enough? I find the air in here almost unbreathable.'

'Then we must go,' Duncan said. 'Come, Miss Bulford, Miss Annabel.' And with a glance towards the others, he ushered the entire party out with only the briefest word of thanks to Madeleine.

'Whew!' Marianne said, when they had gone. 'Did you ever meet anyone more on their dignity than the elder Miss Bulford? And what was that about servants?'

'I don't know,' Madeleine said. 'I think she may have recognised me, guessed who I am.'

'What do you mean, recognised you?' Sir Percy demanded. 'Are you known to her?'

'Oh, yes, she knows me all right, and so does Annabel. It was a long time ago. I had hoped they would not remember me.'

'Go on, gel, you've got this far, you might as well tell us the whole. I won't tattle about it, but I might be able to help.'

'When my mother died, I didn't appear to have any family. Our neighbours took me to an orphanage. When I was old enough to work, they sent me to Bedford Row to be a servant to the Bulfords. I worked in the kitchen there for three years and then they turned me off and I found work as a seamstress and then I came to the theatre and Marianne took me under her wing. That is my history, no more, no less.'

'And the French *comte*?'

Madeleine shrugged and then laughed. 'He is an interesting character, is he not? He has certainly kept the gabblegrinders busy these last few weeks and he has filled theatre seats. We have never had such full houses and as the actors are paid a percentage, they are all pleased.'

'It is not the *comte* who has filled the seats, it is the chance to see two fine actresses bringing the stage to life,' he said firmly. 'The theatre has never been so blessed, not even when Mrs Jordan and Sarah Siddons trod the boards.'

'Why, thank you, kind sir,' Marianne said, curtsying.

'I suppose you are going to tell me to make a clean breast of it,' Madeleine said.

'That is entirely your affair,' he said with a smile. 'But why spoil something that is working so well?'

Madeleine looked from one to the other. 'I do not see how you can make light of it.'

'Best way, m'dear,' he said. 'A merry jest.'

'The Marquis of Risley will not think so. He presented me to the Duke and Duchess. They will be furious.'

'Oh, I do not think so,' he said airily. 'Come, let us go to supper, I am gut-foundered, begging your pardon for the vulgarity.' He offered them an arm each and thus they left the theatre for the short walk to Reid's.

When they arrived Madeleine was horrified to find the Marquis of Risley and his party already seated at one of the tables. She held back, but Sir Percy kept a tight hold on her elbow, as they were ushered to the table he had booked. *'Nil desperandum,'* he whispered in her ear, at the same time nodding a greeting towards those at the other table. 'Remember your grandfather.'

She could not remember her grandfather because she had never known him, and thinking about the fictitious *comte*, made the colour flood to her face. Never had she regretted that Banbury tale more than she did now. Duncan, though pretending to pay attention to his guests, was watching her settle in her seat with a strange light in his eye, almost as if he had guessed the truth. Or perhaps Hortense Bulford had already whispered it to him. She squirmed and turned away, unable to meet that steadfast gaze.

'Now, let me see,' Sir Percy said. 'What shall we have? There is turbot and oysters, which I am partial to, but perhaps they are too commonplace for ladies. Shrimps, perhaps?'

'I am not at all hungry,' Madeleine said. Even with her back to the other table she could feel Duncan's gaze on her. It was making the hairs on the back of her neck prickle.

'Then shrimps in a light sauce should do you very well, my dear.' Percy was determined to keep her attention so that she could not hear what was being said at the other table. 'Followed by partridge and a little roast pork and vegetables. What do you think?'

'That will be plenty for me,' she said.

He ascertained that Marianne was happy with his choice and gave the order to the waiter who hovered at his elbow. 'And wine,' he said. 'The best you have in the cellar.

'Now,' he said, leaning forward, 'we will converse about the play. Until tonight it was not one of my favourites, but now I can see hidden depths. People in disguise wanting to be loved for themselves alone, very good.'

'But they all end up with the right people,' Marianne put in.

'Oh, yes, you see, bloodlines will out. There is something about the way a lady of breeding holds herself, you know. Straight back. Head up. Chin in. And the voice. You cannot disguise the voice.'

Madeleine laughed. 'You can if you are an actress.'

'No, my dear, not even then.'

Duncan, listening to Madeleine laugh so easily, as if she did not have a care in the world, was filled with a kind of fury, that made him want to go over and turn her round and shake her until her eyes popped out. How could she be happy when he was sunk in the depths of despair? He was obliged to make stiff, boring conversation with his guests, who were determined to peg him out on the matrimonial line, when all he wanted was Madeleine. In his arms, in his bed, by his side as his marchioness.

'I heard a rumour that Mr Willoughby had challenged you to a duel,' Hortense said. 'Is it true?'

'Oh, it was nothing but a jest,' he replied, wondering where she had heard it. 'We are the best of friends and have been since our schooldays. And duelling is against the law.'

'It still goes on.'

'Not by me,' he said coldly.

'Why did he challenge you?' Annabel asked.

'Oh, something and nothing. I pray you, forget it.'

'I heard it was over the actress,' Hortense persisted. 'But you are right, she is something and nothing.'

'I wish I could remember where I had seen her before,' Annabel said, while Duncan fumed. He ought to jump up and publicly defend Madeleine, but a glance in her direction told him she had heard what had been said and his intervention would be no more welcome now than it had been when Benedict had been objectionable.

'Of course you have seen her before,' Hortense said impatiently. 'You are always going to the theatre. I told Henry it was not seemly for you to go so often, but he seemed to think it would do no harm. Fancy wanting to go into that smelly, airless dressing room. And to find two of them there half dressed and Sir Percival Ponsonby taking his ease, quite at home. Does he get a perverse pleasure from watching them change their clothes?'

'Sir Percival is a gentleman,' Duncan said, looking towards the other table. 'And a close friend of my family.'

'Don't worry about me, m'boy,' Percy said, loud enough for everyone to hear. 'I can defend myself if the need arises.'

'I did not mean at the theatre,' Annabel put in quickly. 'Somewhere else. Some time ago. It is a memory in the back of my mind and, tease as I might, I cannot bring it to the fore.'

'Duncan, do you remember when we put on a play for Mama's charity?' Lavinia said, in an effort to change the subject. She turned to the Misses Bulford. 'It was *A Midsummer Night's Dream*. We put it on in the ballroom of Stanmore House. Everyone took part, even Duncan and Mr Willoughby.'

'Oh, did you?' Annabel asked Duncan. 'I did not know you were talented in that direction.'

'I am not. I was bullied into it by Lavinia,' he said, blessing his sister for the diversion. 'She was the leading light. And she painted all the scenery.'

'How clever of you!' Annabel said, eyes shining. 'I should so like to do that. It must be great fun.'

'Oh, it is,' Lavinia said. 'But hard work too. We were fortunate to have Mr Greatorex and Miss Doubleday to help us. It was a great success and made several hundred pounds for the charity.'

'When was this?' Hortense asked. 'I do not remember hearing about it.'

'Oh, it was about seven years ago, the year the King tried to divorce the Queen. I do not suppose it was known to anyone except our close circle of friends and the people from the orphanage.'

'Oh, then Annabel would still have been in the schoolroom, too young to know of such things,' Hortense said. 'And amateur theatricals never interested me.'

The conversation continued along the same lines while the next course was brought to the table. They were still sitting there when Sir Percy and his two companions rose to leave. Duncan made a point of bidding them goodnight, wishing he could get up and go too. He desperately wanted to speak to Madeleine.

'Goodnight, ladies,' Sir Percy said, beaming round at them and then nodded to the men. 'Corringham. Stanmore.'

'I wish we could have asked them to join us for the last course,' Annabel said.

'Good gracious, sister, whatever are you thinking of?' Hortense said. 'You cannot be seen with actresses, however devious they are.'

'Devious?'

'Yes. I have just realised where we have seen that one before, the young one. It was in our own kitchen.' Her voice was triumphant. 'Don't you remember Maddy, the skivvy? She was with us three years before Papa threw her out.' She laughed harshly. 'She always was a liar.'

Duncan looked from one to the other and then at Lavinia. His sister was slowly shaking her head, as if to tell him to remain silent. He did not need to be told—he had been struck dumb.

Chapter Seven

How Duncan managed to get through the rest of the evening he did not know. Miss Bulford was gloating and Miss Annabel was innocently excited by the thought that an acclaimed actress had actually spent three years under the same roof as she had, had even talked to her when she went to the kitchen begging sweetmeats from the cook. 'Who would ever have believed she would go on to be so famous?' she said in wonder.

Lavinia had quickly struck up a different topic of conversation and no one noticed that Duncan had become silent. He smiled and agreed to whatever was said and when the party broke up, bade goodbye to his sister and her husband and escorted the Misses Bulford home in his carriage before going home himself. His head was in a whirl. The words, *always was a liar,* went round and round in his head. Miss Madeleine Charron had made a complete cake of him.

210

* * *

The next morning he rose bleary-eyed, put on a dressing gown and went down to find his step-mother, always an early riser, at the breakfast table reading her correspondence which had just been delivered. She looked up. 'Good morning, Duncan,' she said. 'Did you have a pleasant evening?'

'Yes, thank you.'

'And went on to your club afterwards by the look of you.'

'No, Mama, I did not. We had supper at Reid's and afterwards I took the ladies home and came straight back here.'

'Then there is something serious troubling you. Is it Miss Bulford?'

'No. Annabel is a sweet girl, too sweet for me.' He sat down and poured himself a cup of coffee from the pot on the table. There were dishes of food on the sideboard but he did not feel like eating.

'Duncan, my dear boy, you must be very careful if you do not intend to offer for her. You have been seen about with her several times and I know Lady Bulford has expectations. If you should encourage that without perhaps meaning to...' She paused to study his face.

'It was you and Lavinia insisted I should go to Almack's, Mama, and Lady Bulford herself who asked me to escort Miss Annabel to the Tremayne ball. I could not refuse without being uncivil and it was Miss Charron who invited Annabel backstage and Annabel who asked me to accompany her. I felt bound to agree, but I did make a larger party of it, so that she would not find it too intimate. I do not see how I could have acted differently. And last night…' He paused. 'Last night I felt I was being driven into a corner.'

'Is it the idea of marriage you cannot face, or simply marriage to Miss Annabel? She is, after all, entirely suitable.'

'Mama, Miss Annabel Bulford is not for me.'

'Then in all conscience you must make that plain before it goes any further. Take someone else out. There are others…'

'I have been in the company of others and though they are agreeable enough, there is not one with whom I would want to spend the rest of my life.'

Frances looked closely at him. 'No one at all?'

He thought of Lavinia's advice to confide in their stepmother, but that had been given before they heard about Madeleine being a servant in the Bulford household, before she had been uncovered as the liar she was. There was no need to tell the Duchess anything now, no need to keep torturing himself about how to make her acceptable to his father. She never would be. 'No,' he said emphatically. 'There is no one.'

They were interrupted by a footman who came to announce the Countess of Corringham. Almost before he had finished speaking, Lavinia came in, holding Jamie by the hand and carrying the two-year-old Caroline on her hip. In no time at all Jamie had scrambled on to Duncan's lap to show him his new sailing boat and Caroline was nestling in the Duchess's arms.

'We are on our way to the park to sail Jamie's boat on the lake,' Lavinia said. 'I thought perhaps you might like to accompany us, Duncan.'

He agreed to go; the fresh air of the park might help to clear his head. He went up to his room, dressed in dove grey pantaloons and a frockcoat of dark blue superfine, picked up his tall hat and kid gloves and made his way out to the Corringham carriage where Lavinia, the children and their nursemaid waited for him.

Not until the children were toddling ahead of them along the path in the park, clinging to the hands of the nursemaid, did Lavinia speak to him about Madeleine. 'Did you talk to Mama about Miss Charron?' she asked.

'What, that it turns out she was a kitchen maid, after all? Why do that? Everything has changed. There was never a French *comte* and it only goes to show what a corkbrain I was to believe her lies.'

'And the existence of the *comte* was important, was it? He was the key to the whole? You cannot love someone who is not of gentle birth?'

'I cannot love a liar, Vinny.'

'But perhaps she is not lying. If all her family were dead, what else could anyone do with a motherless child but put her in an orphanage? It is a short step from there to a life in service, you should know that from listening to Mama. She has to try and find employment for all her orphans when they are old enough to leave and what else is there? It does not disprove Miss Charron's story. If anything, she should be admired for rising above her misfortunes.'

'I did not think I should find you on her side.'

'I am only playing the devil's advocate, Duncan. And Hortense Bulford could be mistaken.'

He smiled crookedly. 'Is that why you came over today, Vinny, simply to play the devil's advocate?'

'Yes, why not? I could see how Miss Bulford's revelation had hit you. You went pale as a ghost and you were grinding your teeth like you used to do when you were little and could not have your own way. I was afraid you might do something foolish.'

'I wanted to bundle the interfering witch out of the door.'

'It is as well you did not. It would have caused a dreadful scandal.' She paused. 'Duncan, I do believe that, in spite of what Miss Bulford said, you are still enamoured of Miss Charron.'

'No, it is over. It was over before last night. She holds me in aversion and now it is mutual.'

She sighed. 'I am sorry for you, Duncan, truly sorry, but you will get over it.'

It was easy for Lavinia to say that. James, Earl of Corringham, had never been unacceptable;

Frances had been his stepmother before she had been theirs and James and the Duke dealt very well with each other. But this was different. He was not one to treat love lightly; once his heart was given, it stayed that way and if he said anything to the contrary, he was lying.

Unwilling to endure any more quizzing, he dashed away from her and caught up with the children who had drawn ahead of them. 'Come on, Jamie,' he cried. 'Let us see what this vessel of yours is made of.'

They spent an hour sailing the boat, at the end of which Duncan's cuffs were soaked and his knees green from kneeling on the grass. He sat back on his heels beside the water and looked at the children, laughing at the antics of the ducks who came in search of food. Jamie would carry on the Corringham name but who was there to continue the Stanmore line? Who, after he had gone, would take over the Risley estate and all the other properties which provided a home and livelihood for so many people? He had a duty to marry and, at twenty-five years old, he could not leave it much longer.

He looked up when Lavinia's shadow fell over him. 'I think what you need, Duncan, is a family,' she said. 'You are so good with my little ones.'

He smiled and got to his feet. 'Before I can do that, I have to find a wife.'

'There I cannot help you. But I do think you could do with a change of scene and some different company. I am going to hold a little supper party next Thursday and then, if the weather is still fine, we will all go on to Vauxhall Gardens. There is to be a concert of Handel's *Water Music* and fireworks.'

Now that it had been scourged of its rowdy reputation, Vauxhall Gardens, a vast pleasure ground situated on the south side of the river, was a favourite meeting place for the citizens of London from the lowest to the highest. Even the King, when he had been Prince of Wales, had been a frequent visitor. 'I am not sure…'

'There will be no Misses Bulford, I promise. It will do you good to be with other young people, put a stop to the gabblegrinders. What do you say?'

'Always the big sister looking after me,' he said, with a laugh, as he hoisted Jamie on to his shoulder to take him back to the carriage. 'Very well, if you insist.'

They set him down at Stanmore House and he went indoors to change into his old drab coat and stuff trousers before setting off on foot to visit Bow Street and Newgate. If anything could bring him down to earth, that could.

He was on his way out when he was met on the step by a figure in a green riding coat and blue breeches tucked into black tasselled knee boots.

'Morning, Sir Percy,' he said. 'You are up betimes. Did someone set your bed afire?'

'No laughing matter, Stanmore. I ain't at me best in the morning, but needs must.'

'Have you come to see Stepmama?'

'No, came to see you. Promised.'

'That sounds ominous. Walk with me.'

'Where are you going dressed like that?' Sir Percy demanded. 'You look as though you are off to dig up the roads.'

Duncan laughed. 'No, I am going to prison.'

'Prison? My boy, what have you done?' Percy asked in alarm, as he fell in beside his young friend.

'Nothing. I visit occasionally.'

'Rum sort of thing for a fellow to do when he don't have to, don't you think?'

'I like to do what I can to help the poor fellows there.'

'But they're criminals!' Sir Percy was aghast.

'There but for the grace of God…'

'Now, you are being perverse. You would never land up there, whatever you had done, your papa would see to that.'

'That's just why I go. Wealth and privilege are all very well, Sir Percy, but they bring responsibilities, you know.'

'Talking of that, reminds me why I came to see you.' Sir Percy, unused to walking anywhere, was almost running to keep up with Duncan. 'Do slow down, me boy, I'm not as young as I was.'

Duncan moderated his pace. 'Go on.'

'Is it true Willoughby has challenged you to a duel?'

'Yes, but he was in his cups at the time and I doubt he'll insist on it.'

'I hope you're right, but if he does, what will you do?'

'Choose pistols and miss.'

'But can you be sure he will miss you?'

That crazy duel was the last thing on his mind and he did not see why Sir Percy was quizzing him about it. 'No, but what else do you suggest I do?'

'It's illegal. If you tell me where and when, then I can make sure the law is on hand to stop it.'

Duncan laughed. 'And that really would put me behind bars.'

'You know very well it would not. Young gentlemen will have their little fallings out. No harm done. That's what I'd say if I were the beak you came before.' He paused. 'The lady concerned is very anxious you should not put yourself at risk.'

'The lady being Miss Madeleine Charron, I suppose. You may tell Miss Charron I am not fighting a duel over her, she is not worth the expenditure of energy.'

'I say, Stanmore, that's a bit brown, ain't it? Thought you were sweet on her.'

'I do not like liars and she is a master.' He gave a cracked laugh. 'Or should I say mistress.'

'Have you never told a white lie? Never twisted the truth to suit yourself?'

'That's different.'

'No, it isn't. She is a lonely young lady whom Society discarded, threw out to fend for herself when she should have been in the bosom of a loving family. You talk of visiting prisoners and helping them, she has been a prisoner of a kind herself, a prisoner of the way Society works.' It was a very long and articulate speech for Sir Percy.

'She was a kitchen maid, of all things, and worse, it was in the Bulford household.'

'Yes, I know.'

'Why didn't you tell me?'

'Didn't know till last night. An' I ain't one to betray a confidence. If she did not tell you about it, you may be sure she had a very good reason.'

'What reason?'

'I think you should ask her that yourself.' He looked around him; they had left the Strand behind and were halfway down Fleet Street. 'Boy, where are you taking me?'

Duncan stopped. 'I am sorry, I am so used to coming this way, I did not think. Come, I will escort you back to civilisation.'

They turned to retrace their steps and were approaching St James's when they came face to face with Benedict Willoughby. It was obvious from his scowling countenance he did not mean to acknowledge his erstwhile friend, but Sir Percy stopped right in front of him, obliging him to halt.

'Good morning, Mr Willoughby,' he said cheerfully. 'We are well met.'

'Good morning, Sir Percy. I would stop and pass the time of day, but I do not like the company you keep.' Benedict looked pointedly at Duncan who stood a few steps away, silently awaiting developments.

'Stanmore is my friend.'

'Then has he asked you to represent him?'

'No, wouldn't if he had. Contrary to law, don't you know.'

'What's that to the point? He knocked me down and I demand satisfaction.'

'Then fight it out at Jackson's.'

'He knows perfectly well I never could abide pugilism and he's well versed in the art.'

'So you fancy pistols at dawn, do you?' Sir Percy went on, standing his ground. 'One of you could be seriously hurt, killed even, and it would probably be you. I collect Stanmore would have the edge on you there too. Why don't you both shake hands and be done with it?'

'If he makes a public apology.'

'That I will never do,' Duncan put in before Sir Percy could stop him. 'He was the one in the wrong.'

'Then it will be gaol for the pair of you and who will get the lady then, I wonder?'

They turned to look at him and then both laughed. 'Do you want her?' Benedict asked, addressing Duncan for the first time.

'No, do you?'

'No, I have suddenly lost interest. She is nothing like as vivacious as she is on stage. Beautiful, yes, but decidedly frosty. But that don't mean I'm backing out. No one is going to call me a coward.'

'Tell you what,' Duncan said with sudden inspiration. 'Come with me now and I'll show you something. And if you still want to fight me, then go ahead, I promise not to defend myself.'

'Show me what?'

'Wait and see.'

He called a cab which took them as far as Ludgate Hill, where he told the cabman to wait. Then they set off on foot up Old Bailey. 'My God, Stanmore, where the devil are you taking me?' Benedict demanded.

'To hell,' he said. 'Euphemistically called Akerman's Hotel. In other words, Newgate prison.'

'What for?' Benedict was already gagging on his handkerchief from the vile stench which seemed to ooze up from the very cobbles.

'I thought it might open your eyes to what to expect if we go through with that duel. Sir Percy will not stand by and let it happen, you know. We are sure to be apprehended.'

It was as well they had left the cab at the end of the street; there had recently been a hanging and

Bow Street was blocked to traffic while the crowd dispersed and the scaffold was dismantled. The stench of death was overpowering. Hawkers with trays were selling off short pieces of the rope used for the hanging and items of clothing from the corpses. Waiters from the nearby tavern were carrying food in to those prisoners who had money to buy it.

They approached the door where a seedy individual sat on the step, whittling a stick He stood up when he saw Duncan. 'Good day, your honour. You just missed a fine hanging, a very fine hanging, danced like Morris men they did. Took ten minutes a-dyin'.'

Duncan grimaced. 'I can't do anything for those poor creatures whoever they were. I am more concerned with the living. Who else have you got for me to see today?'

'There's a cut-purse, got five years, and a fogle hunter, though why anyone bothers stealing handkerchiefs I never could fathom. Only a bantling. He got a year...'

'You're never going inside?' muttered Benedict in disbelief.

'Course he is, his lordship is a reg'lar visitor,' the man said. 'An' wery welcome, he is too.'

'Then you can go alone,' Benedict said. 'I'd die before I ventured in there.'

'Well, that's where you'll go if you insist on fighting that duel,' Duncan said. 'I thought I'd show you what to expect.'

Benedict hardly heard him, he had turned away to be sick in the gutter. 'Come away, man, for God's sake,' he said, wiping his mouth.

Duncan smiled at the doorkeeper; he was hardly a turnkey, for the door was not locked and there were people coming and going all the time. 'Seems my friend does not have the stomach for it,' he said. 'Another day, perhaps. Is the bantling manacled?'

'To be sure he is.'

Duncan dropped a few small coins into his filthy hand. 'See the chains are eased. I shall check next time I come.' Then he turned and put his hand under Benedict's elbow to help him back to the cab.

They had been travelling in silence several minutes when Benedict finally spoke. 'What sick thrill do you get from visiting a place like that?'

'I get no thrill at all from it, my friend. I go because I feel it is my duty to do what I can for those poor souls incarcerated there. Many of them have committed no crime, or if they have, it was a minor one. They are chained to a stone floor, flogged and half-starved if they don't have the blunt to pay for easement of irons and extra food. The only thing that is cheap and plentiful is rotten gin. I do what I can and when they are released I try to find them gainful employment.'

Benedict turned to stare at him. 'I never knew that.'

'No reason why you should have.' He was thankful that Benedict was talking to him normally again. 'It's not something I want noised abroad. Those poor people would never trust me again if I made a song and dance about it and I trust you to say nothing. You are, after all, my oldest friend.'

'Oldest friend!' Benedict started to laugh. It began as a chuckle and ended as a full-throated roar and Duncan joined in, still a little unsure whether his friend was having hysterics or was genuinely amused by the situation.

'Pax?' Benedict said, holding out his hand.

Duncan grasped it. 'Pax.'

'I could do with something to take the vile taste of that place from my mouth. What say you we find something to eat and drink?'

'Good idea.' Duncan paid off the cab and they found an eating house where his strange garb would not be considered out of the way and ordered salmagundi—a mixture of cooked meats, anchovies, hard-boiled eggs and onions—for which Duncan paid. It was the least he could do.

'I'm going shopping,' Marianne announced. 'I want a new dress for the concert. Are you coming?'

'Concert? What concert?' Madeleine asked. They had just finished rehearsals and were free until the evening performance. Madeleine had planned to go back to their lodgings and catch up on lost sleep. She had had none the night before and had hardly been able to keep her eyes open during rehearsal. Unless she had some rest, she would be a dishrag by the evening.

'The concert at Vauxhall Gardens on Thursday. Sir Percy has asked us to join him. Don't you remember? Last night.'

She hardly remembered anything of the previous night except snatches of conversation going on at the adjoining table and Duncan's back whenever she dared venture to turn and look at it. His dark hair curled into the nape of his neck and over the top of his collar and his broad shoulders filled the width of his coat, so that it lifted a little whenever he raised his arm to drink or make some point while he spoke. Unable to see his face, she had tried to imagine it. It was not difficult, for every feature was ingrained in her memory.

It was an immobile kind of face, the contours classically sculpted, the nose straight and narrow, but it was his dark eyes that betrayed his feelings. Sometimes the irises were dark with anger as they had been when he had said she was no better than a whore. Sometimes, they were a soft, almost liquid amber when he was being tender. And he was capable of great tenderness. Was that the side he showed to Miss Annabel Bulford? Could he ever be angry with that insipid schoolgirl? Had she ever seen the fire of desire in his eyes?

She shook herself. 'No, I could not have heard him. Have you accepted?'

'Of course I have, why not?'

'No reason. Did he say if the Marquis of Risley would be there?'

'No. Can you not think of anything else, Maddy? Duncan Stanmore is not the only fish in the sea, you know. You really must snap out of it before it affects your work. You know Lancelot will not put up with the vapours from anyone.'

Madeleine knew her friend was right, but it was difficult when your body was so tired and all your brain would do was go over and over again every word Duncan had ever uttered, every nuance of phrase, every gesture, trying to understand what went on in that enigmatic head of his. She made an effort to pull herself together. 'Right, shopping it shall be. What have you in mind to buy?'

'Oh, something colourful, I think.'

Madeleine laughed. 'You do not mean to vie with Sir Percy in the matter of the hues you wear, do you?'

'Goodness, no! But I like red. What about you? We have a nice little nest egg from our last production, are you going to spend some of yours?'

She was about to say she could see no point, her present wardrobe was more than adequate for her needs, but perhaps a new dress would cheer her up. And so they spent the afternoon ranging up and down Bond Street and Oxford Street, and going into Pantheon's Bazaar where almost anything could be had from a pin to a ready-made ballgown. Here Madeleine chose a blue velvet, as dark as the night sky, its skirt scattered with shining glass beads, its bodice daringly décolleté. Used to making her own clothes, she balked at the price, but Marianne was there to urge her on. She did not know why she succumbed. As far as she was concerned no one who really mattered would see it, certainly not the one who was forever in her thoughts.

They went on to the Burlington Arcade on the corner of Piccadilly and Old Bond Street where Marianne found just the gown she was looking for, a crimson-and-cream striped satin with the biggest leg o' mutton sleeves Madeleine had ever seen. They were so large they were stuffed with horsehair to hold them out; there was no way she could wear a coat over them and was obliged to buy a sleeveless pelisse in burgundy taffeta trimmed with swansdown to go over it.

Happy with their purchases, they left the shop, making for Piccadilly where they hoped to find a cruising cab. It was here, with their arms full of parcels, that they rounded a corner and bumped into Duncan and Benedict. The two young men, having dined well and drunk more than was usual, even for them, had their arms on each other's shoulders and were laughing immoderately.

Duncan, the more sober of the two, stopped laughing immediately and began picking up Madeleine's parcels, which had fallen from her hands. 'I am sorry,' he said, piling them back into her arms. 'Clumsy of me. I do hope nothing has been damaged.'

'Oh, it is only a few fripperies,' she said lightly. 'No harm done.' She did not want to look at him, afraid that he would see the misery and longing in her eyes. She hoped he was not going to make conversation, because there was nothing they could say to each other which would not make matters worse. She had never seen him even slightly tipsy before and wondered what had caused it. He was not worrying about that duel, that much was plain, for he and Mr Willoughby appeared to have made it up. And that only proved how little real feeling he had for her. She knew she was being capricious, but she could not help herself.

She turned to look at Benedict who, deprived of his friend's support, stood swaying dangerously. 'Why, if it isn't the toast of London town,' he said, grinning at her.

'My friend is a little disguised, ladies,' Duncan said quickly, grabbing Benedict's arm and putting it round his own neck. 'I apologise on his behalf.'

'Friends…sh, that's what we are,' Benedict mumbled. 'In…ins…shep…arable.'

'Come on, Ben, let's get you home,' Duncan said. 'Excuse us, ladies.'

'Got to fight a duel, don't you know,' Benedict mumbled as Duncan dragged him away.

Duncan hoped Madeleine had not heard. 'I thought we had decided not to bother?'

'Can't. Matter of honour, don't you know. Everyone knows…sh I challenged you. Up to you to choos…sh the weapons.'

Duncan sighed. It was going to take more than a sight of the outside of Newgate to put Benedict off; he wished now he had insisted on going inside and visiting the cells, a much stronger incentive. If he had to fight a duel, what he needed was a weapon that could do no harm. He smiled suddenly. 'Then we'll fight with pillows.'

'Oh, very apt!' Benedict cried. 'Pillows it shall be. Let's make it worthwhile and do it on a pole over water.'

'Like we used to do at school, you mean?'

'Yes, what do you say?'

'I accept.'

'Then let's drink to it.' They were passing White's at the time and Benedict stumbled towards the door.

Duncan hauled him back. 'No, my friend, they'll not let me in dressed like this and we've had enough for one day.'

He took a firmer grip on Benedict and hailed a passing cab. Once he had bundled his friend inside and told the jarvey the address, he turned for home. It was a long time since he had been so cup-shot and already he was regretting it. Had he really agreed to a pillow fight? Was that all Madeleine was worth, a bag of feathers and a possible ducking? Had Benedict been drunk enough not to remember it tomorrow?

But Benedict did remember. It was all round town the following day. Not only had his friend taken great glee in publicising it, he had chosen the time and place. Not some quiet backwater at dawn, but one of the lakes at Vauxhall Gardens and at ten o'clock at night when the place would be crammed with people. It was something he had never intended when he agreed to it. Now what should he do? He could not back out without losing face. Benedict might even reissue his original challenge. The only way was to make a jest of the whole thing and make it look like a ruse put up for the amusement of their friends. But what would Madeleine say, if she heard about it?

Lavinia was as good as her word and the company at her little supper party consisted of a mixed group of old and new friends, young ladies and gentlemen from the arts and politics. There was a Member of Parliament with very radical views, a couple of young portrait painters, two lady novelists, a diplomat, a manufacturer and a judge, together with their wives and daughters, Benedict and Major Donald Greenaway, who had arrived dressed in his regimentals, and the Duke and Duchess of Loscoe.

The conversation was lively and informed and for an hour or two Duncan was able to take his mind off his most pressing problems, though Madeleine was never far from his thoughts. Sir Percy, who had declined Lavinia's invitation on the grounds that he had a prior engagement, had advised him to ask her why she had lied to him, but he was not at all sure he wanted to know. He had told his sister it was all over and so it had to be.

He pulled himself together to pay attention to the conversation, which ranged from the Greeks' struggle for independence from their Turkish oppressors and the relative merits of the new works of Turner and Constable on which the Duchess was very knowledgeable, to the latest state of the prisons, a subject close to Duncan's heart.

'Full to overcrowding,' the judge said. 'But what do you expect when the law won't let us hang 'em any more.'

'A great many are still hanged,' Duncan said. 'The Home Secretary has only tidied up an archaic law.'

'I collect you are one of those who would abolish it altogether.'

'Oh, I wouldn't go as far as to say that,' Duncan said laconically. 'Murder and treason should still carry the death sentence, but not theft, never theft.'

'Then how can we deter the thieves, sir, tell me that?'

'Prison is bad enough. Have you ever been inside Newgate, my lord?'

'No. Nor want to.'

The conversation threatened to become acrimonious and Lavinia stepped in to avert it. 'What great mystery are you working on now, Major?' she asked Donald.

'Making more work for me, I shouldn't wonder,' the judge said with a laugh.

Duncan held his breath, hoping that Donald would not mention Madeleine Charron. In view of the latest development, he would have to tell him not to proceed.

'Oh, it is not only criminals I seek, my lord,' the Major said. 'Sometimes people become lost: parents, children, grandchildren. At present, among other commissions, I am looking for the daughter of Viscount Armitage.'

'I have never heard of him,' the manufacturer said.

'He has become something of a recluse and is in poor health so he never comes to Town.'

'I remember his daughter,' Frances said. 'She was a pupil of my art master. I did a small portrait of her. But that must have been more than twenty years ago.'

'Twenty-five,' the Major said. 'Do you remember anything else about her? It might help.'

'She was very beautiful, as I recall, but I was not clever enough to transfer that to canvas. Whatever was her Christian name?'

'Arabella,' Donald said.

'Yes, that was it! I remember we called her Bella. But how did she come to be lost?'

'It is a sad story, but not an unusual one,' Donald told them. 'When she was only seventeen she wanted to marry a nobody of whom the Viscount did not approve and when she insisted she was going to do it anyway, he delivered an ultimatum, telling her not to go whining to him when it all went wrong, for he was sure it would. He did not think she would defy him, but when she did, he disowned her, said he never wanted to see her again. She left with her new husband and he has not seen or heard of her from that day to this.'

'What was so unsuitable about the man to make him unacceptable to the Viscount?' Duncan asked.

'He was a common soldier. Not even an officer of good family. He did not have the means to keep her in the style she was accustomed to, not in any style at all.'

'And now?'

'It is preying on the Viscount's mind. He finds himself wondering if she is well and happy and if he has grandchildren he knows nothing of. A grandson would be his heir. And he is ill and afraid he will die without being reunited with his daughter. He tried to make enquiries himself but to no avail and so he called me in.'

'And have you made any progress?'

'Very little. There are so few clues. I have been able to discover where the marriage took place, but after that nothing. I have the man's name, of course, but they seem to have disappeared completely. If he was a soldier, they could have gone anywhere in the world. He might have been killed and his wife left to fend for herself. She might have married again.'

'But if he did survive,' one of the lady novelists said, 'he would be long past military age now and have come home and his family with him.'

'That is what I am hoping. Unfortunately, I have no idea what she looked like twenty-five years ago, let alone what the passage of time might have done to her appearance.'

'You know, Major, I might still have that portrait,' Frances said. 'Would you like me to try to find it for you?'

'Indeed, I would. I would be grateful for any help.'

'You have an impossible task, my friend,' Marcus said. 'Perhaps Armitage should have had his pangs of remorse sooner. He has left it a little late to make amends now.'

Duncan looked sharply at his father. It did not sound as if he agreed with the Viscount's obstinate stand. 'I assume you would not have cut her off, Sir.'

'No, I should have handled it differently, I think. Bought the young man out and found him employment, tested him. Asked them to wait a little. She was young. Nothing is ever gained by putting one's foot down in such cases, except misery and alienation.'

Duncan was reminded of Lavinia's assertion that their father had suffered from being forced into a marriage he did not want and perhaps one day he might ask him about it, but for now, he was comforted. If only Madeleine had not been a servant of the Bulfords! He decided to take Sir Percy's advice and ask her about it, if only for his own satisfaction.

Sir Percy called for Madeleine and Marianne in his carriage, gallantly told them he would be the envy of the *ton* with two such beauties to escort, and took them to supper at Clarendon's which was a huge extravagance. After a gourmet meal and a shared bottle of wine, they set off for Vauxhall Gardens, reached by driving over Westminster Bridge to the south side of the Thames. The bridge was regularly clogged with traffic and tonight was no exception; it took over an hour to make their way across it.

Once they had arrived at the entrance to the gardens, Sir Percy sent his carriage home with instructions to return at midnight, paid their entrance fee and offered his arm to escort them through the shady walks, dotted with statuary, pergolas and fountains, all illuminated by hundreds of lamps, to the huge circular music room where the orchestra was already assembling.

They were soon absorbed into the crowds that were gathering, promenading about the vast central room, waiting for the music to begin. There was an air of expectancy, excitement even. Handel's *Water Music* had first been performed here over seventy years before and had been a regular offering ever since. It lent itself so well to the setting, the leafy bowers, the quietly lapping river, the warm evening and wide sky; the sense of timelessness.

'So romantical,' Marianne said, with a sigh. 'Don't you feel it, Maddy? As if the ghosts of all the lovers that ever were are gathered here. What a setting it would make for *Love's Labour's Lost*.'

The play was set in a park outside a palace and Madeleine agreed that, yes, it would. 'But I doubt we could make ourselves heard out of doors,' she added.

'Oh, you have no soul,' Marianne said, laughing. 'I wonder who is here that we know.'

'Everybody, I should think,' Sir Percy said drily. 'Hang on to me or we shall become separated.'

Madeleine did her best, but when the orchestra finished tuning their instruments and the conductor came forward to begin the recital, everyone surged forward and she found herself being pushed from behind and in the mêlée became separated from her companions. There was nothing she could do about it and so she settled down to enjoy the music, wedged between an overdressed tulip who was what was termed a beau nasty, judging by the odour of his unwashed body, and an equally ostentatious woman. The feather that curled round her turban was so long it was tickling Madeleine's nose.

'Hats!' someone yelled from behind her and the woman, along with everyone else, removed her headgear and Madeleine was able to see a little better.

Once the recital began, Madeleine stood enthralled. The stuffy atmosphere and the fact that her shoes were pinching faded from her mind, until the last note of music died away, to the accompaniment of thunderous applause. After several encores, the audience turned almost in unison to find the best place to view the fireworks. Madeleine searched about her for Sir Percy and Marianne; though she could see no sign of them, she saw no reason to worry. She had heard Sir Percy tell his coachman to return at midnight; all she had to do was make her way to the gate by the appointed time and she would find them there.

The crowds were still so thick that she could not have made her way against the general flow even if she had wanted to. She allowed herself to be carried along and found herself near the river bank. It was a good spot to view the fireworks, which were being set off across the river, and people were congregating all along its banks. The crowd fell silent as the sky was lit by fountains of coloured light and the air punctuated by the sharp crack of explosions.

When the last of the drops of colour fell to earth, there was a concerted sigh and then Madeleine suddenly saw Benedict Willoughby, outlined by the dying embers, standing beside a small inlet of the river in pantaloons and shirt and nothing else. And beside him, similarly dressed, was Duncan Stanmore. Both men were fit, but Duncan's torso rippled with muscle and his tight trousers left little to the imagination. She was too far away to see his expression, but he seemed very intense, concentrating on watching half a dozen men lay a smooth, round pole from bank to bank across the stream that fed into the main river.

Madeleine craned forward as the crowd, now there were no fireworks to see, gathered about them in curiosity. A whisper was carried from person to person, from one small group of people to the next, growing in volume until it reached the spot where Madeleine stood. 'They are going to fight a duel.' The crowd rushed forward, running to be nearest the action, taking Madeleine with them.

Her heart was in her mouth. Sir Percy had told her he did not think either man was in a mood to proceed with that foolhardy challenge and having seen them with their arms about each other only the day before, she had assumed all danger has passed. How wrong she had been!

She struggled through the crowd, using her elbows when necessary, until she was very close to the open space that had been made around the men by their seconds. Her intention was to try to stop it, but before she could do so, the two men bowed formally to each other and were each handed a pillow. The crowd began to roar with laughter as they both climbed astride the pole and inched their way out to the middle, facing each other.

'They are going to fight a duel with pillows!' the onlookers shouted. 'To be sure they will never kill each other with feathers.'

James Corringham, who was acting as one of Duncan's seconds, went over the rules in a loud voice so that those nearby could hear. They were not to touch each other with anything other than the pillows and no one from either side was to touch the poles or assist in any way until one or the other was in the river. He asked them both if they were ready and, when they nodded, fired a pistol into the air and they set to, clinging to the pole with their knees and one hand while battering their opponent with the pillow held in the other.

'What are they fighting over?' someone behind Madeleine asked a companion.

'To be sure it can only be a wench.'

The first man laughed. 'Then they must count her worth in feathers, not enough to risk getting hurt for. Do you know who she is?'

'No. But I know those two. Best of friends they are, so it can only be a jape to amuse the crowd.'

Madeleine had heard all she wanted to hear and would have liked to leave, but she could not make her way out of the press of people around her and was obliged to stay in her place. Both men were still wielding their pillows, but there were feathers everywhere and they would soon only have the cases in their hands. Besides, they could hardly go on for laughing.

'Go to it, Stanmore!' someone shouted.

'Have at it, Ben!' yelled someone else.

It took all their concentration to remain on the pole and they had eyes only for each other, but when Benedict slipped and had to put both hands down to recover his balance, Duncan momentarily looked up. He saw Madeleine, standing watching them. She was not laughing like everyone else; in fact, she looked decidedly miffed, standing alone in a dark gown studded with brilliants, which made her look like a goddess. How could a kitchen maid show such a commanding presence?

It was almost enough to unseat him. Luckily Benedict was busy settling himself again and he had time to recover his balance. But it was no longer funny and he wanted to finish it off as quickly as possible and hitched himself forward to get in closer to his opponent. One furious swing and Benedict was hanging upside down under the pole, held there by his crossed legs and scrabbling hands. He was not yet in the river and tried to pull himself back, but Duncan thrashed him again and again with the remains of his pillow, to the accompaniment of the roars of the crowd. At last Benedict's legs gave way and he fell with a splash into a couple of feet of water.

The crowd cheered and Duncan held up the pillow in salute and that was his undoing. The pole was wet and slippery and he joined his friend in the water. They were helped out by their laughing seconds, who stood by with blankets to wrap round them. 'Well done!' Donald shouted, shaking Duncan by the hand. Duncan strode over to Benedict and offered his hand, but when he looked up again for Madeleine, she had gone.

Chapter Eight

Madeleine had taken the opportunity to escape as soon as the fight was over and the crowd began to disperse. She found Sir Percy and Marianne walking arm in arm down the main avenue towards the entrance. They were laughing.

'Where have you been?' Marianne asked.

'Watching two grown men make cakes of themselves.'

'Oh, so you saw them too?'

'I should think half of London witnessed it and if they did not, they will hear all about it in the morning.'

'Better that than kill each other,' Sir Percy said. 'I think it was rather clever of them. Honour is satisfied and no one hurt. A good way to round off the evening's entertainment, though what the Duke will say when he hears, I do not know.'

'Doubtless he will agree with you,' Marianne said.

Madeleine was silent. In her heart she knew they were right, but she could not help remembering the comment of the man standing behind her: *They must count her worth in feathers, not enough to risk getting hurt for.* She did not know whether to be furious or thankful.

She supposed she had seen the last of both of them, but she was wrong. Duncan was in the audience the following evening and was waiting at the stage door when she left the theatre at the end of the evening. She pretended not to notice him, but he stepped in front of her, magnificent in a black evening suit with a snowy white frilled shirt. 'Miss Charron, good evening.'

'Good evening, my lord.'

She went to pass him, but he took her arm. 'Allow me to take you home. My carriage is outside.'

'What makes you think I have any desire to ride in your carriage, my lord Marquis? I have nothing to say to you.' She tried to sound haughty and indifferent, but inside she was quaking. For all he had made a fool of her, pretending to have feelings for her when all the time it was a great game to him, she still loved him. Hurt as she was, nothing could change that.

'But I have a great deal to say to you and unless you want it said here and now, for anyone passing to hear, you will get into the carriage. I will take you straight home, have no fear.'

It did not sound as if he intended to make protestations of love or suggestions she should become his paramour. His voice was cold, as indifferent as she had hoped hers sounded. 'I am not afraid,' she said. 'And as you have so kindly offered, I will save myself the price of a cab.' She did not wait for him to escort her, but strode out, head high, and stepped up into the carriage. He climbed in beside her.

'I did not know you would be at the fireworks,' he said when they were under way.

'There is no reason why you should, my lord. I go where I please, with whom I please.'

'You appeared to be alone.'

'I was not. I had become temporarily separated from my companions. It was of no consequence, I soon found them again.'

'I looked for you, you know. Afterwards.'

'Why? Did you imagine that I would be amused by your antics?'

'It wasn't done for your amusement, Miss Charron, but in order to save bloodshed.'

'You could simply have refused Mr Willoughby's challenge.'

'And be known for a coward! No, Miss Charron, that was not to be thought of, honour had to be satisfied. Now Willoughby and I can be friends again and no harm done.'

'Is that why you stopped me tonight, simply to tell me that? Because if you did, I must tell you I am entirely indifferent.'

'I do not think you are indifferent. I think you are angry.'

He could read her mind too easily for her comfort. 'Not at all,' she said. 'But do you know what they were saying, those people gathered round you? They said that I was valued at a handful of feathers.' She spoke bitterly, realising that she was being unjust but unable to stop herself.

'You would rather we fought to the death?' he queried, angry himself now. 'I might have known that would tickle your prodigious vanity.'

'My vanity! What do you know of my vanity, or my humility come to that? You do not know me.'

'No, and that's a fact,' he snapped. 'Why did you not tell me you had been a servant in Lord Bulford's household?'

So he had heard. She was not surprised; it could only have been a matter of time before one of the Bulford girls, if not Henry himself, remembered her. 'Is there any reason why I should have?'

'You knew that I… I was growing fond of you. You led me on to believe…'

'I did nothing of the sort. I told you plainly that I would not become your *chère amie.*'

'I did not suggest you should.'

'You did not have to, it was what you meant. I am not a fool, you know.'

'No, but you *are* a liar.'

Unable to deny it, she was silent. The carriage rolled on through the streets of London, now in the

light of street lamps, now in darkness. Occasionally
he caught a glimpse of her face. It was not defiance
he saw there, nor truculence, but infinite sadness.
His anger melted away.

'Will you tell me why?' he asked softly.

She forced herself to sound normal, though there
was a catch in her voice. 'You mean why I did not
tell you I had been a servant? My lord, you knew
I had been in an orphanage, surely you realised I
had not gone straight from there to the stage? I was
put to work at Lord Bulford's residence and very
hard I had to work too. After that I earned my living as a seamstress before I met Mr Greatorex and
he saw my potential as an actress. I did not lie, I
simply did not go into detail, that's all.'

He sighed. Lavinia had been right and he ought
to admire her, not condemn her.

'And the French grandfather?'

She gave a strangled laugh. 'Now we are getting
to the hub of the matter.'

'No, it is of no importance to me, my dear. I
would love you whoever your grandfather was, but
Society has its own funny ways.'

Her heart soared. He loved her. He had said he
did. But there were obviously conditions and he
still did not know the extent of her deception. She
ought to make a clean breast of it, but just for a
moment she wanted to savour the idea of loving
him and being loved by him, as if there was no
great obstacle blocking their path. She was re-

minded of the little lecture Sir Percy had given her about a landowner's responsibilities and the need to have the respect of those around him. Was he being torn two ways?

'So I have discovered,' she said. 'But you spoke of love. Love does not admit of barriers, does it? If Society's opinion is so important to you, then it cannot be love you feel.'

'You do not understand.'

'Oh, I understand only too well. If I were of noble birth and stopped earning my living on the boards, then I might, at a pinch, be accepted by this Society you set such store by. I tell you this, my lord, I will not pretend to be other than the actress I am and if you cannot accept that, then there is no more to be said.'

He turned towards her as the carriage drew to a stop outside her lodgings and took both her hands in his. 'Madeleine, why are we quarrelling? I did not mean to disparage you. I love you. I thought you loved me. Tell me if I was wrong.'

Steeped in misery, she could not give him an answer, though he was evidently waiting for one because he made no move to get out and help her down but continued to hold both her hands. If she had any sense, she told herself, she would pull away, open the door and jump down herself, but she was shaking so much, she doubted if her legs would support her.

'Well, my dear, shall I assume you are not going to deny it?'

'If I say you are wrong, you will only call me a liar again,' she said miserably.

'Then you do.' He turned her hands over and raised the palms to his lips. She shuddered with an exquisite pleasure which sent ripples of desire running through her body. She lifted her face to look into his for one long searching moment, during which his eyes never left her face, then slowly he lowered his head and kissed her lips. His mouth on hers was gentle at first, tentative almost, but when she did nothing to resist it, the pressure of his lips intensified and became more demanding until she was screaming inside for him to make love to her.

When at last he let her go, the tears were streaming down her face and she could not stop them. 'Oh, my dearest love,' he said, handing her his handkerchief. 'You do, you really do.'

She scrubbed at her face and pulled herself together. 'It makes no difference. I will never be your mistress, I will never be anyone's mistress.'

'Not my mistress, my wife. We could be married if only—'

Her laughter sounded harsh in her own ears and it startled him. 'Oh, yes, my lord, if only someone were to wave a magic wand and obliterate my past and make me one of the nobility. Pigs will fly first. I have no past except the one you know and now that Miss Bulford has recognised me, the whole world will soon know it.' She took a deep breath determined to finish. 'Far from having a noble background, I am a child of the people. I do not know who my grandfather was. I invented him. I do not even know who my father was, presumably one of the Duke of Wellington's scum…' Her voice was full of bitterness. 'There! Are you satisfied now? It's what you wanted to hear, isn't it?'

His look of horror was enough to bring her back to sanity. He did nothing to stop her when she opened the door, flung herself from the carriage and rushed into the house.

It was all over. Their love had never had time to blossom. It had never stood a chance. And she had brought her troubles on herself. She should never have invented the *comte*, never pretended to be other than what she was. This was her punishment, to love without hope, to be spurned by Society. Why had she been so foolish as to think she could get away with it?

But as she toiled up the stairs to her room, thankful that Marianne was out and could not quiz her, she wondered why her mother had not told her about her father. If he was a soldier and had died on some foreign battlefield, surely that was something to be proud of? Would it help if she knew? She went to the window to look down into the street. Duncan's carriage, driving away down the street, was a blur, seen through tears. 'Fool!' she berated herself. 'Idiot!'

She scrubbed at her face, undressed and climbed into bed, though she knew sleep was impossible. Something had to be done to cure the ache inside her. Somehow her life had to be changed. She thought of leaving town, finding work in a provincial theatre, but whatever she was, she was a professional and could not leave the play in the middle of a run. And nothing and no one could be allowed to affect her work, that must be paramount. It had taken years and years to reach the standing she enjoyed now and she would be a fool to throw it away. She was stuck.

Having talked herself into a more positive frame of mind, she fell asleep at last.

She woke the next morning still determined to make a new start. That afternoon she insisted on a fresh rehearsal to change one or two aspects of her performance she felt could be improved, one of which was her French accent. 'I am supposed to be a Princess of France,' she told Lancelot. 'I don't sound French at all.'

He laughed. 'And you with a French name and a French granddaddy! Very well, I'll ask a friend of mine who speaks the language to coach you, but don't overdo it, will you? You are playing to an English audience, they must be able to understand you.'

Ironically, Pierre Valois, who arrived at the theatre the following afternoon, was the son of a

French *émigré*, who had come to England in 1793 to escape the guillotine. Although Pierre had been born in London a year later and English was his native tongue, his father had insisted on bringing him up to speak French and now he earned his living teaching young ladies to speak the language. Though he was older than Madeleine by nine years, his background was so like the one she had invented for herself, that she could only wonder at the vagaries of fate which had brought them together.

He was handsome and he knew it, but he was also charming company and he soon had her laughing at her attempts to put a French accent on Shakespeare's English words. 'Did your mama never speak French?' he asked her.

'Not that I know of. Why?'

'I heard your papa was French. Or was it your grandpapa?'

'I never knew either of them,' she said, and closed her mouth firmly on the subject. But it made her realise the story had not gone away. Duncan had not seen fit to broadcast her deception, probably because it would make him look a fool. The *comte* was still dogging her footsteps.

'Well never mind, even if you never knew your ancestors, I think there is something of the Frenchwoman in you. You are so, so...*je ne sais quoi*...elegant and self-possessed. Your demeanour proclaims you every inch a Gallic princess.'

She laughed. 'That is the actress in me.'

'Perhaps. But as the saying goes, "What's bred in the bone will come out in the flesh."'

'You are not the first person to say that to me,' she said, thinking of Duncan. But Duncan knew the truth now and she must put him from her mind. 'Now, do you think we can proceed? I want to try out my new accent at tonight's performance.'

She was an apt pupil; that evening she had a delightful French accent, which enchanted her audience. The applause at the end was a fitting tribute to her dedication and hard work and she acknowledged it by dropping into a full curtsy. This was what she had been born for and she would do well not to forget it. She took several curtain calls and accepted the many bouquets sent up to her with charming graciousness, but when she returned to her dressing room it was to the knowledge that nothing had really changed.

Pierre was waiting for her, sitting at his elegant ease, talking to her dresser. He rose when she entered. 'My congratulations, *ma'amselle*. You were magnificent.'

She smiled. 'I did not let you down, did I?'

'I never thought you would. But I was not referring to your accent, but your whole performance. I was transported with delight.'

'Thank you, kind sir.'

'We must celebrate. Will you do me the honour of supping with me?'

She paused, thinking of Duncan, but Duncan was gone, a small part of the past she had decided to turn her back on. And Pierre Valois had no connection with the *haut monde* or anyone from it. She would be safe with him. 'I shall be delighted,' she said. 'Give me a minute to change.' She disappeared behind the screen with her dresser and after a few minutes emerged dressed in the blue velvet dress she had worn to Vauxhall Gardens.

'Magnifique!' he said, stepping forward to take both her hands and hold her at arm's length to look her up and down. 'The brightest star in the firmament. I shall be the envy of the whole city, no, the whole country.'

Laughing, she flung a cloak round her shoulders and declared herself ready to go.

He took her to Stephen's in Bond Street, an eating establishment much favoured by army officers, where the food was very good but not up to the Clarendon's standards nor its prices, where a meal could cost as much as four pounds a head. She did not suppose for a minute he had the resources of Sir Percival Ponsonby and to be truthful she was glad not to be on show at the dining rooms frequented by the Marquis of Risley and his kind. No doubt they were still laughing over that parody of a duel.

The eating house was a popular place, but a table was soon found for them. After consulting her, Pierre ordered sole *bonne femme*, saddle of lamb with several different vegetables, including salsify fried in butter and broiled mushrooms. 'And champagne to go with it,' he told the waiter. 'We are celebrating.'

'Why did you say that?' she asked, as the waiter went away smiling.

'Celebrating, you mean? We are, aren't we? The success of a joint enterprise. And my delight in the part I played in it. I would rather teach you than half a dozen school misses, who simper and giggle and have no idea how a real lady conducts herself.'

'And how does a real lady conduct herself?'

'Like you do, my dear, with grace and charm.'

She smiled at his gallantry. *'Merci, monsieur.'*

Their food and wine arrived. The champagne was poured by the waiter who wished them *'Bon appétit'* and left them.

'To the most beautiful woman in England, who also happens to be an incomparable actress,' Pierre said, raising his glass to her. 'May she long continue to enchant us.'

She laughed and picked up her glass. 'To a French teacher *par excellence* who is also an accomplished flirt.'

'What's wrong with that?' he demanded. 'How dull life would be if we could not enjoy a little flirtation now and again. Don't you agree?'

'Oh, I agree.'

'Then let us continue, shall we?'

'Eating, drinking or flirting?'

'Why, all three, my dear lady, all three.'

She laughed. So long as the conversation did not flag, giving her time to think, she was almost content. He was outrageous in his comments about the latest *on dit*, paid her extravagant compliments, which she accepted in the spirit in which they were given, light-heartedly and with no undercurrents to trap her. She responded in kind and the evening passed very pleasantly.

It was when they were getting ready to leave and he was putting her burnoose about her shoulders that she noticed Major Greenaway, sitting at a table alone. He stood up as she passed him on her way out. 'Miss Charron, your obedient,' he said, bowing.

'Major Greenaway. Good evening.'

With her escort's hand under her elbow to guide her, she continued past his table and out into the street where the cab Pierre had ordered was waiting for them. The presence of Major Greenaway had not exactly spoiled the evening, but it had brought a sharp reminder that she was not as tough as she liked to think and that Duncan Stanmore had been a presence at the table the whole way through the evening. It was very unfair on her companion, but she hoped he had not noticed.

She had wondered if she might have to fight him off at the end of the evening, but he behaved perfectly, taking her to her door and kissing her hand with exaggerated courtesy. 'I have had an enchanted evening, from the time the French princess came into view on the stage until this minute.' He sighed dramatically. 'And now, I suppose, it must come to an end.'

'I am afraid so,' she said, retrieving her hand. 'But I thank you for your escort.'

'Then take pity on me. Come out with me again.'

'Perhaps,' she said. 'You know where to find me.'

'Then I shall be in the audience again tomorrow night.' He smiled and kissed the tips of his fingers to her. '*A bientôt.*'

Had she meant that? she asked herself, as she went indoors. He had been very helpful over the French accent and an amusing supper companion, but did she really want to encourage him? She smiled to herself; his extravagant compliments meant no more to him than they did to her and where was the harm? If it helped to take her mind off a certain Marquis, then so much the better.

'Stanmore, there you are.'

Duncan, in the act of stripping off for a sparring bout at Jackson's, turned to find Donald Greenaway at his elbow. 'Hallo, Major. What brings you here?'

'Bedevilled, my friend. I can make no headway with the Viscount's commission and so I decided to turn my attention to the matter of Miss Charron's grandfather. I thought I'd pursue the army connection, so I arranged to meet a friend from the Department of Military Knowledge at the Horse Guards last week at Stephen's. He has access to the casualty lists. Strange I should see her there.'

'Who?'

'Miss Charron. She was with a fellow I had never seen before. I asked the proprietor if he knew him. His name is Pierre Valois and he is the son of a French *émigré* who came over in the nineties, so it seems the lady is making her own enquiries.'

'Making her own enquiries, why should she do that?' Duncan demanded. She had taken him for a gull with her lies and pretence and he had simmered with anger and resentment for days before he could convince himself that she was not worth the heartache.

'Why not? If you had never known your father and grandfather, wouldn't you be curious about them? Especially if it makes a difference to how you are received in Society.'

It was on the tip of his tongue to tell his friend that Madeleine had lied, but he decided to say nothing. She would be the object of scorn and derision and he could not do that to her, whatever she had done. 'Yes, I suppose I would, but as she seems to be managing very well on her own, there is no need for us to pursue the matter.'

'Not pursue it?'

'That's what I said. I have decided not to proceed. I'll pay for what you have already done, of course.'

Donald looked closely at his friend, wondering what had brought on his change of mind, but decided not to comment. 'Apart from a little golden grease to smooth my path at Whitehall, I haven't done much, been too busy with the Viscount's problem.' He paused. 'How long are you going to be here?'

'An hour or so, why?'

'I thought we might go together to visit Lady Loscoe. She promised to try and find that portrait of Viscount Armitage's daughter, if you remember.'

'Wait for me then. Or strip off and go a few rounds.'

'No, thanks. Like your friend, Willoughby, I'm no pugilist.'

'Oh, you heard about that, did you?'

Donald grinned. 'Who hasn't? The whole of London knows.'

'What are they saying?'

'That it was capital sport and a very fitting end to Willoughby's pretensions.'

'What are they saying about the reasons for the challenge?'

'Oh, that there is sure to be a lady in the case, but as to her identity, they are only guessing.'

'Then they may go on guessing.'

Duncan's sparring partner arrived and he left Donald to watch while he weaved and ducked and threw punches with practised ease. Donald, whose knowledge of the noble art was limited to acting as a sparring partner to the Duke of Loscoe when they were both much younger, was full of admiration for the speed of Duncan's footwork and the way he defended himself against his opponent's onslaught, while finding his target himself. At the end of the bout Duncan came over to him, rubbing himself with a towel. His body was gleaming and he was breathing quite heavily, but there wasn't a mark on him.

'I can see why Willoughby did not want to meet you in the ring,' Donald said. 'When did you first take up pugilism?'

'Oh, years ago. My father introduced me to it when I was no more than a bantling.'

'And he was one of the best, as I can vouch. I've had bumps and bruises by the score given in the cause of friendship. That's when I decided the sport was not for me.'

Duncan smiled. 'I've had a few myself. If you give me a few minutes to bathe and dress, I'll be ready to go.'

* * *

They walked in companionable silence, but Duncan was thinking about Madeleine dining with the Frenchman. Who was he? Where had she met him? She wasn't trying to find out about her grandfather, because she had admitted he never existed, so what was she up to? And why did he feel like finding the man and tapping his claret for him? He smiled inwardly. He had done that to Benedict and look what had happened. And next time, the result might not be so amenable. Besides, she was not worth it.

'Did you find out anything about Charron from the army casualty lists?' he asked, trying to sound casual.

Donald turned towards him, smiling. 'Thought you didn't want to know?'

'Curious, that's all.'

'Nothing. No Charron on the lists as far as my friend could tell.'

'He might not have been a casualty. Could have come home in one piece.'

'Not on the strength either. At least not under that name.'

'Oh. Could he have been in one of the German regiments?'

'Possible, I suppose. That's why I thought she might know something she has omitted to tell anyone. It could be something important like a change of name or some little thing like a dim memory of a place or something said by her mama. I thought you might have learned more…'

'No, afraid not. But it's of no consequence now, since my interest in the lady has waned.'

'Then I must go back to the Viscount's problem. I wish I could help the old man, he is getting weaker all the time and I hate having nothing to tell him.'

'He should not have turned his daughter out. I could never do that. Children are precious…'

The Major laughed. 'And there speaks someone who has never known the joys or the responsibilities of fatherhood!'

Duncan gave a wry smile at his friend's teasing. If he did not make a push towards matrimony, he never would know. The thought of spending the rest of his life as a bachelor with no young people, like his nephew and niece, around him, was not to be contemplated. He loved children and Vinny had been right; he ought to have some of his own. 'One day,' he said. 'Give me time.'

They arrived at Stanmore House and were shown into the drawing room, which was crowded with the Duchess's friends. 'Oh, goodness, I had forgot it was one of Stepmama's at-homes,' he said. 'Now we shall have to act the agreeable until they have all gone.'

The two men went forward to greet the Duchess and then began to circulate as was expected of them. It did not take them long to discover that Lady Bulford was present with Miss Bulford and Miss Annabel.

'Why, how agreeable we are met again so soon,' Lady Bulford said, fluttering her fan at him. 'Annabel, is that not so?'

'Oh, indeed yes.' Annabel blushed to the roots of her fair hair and refused to meet Duncan's eyes.

'May I present my friend, Major Greenaway?' Duncan said. 'Major, this is Lady Bulford and her sisters-in-law, Miss Bulford and Miss Annabel Bulford.'

They acknowledged him and he bowed formally. 'Your servant, ladies.'

'I am trying to place you,' Lady Bulford said. 'I do not seem able to recall the name. From the country, are you?'

'Major Greenaway is an old friend of my family,' Duncan put in, afraid that Donald was about to give the lady a put down.

'Any friend of the dear Duke is a friend of mine,' she said, recovering herself quickly.

'I heard you had been in a scrape since we last met,' Hortense said to Duncan.

'Scrape?'

'Oh, Hortense, you must not quiz the Marquis about it,' Annabel put in. 'It is only tattle, after all, and we do not want him to think we put any store by it.'

'Tattle?' he queried, pretending innocence. 'About me?'

'Oh, it is nothing,' Annabel said. 'They say Mr Benedict Willoughby challenged you to a duel and you fought with...'

'Fought with what?' Duncan could not prevent the smile which played about his lips. 'Pistols or swords? I am considered a prime hand with both.'

'You know very well, my lord, that it was with pillows. Everyone is laughing about it.'

'Surely, my dear Miss Bulford, it is better to be laughing than crying? And someone would certainly have been weeping if we had used orthodox weapons. It was a ruse to amuse our friends, not to be taken seriously at all.'

'Oh, but the lady...'

'Lady?' he queried. 'Whoever said anything about a lady?'

'No, of course there was no lady,' Hortense said. 'What man of breeding is going to sully his reputation fighting over a kitchen maid? Do be sensible, Annabel.'

Duncan opened his mouth to give her a sharp retort, then shut it again. 'Excuse me ladies,' he said, bowing stiffly. 'There is someone I must speak to.' And with that, he turned on his heel and left them.

How dare they? How dare that...that termagant speak so disparagingly of the woman he loved? Hortense Bulford could not hold a candle to Madeleine Charron. Madeleine was more of a lady than she would ever be. He gave a twisted smile.

Less than an hour ago he had denied all interest in the actress, promised himself he would put her from his mind and find himself another wife, which only proved how inconsistent he was. But if he ever married Annabel Bulford, he would make damned sure her sister was never invited to stay.

Since he had told his stepmother very firmly that he was not considering making an offer for Annabel Bulford, this thought took him by surprise. He was not ready for that. Not yet. He needed a drink. He strode across the hall to the library where he knew his father kept a decanter of brandy and some glasses. He was in the act of helping himself when the door opened and the Duke came in. 'Have the prattling women driven you out, Duncan?'

'Something like that.' He held up the decanter. 'You don't mind, do you?'

'No, help yourself. Pour me one too.' He sat down in one of the armchairs by the hearth. 'We should have a little talk.'

'Oh, that sounds as if you are going to deliver a jobation.'

'Not at all,' he said, accepting a glass of brandy from his son and nodding towards the opposite chair. 'You are too old to scold like a child. But your reaction inclines me to think you have something on your conscience.'

Duncan sat down and took a mouthful from his own glass. 'No, sir, my conscience is clear.' He paused, wondering whether his father had heard about the duel. 'I suppose you are referring to that *contretemps* with Ben Willoughby.'

'What made you do it?'

'Willoughby demanded satisfaction, so what could I do? He is no match for me with pistols or swords and I did not want to hurt him.'

The Duke smiled. 'You did not consider that you might have been the one to eat grass?'

'Yes, of course I did. No one is infallible.'

'Very true. The idea of pillows was a stroke of genius, but why in so public a place?'

'That was his choice, not mine. I could do nothing about it. I think he wanted to humiliate me. It is done with now and will soon be forgotten.'

'Let us hope so. What was it all about?'

'I would rather not say. But he deserved the ducking.'

'Then I will not pry, so long as you have done nothing to bring shame on yourself or your family.'

'No, Father, I have not.'

'Good.' He paused, swilling his drink round in its glass, as if considering what to say next. 'When are we going to see you married, Duncan?'

'Oh, no, not you too. It is enough that I have to endure it from Vinny, who is so happy in her marriage she thinks anyone who chooses to be single must be short of a sheet.'

'I hope this desire to stay single is not a permanent state of affairs. I do not wish to push you into matrimony, my boy, but it is time, you know.

I can thoroughly recommend it.' He paused and lifted his glass. 'To the right woman, naturally.'

'I am giving it some thought.'

'Lord Bulford has indicated his younger sister would entertain an offer.'

'He has spoken to you? Papa, I thought the days when parents and guardians arranged their children's marriages were long gone.'

'I think he was sounding me out, to see if I would put any obstacles in your way.'

'And what did you say?'

'I said you were of age and the decision when and whom to marry was yours and yours alone.'

'And did you mean it?'

'I am not in the habit of saying things I do not mean, Duncan, although I hope you would be sensible—'

'And not marry a kitchen maid,' Duncan finished for him. 'Don't worry, Father, it is not likely to happen.' He noticed the puzzled look on his father's face as he drained his glass and realised he had not heard that particular *on dit*. 'Will you excuse me? I must find Major Greenaway. He came with me to see Mama. She said she would try and find the portrait she painted of Viscount Armitage's daughter.'

'Of course.'

When he returned to the drawing room, he found Donald was still talking to the Bulfords, which surprised him. He went to join them, realising it behoved him to make amends for his abrupt departure. He smiled. 'I am sorry I had to hurry away,' he said.

'No matter, my lord, you are back now,' Annabel said. 'Major Greenaway has been entertaining us with stories of his adventures.'

'Indeed?' he queried, raising his eyebrow at Donald. 'I shall have to persuade him to tell them to me sometime.'

'Did you know he is familiar with all the Bow Street Runners and often uses them to help him find people who are lost to their relatives?'

'Yes, I did know that. He also finds lost or stolen jewellery and apprehends criminals. And twice he has rescued ladies who were kidnapped.'

'What interesting friends you have, my lord,' Hortense put in. 'Do you perhaps dabble in mysteries yourself?'

It was a direct reference to Madeleine, but he refused to rise to the bait. He smiled. 'Occasionally, Miss Bulford, if the Major needs some help.'

Annabel looked relieved. 'Oh, that must be why—' She stopped in confusion. 'Oh, I am sorry. Major Greenaway says a lot of his work is confidential, so I must not ask. Suffice it to say, I do understand.'

Puzzled, he looked towards Donald, who was grinning. What had the idiot been saying to them? He was at a loss to find an answer, but was saved by the arrival of Lord Bulford come to take the ladies home. There was a flurry of goodbyes and from Annabel a reminder that her come-out ball was only two weeks away and she was looking forward to seeing him there, and then they were gone.

'Well,' Duncan demanded of his friend. 'What the devil have you been saying to them?'

'Oh, something and nothing. All a closely guarded secret, of course.'

'Of course. Your secret will be as safe as water in a bucket full of holes.'

'That's what I thought.'

'So?'

'I told them that I was very near to solving the riddle surrounding a well-known actress.'

'But you aren't.'

'No, but they don't know that, do they? I said if they repeated the story of the kitchen maid, it could go very ill for them, when the full truth was revealed. I also said I had enrolled you to help me…'

'Oh, Lord, Donald, you've cooked my goose now. Madeleine confessed she had made the whole story up. There never was a French *comte*.' He saw the Major's eyes widen in surprise and added, 'But I shall call you a liar if you ever repeat that.'

'Oh, Stanmore, I am sorry. I thought I was helping. Why didn't you tell me when we spoke of her before instead of simply saying you had changed your mind?'

'It is not something I want the gabblegrinders to get their teeth into; the Marquis of Risley made a complete flat by a nobody of an actress.'

'I see,' he said, though it was clear he did not see at all.

'Let's go and find my stepmother. I've hardly spoken two words to her all afternoon and you need that portrait.'

The Duchess had been standing by the door, saying goodbye to all her guests, but now they had all gone and the servants were clearing away the tea cups and crumb-laden plates from almost every flat surface, she came across the room to join them. 'Duncan, I am honoured,' she said, smiling. 'You have attended two at-homes in as many weeks. What have I done to deserve it? Or has it something to do with the presence of Miss Annabel Bulford?'

'I did not know she would be here, Mama.'

'No? She evidently expected to see you.'

'Did she? I said nothing to her about coming. Or was it simply curiosity to know what you had to say about that so-called duel?'

'If it was, I am afraid she must have been disappointed. I professed ignorance on the subject.' She did not wait for a reply but turned to Donald. 'And you, Major, I collect have come for that portrait of Bella Armitage?'

He bowed his head. 'If you would be so kind, my lady.'

'I found it yesterday up in the attic with all the lumber, covered in cobwebs. Luckily it cleaned up nicely. I left it in my studio. I'll go and fetch it.'

'She won't let the servants anywhere near her studio,' Duncan said, noticing the look of surprise on the Major's face as she disappeared on her own errand. 'Sacrosanct, it is. Even I am only allowed in by invitation.'

He walked over to the window, which looked out on to St James's Square. The street was busy with traffic; a dog was chasing a ball in the park, thrown by a little boy, one of three children in the charge of a nursemaid. He watched the dog return with the ball and drop it at the boy's feet. One of the little girls scooped the dog up and it licked her face. They were all laughing. He felt an almost irresistible urge to run out and join them. Sooner, rather than later, he must set up his own nursery or he was in danger of becoming an old bachelor like Sir Percival.

'Here it is.' He turned away from the window as the Duchess returned, carrying a small canvas about a foot square. 'I never did finish it. I think she may have disappeared about then, but I have no recollection of hearing that at the time.'

Duncan walked over to join them as the Major took the picture from her. 'She was beautiful. Don't you think so, Stanmore?' He held the canvas towards Duncan.

'My God, it's Madeleine. Miss Charron.'

'Don't be silly,' Frances said. 'I painted that over twenty-five years ago. It's been gathering dust ever since.'

'But it's her likeness. Can't you see it? Those eyes. And the chin.'

'There is a faint resemblance, I agree, but no more. If I had had time to finish it, it might look entirely different.' She turned to Major Greenaway. 'I am afraid it is not going to be much help to you. I am sure the flesh tones are not right and I had hardly started on the hair. It was very dark, as I recall.'

'It is better than nothing,' he said. 'At least, I will have something to show anyone who might remember her.'

'Where was she last sighted?' Duncan asked. He was still looking at the picture. On closer examination, of course it was not Miss Charron. As his stepmother had pointed out, the likeness was only superficial, but for one heart-stopping moment he thought he had been looking at a picture of Madeleine. Had she become so ingrained in his heart and soul that he was seeing her wherever he looked?

'She was living over a bakery in St Albans with her husband. It was only a year after they were married. One person I spoke to said they were a strange couple. He was a big man, very domineering, and she seemed exceptionally shy, wouldn't say boo to a goose. She might have been afraid of him. They went out very little and lived very frugally. They moved away, no one seems to know where they went nor exactly when.'

'Poor thing, she would have found life extremely difficult after being used to servants and a comfortable home with meals put on the table for her,' Frances said. 'She was not robust, as I recall, but rather delicate. Do you think she could have died?'

'It is possible. I have been searching through hundreds of church records for a burial but, not knowing exactly where to look, it is a laborious task and so far I have found nothing. Nor any evidence of a child, though that is not to say there wasn't one. One woman I talked to in St Albans said she thought Mrs Cartwright was *enceinte* when she left.'

'Cartwright?' queried Duncan.

'Yes. That was the fellow's name. John Cartwright.'

'I'll ask around,' Duncan said, knowing that if the name had been Charron, Donald would have said so long before, but disappointed, just the same.

'They are unlikely to have mixed with the *haut monde*,' the Major pointed out. 'He was one of the lower orders, according to Viscount Armitage.'

Duncan gave a wry smile. 'My acquaintances are not all from the top hundred, Major.'

'No. Do what you can. I shall be obliged.'

'And I could enquire at the orphanage,' Frances said. 'If there was a child...'

Mention of the orphanage reminded Duncan so forcefully of Madeleine that he wondered why he had not pursued that line of enquiry before. But it was too late. Madeleine Charron had admitted a reprehensible deception and must be put firmly from his mind.

Chapter Nine

Pierre haunted the theatre after that first meeting. He was in the audience every night leading the applause, he sent her extravagant bouquets of flowers, he sat in her dressing room after the performance waiting for her to change and go out to supper with him. Sometimes she agreed, sometimes she turned him down, but then he simply smiled and returned the following night.

'He is much more your style than the Marquis of Risley,' Marianne told her, when they were preparing for the evening performance about a week later. 'He is of good family, his antecedents are known and accepted and though he is not exactly a top sawyer, he is not so far adrift that he would not make you a perfectly acceptable husband.'

'The subject has never been broached,' Madeleine said.

'It will.'

'Gammon!' Madeleine laughed, though it was a little strained. 'I hardly know him.'

'I'll lay odds on a proposal before the month is out.'

'Oh, Marianne, what shall I do?'

'Do? You could accept him.'

'But supposing I do not want a husband? You have never had one.'

'I am different. I enjoy my life as it is. I have my friends and my work and that is enough for me, but that does not mean it would be so for you. You are made for marriage and a family. You need a family. It is the only way you will overcome the hobgoblins that haunt you.'

'Am I haunted by hobgoblins?'

'You know you are. This obsession to become a lady and be accepted by the *haut monde*, is not healthy, you know. If you are not careful, you will become an embittered ape-leader and goodness knows what that will do to your work. Can you not see that?'

'I suppose so,' she said doubtfully. 'But I do not love Pierre and he doesn't know there is no *comte* either.' It had worried her at first that the story of her French grandfather had not been revealed as a deception. Every day she had expected some titbit of gossip to reach her that meant she had been exposed. But far from that happening, the tale seemed to have strengthened without her doing anything to advance it. What she had dreamed of all the years of her struggle to survive and her life before she met the Marquis had happened. She had been accepted.

Oh, not in the inner circles, the true top one hundred, but near enough. She was listened to, deferred to and often addressed as 'my lady', a title she was certainly not entitled to use, even if her grandfather had been a *comte*. Tradespeople, dressmakers, shoemakers, hairdressers, cab drivers, vied with each other for her custom and were all too ready to allow her to run up bills. She was invited to soirées, routs and picnics and was not expected to perform for her supper, though she occasionally did *tableaux vivants* or what Lady Hamilton had called 'attitudes' to entertain her hostess's guests.

But it had all gone sour. It had gone sour because it was built on a lie and because she had fallen in love with one of the hated aristocracy when all she had intended was to use him.

She told herself she was over the Marquis of Risley and that he had turned out true to his class after all, an overweening, top-lofty, vain member of a section of society who did not know what a day's work was like, nor what it was to feel cold and hungry and who thought money could buy anything. And when her strict sense of justice reminded her that he did a great deal of good among the inmates of the prisons, she countered this by arguing that he associated with criminals because it made him feel virtuous, not because he had any real idea of what they thought or felt.

The trouble was that he was so enmeshed in her heart, it was almost as if he was the reason it continued to beat. Pierre Valois did not affect her in that way. Pierre was comfortable to be with; he made her laugh and he made no demands on her intellect but there was something missing, something that was always present when she was with Duncan. It was passion, fire, an overpowering need to be close to him, even when they were quarrelling.

'Tell Monsieur Valois the truth,' Marianne said, with her usual bluntness. 'I do not suppose he will care in the least. He might even find it amusing.'

And so she told him everything two evenings later when they were dining at Fladong's in Oxford Street. And Marianne was right, he laughed. 'Oh, how clever of you, my love, but why choose a Frenchman?'

'Harder to trace,' she said. 'The English aristocracy are all known to each other. The location of every great house is common knowledge. I would never have got away with an English grandfather, but the progeny of French aristos are as numerous as sparrows. You are one yourself.'

'I do not think I like being compared to a sparrow,' he said, grinning at her. 'An eagle, now that would be more like it.'

'You do not condemn me?'

'No, why should I? But are you sure there is not even a grain of truth in the story? After all Charron sounds French and Madeleine is a French name.'

'My mother invented Charron for a name because she thought it would be good for business. She was a modiste, you see.' She smiled. 'Like chefs and fencing masters who have never been anywhere near France give themselves French names.'

'I still say there must be something in it. You have good breeding and that is something you cannot learn.' He held up his hand when she opened her mouth to protest. 'Oh, I know you are the finest actress that ever trod the boards, but even you could not assume what was never there. I think we should do some delving.'

'Oh, not you too!' she exclaimed, laughing at his flattery. 'I did not think it would matter to you, unlike some I could name.'

'Oh, it doesn't, but like is attracted to like, don't you think? I think that is why I feel we were meant for each other.'

'Fustian!'

'Oh, do not tell me you do not feel it too, this *rapport* we have.'

'*Rapport*,' she said. 'I give you *rapport*, but that could happen to any two people at any time, that is not to say—' She stopped, floundering. 'You don't have to be French.'

'True,' he said thoughtfully. 'Maddy, don't you know I adore you? I want to marry you.'

'Oh, Pierre, I wish you hadn't said that.'

'Why? You are not going to turn me down, are you?'

'I'm sorry. We have a great deal in common and I am very fond of you, but…'

'You are still wearing the willow for the English Marquis,' he said bitterly.

'Who told you that?'

'I do not need to be told. Whenever his name is mentioned, your eyes become blank as if you are far away in a dream of your own, and when he is present, as he was the other day at Lady Graham's musical evening, you could not take your eyes off him. They glow when you see him, as if someone had turned up a lamp.'

'That's humbug.' She wished he had not mentioned Lady Graham's concert. She had not expected Duncan to be there and the sight of his tall figure in immaculate evening wear, standing at the back of the room, made her heart skip a beat. He had bowed to her as she passed on Pierre's arm, murmuring, 'Miss Charron, your obedient,' but he had not smiled.

She had spent the remainder of the evening not listening to the music but thinking of him, knowing from where he stood he could see her sitting in the middle of the audience. Once she had ventured to turn in her seat and found him looking at her, but his thoughts she could not fathom and quickly turned away again, knowing her face was on fire.

'Oh, I know you tried to pretend indifference,' Pierre went on. 'And anyone less in tune with your sensibilities might have been taken in, but I was not. Maddy, he will not marry you, you know that very well and you are deceiving yourself if you think he will. Besides, I have it on good authority, he is as good as promised to Annabel Bulford.' He seized her hand across the table and nearly knocked her wine glass over. 'Forget him. Look at me. Am I not here? Am I not languishing for love of you?'

'Are you? You have only known me a couple of weeks, not long enough to be sure of anything.' She was aware, as she spoke, that she had fallen in love with Duncan Stanmore in less time than that. She could not stop herself comparing the two men. They were both handsome and both had impeccable manners, both were good company and both were generous, though Pierre was unable to spend as freely as Duncan, which would not have counted in the least if she had truly been in love with him. In the end it came down to how she felt in her heart and here there was no comparison. Duncan stirred her limbs, made her quiver with desire, sent her heart racing. But it was more than that; she admired his courtesy, his compassion, his tenderness for others, his intellect. Everything about him except his arrogance. And that, she decided, was bred in the bone.

'It seems like forever.'

'Pierre, I think it is not me you love, but the actress.'

He sighed dramatically and blew his nose on a spotted silk handkerchief which, until that moment, had been dangling from his coat pocket. 'You leave me desolate, a broken man.'

'Who is the actor now?' she demanded, laughing.

He recovered astonishingly quickly and they finished their meal and were bowed out by the proprietor who was calculating how much extra business he could milk out of the fact that the great actress and her Corinthian friend had dignified his establishment. A cab was fetched for the short journey to her lodgings and he left her there with the admonishment, 'I meant it, you know. Forget what you cannot have and settle for me.'

Was he right? 'I'll think about it,' she said.

Duncan was trying his best to forget a pair of violet eyes which were as expressive as any words. Eyes that had been either blazing at him with fury or full of tears that sparkled on long dark lashes like diamonds, wringing his heart. An actress's trick, of course, just as that sob story about the French *comte* had been a trick to gain his sympathy. She had used him and he did not like being used.

He threw himself into the Social whirl, accepting almost every invitation that came his way in order to expunge her from his mind. He was the catch of the Season and to be seen in his company was the height of bliss for the year's young hopefuls and so the gold-edged invitation cards poured in. He found himself attending routs and balls, concerts and lectures and going for picnics and carriage rides in the park.

He tried to be even-handed, but that was becoming increasingly difficult because the word had gone round that he was dangling after Miss Annabel Bulford and she was at almost every function he attended and, according to Lavinia, being urged by her sister-in-law to make a push to bring him to a proposal. He supposed he could do worse. But that was damning with faint praise and was not a good basis for a happy marriage.

Seeing Madeleine at Lady Graham's with her new escort was a sharp reminder that his efforts to put her from his mind had failed. The story of her grandfather, the *comte*, had been accepted and was now being strengthened by the fact that her latest admirer was the son of a French *émigré*. The young man was too flamboyant for Duncan's taste, both in dress and manners, but he would not admit he was prejudiced. He wondered if the man knew the truth about his lady love, a question echoed by Donald Greenaway.

They were standing in Hyde Park in a huge crowd that had come to watch a balloon ascent. Duncan had offered to take Lavinia's children and that had resulted in all the children in the family clamouring to accompany him. Besides Lavinia's two, there was his fourteen-year-old cousin Jack, home from school for the summer holiday, his half-brother Freddie, now a sturdy nine-year-old and the apple of the Duchess's eye, and Andrew and Beth, the children of James Corringham's sister Augusta.

Surrounded by the older children, with the two youngest perched one on each shoulder, he looked like a veritable Pied Piper, as Donald had told him when he had come upon him and laughingly taken Jamie from him to sit him astride his own shoulders. Relieved of the boy, Duncan had put Caroline's tubby legs about his neck and taken her hands firmly in his own.

'I've been thinking about Miss Charron,' the Major said.

'Oh.' Duncan's tone was guarded.

'I've a mind to go and talk to her.'

'Why? You are not planning to expose her, are you?'

'No, but I was looking at that portrait the other day and I think you were right, it does bear some resemblance to Miss Charron. It's a long shot, but I thought I'd show it to her. Have you any objections?'

'Why should I?'

'It might blow her story sky high and you said—'

'Major, you have a job to do and how you do it is your affair. Besides, I do not think Miss Charron can have any connection with an English aristocrat or she would certainly have made use of it long before now. She would not have needed the French *comte*, would she?'

'True. You'd think under the circumstances, she would keep away from all things French, wouldn't you? Do you think Valois knows the truth?'

'No idea. None of my business.' His tone was curt and Donald fell silent.

The preparations for the ascent going on in the open space that had been roped off from the public were proceeding apace and the balloon was almost fully inflated. Caroline, on his shoulder, was wriggling up and down in her excitement. 'Sit still, Carrie,' he said. 'If you fall, you will be hurt and you won't be able to see the balloon go up into the sky.'

Intent on helping his small relatives to a good view as the intrepid flyers climbed into the basket and those holding the ropes prepared to release it, he did not see Madeleine. But she saw him. Standing beside Major Greenaway, surrounded by excited children, he seemed perfectly at ease. He was hatless and the child on his shoulders had ruffled his dark curls, his cravat had come awry and her dusty shoes had marked his green superfine frockcoat, but he seemed oblivious of it. Watching him and not the spectacle she and Marianne had come to see, her heart ached so much she wanted to burst into tears. He would make a wonderful family man. But not with her. If anything was needed to convince her, it was that happy group.

'Who are they all?' she asked Marianne, as the balloon began to ascend slowly, accompanied by cheers from the spectators.

'Who?' Marianne had not seen them.

She used her frilled silk parasol as a pointer. 'All those children with the Marquis.'

'The tall young man is Jack, son of the Duke's brother, though the Duke and Duchess have adopted him, the bantling beside him is Freddie, the Duke and Duchess's son, and there is Andrew and Beth, who belong to the Earl of Corringham's sister, Lady Augusta Harnham. And the two sitting on the men's shoulders are Lady Lavinia Corringham's children, Jamie and Caroline. James Corringham and Augusta are the Duchess's step-children from her first marriage to the Earl of Corringham's father, did you know that?'

'No, I didn't.'

'They are all very close. I met the older ones when they took part in that play I told you about. It looks as though they adore the Marquis.'

'Yes.' She understood now why his family was so important to him and why he would never cut himself off from them, not even for love of a woman. She had never stood a chance.

Some of the crowd began running after the balloon, intent on seeing it come down, but it soared up over the trees and was soon lost to sight. Others crowded into vehicles and tried to follow it, while the rest slowly dispersed. Duncan said goodbye to the Major whose business took him in a different direction, and turned to take the children home. It was then that he saw Madeleine standing not ten yards away. Dressed very simply in a pink muslin gown trimmed with silk rosebuds and wearing a fetching straw bonnet tied with a pink ribbon, she looked so modestly beautiful, it was difficult to believe she was capable of blatant deception. And yet she was.

They stared at each other for several seconds, while the crowd milled about them. She could not move either towards him or away from him, or even curtsy. Neither could he bow to her because he still had Caroline perched on his shoulders, nor even doff his hat since he was not wearing one. 'Miss Doubleday. Miss Charron. Goodday.'

'Good afternoon, my lord.' Marianne greeted him with a smile. 'Have you ventured into running a kindergarten now?'

He returned her smile, aware that Madeleine, standing beside her, had not moved. 'Children are so rewarding, don't you think? Give them your trust and they play you straight. These...' he waved his hand about him, but he was looking at

Madeleine as he spoke '…are my family, the rock on which my life is built.'

'You are indeed fortunate to have such a family, my lord,' Madeleine managed at last. 'But they grow restive and we must not keep you from them.'

He knew he deserved the put down, if put down it was. It was unkind of him to have made that comment about the children and his family. Madeleine had no family and perhaps that was why she needed to invent one. He could find sympathy for beggars and thieves and go out of his way to help them, yet he could not forgive her for her deception. But she had not asked for forgiveness; as far as he could tell she was utterly unrepentant.

His smile was fixed and did not reach his dark eyes. 'Then I bid you goodbye.'

She watched him walk away, not quickly because the smaller children could not keep up, but shepherding them carefully.

'Goodbye,' she murmured, as she and Marianne turned to leave by the Stanhope Gate. She was seized with an urge to look back, but schooled herself to look straight ahead, twirling her parasol nonchalantly. But that goodbye was as final as anything could be.

'Lancelot has decided this will be the last week of *Love's Labour's Lost*,' Marianne said, as they walked. 'Everyone in London who wanted to see it has surely been by now.'

'I suppose so, we've had some very full houses. What is he going to do next?'

'He hasn't decided. He asked me what I thought.'

'What did you say?' If the play's run was ending, now was the time to leave, now while she had the chance. She needed time, time to adjust, time to forget, time to build a new life. And not with Pierre Valois. If she stayed in London he would continue to importune her and she might weaken and that would be a disaster for both of them. Seeing Duncan with his family had finally decided her. She could not marry him, so she would remain single, but being single in London, reading about his wedding, perhaps even seeing him married, and watching his family grow around him would be unbearable.

'I said we ought to have a change from Shakespeare.' Marianne went on. 'We've had three of his plays in succession and the public deserve a change. I suggested a farce. What do you think?'

'It's all one to me. I shall not be here.'

'Not here? Where are you going?'

'I don't know yet, a provincial theatre somewhere.'

'Have you told Lancelot?'

'Not yet, but he won't mind if he's going to run a farce. It is not my style. I will tell him I need a rest.'

'He won't like it.'

'My mind's made up.'

'What about Pierre? He has asked you to marry him, hasn't he?'

'Yes. I turned him down. It would not serve.'

'Oh, Maddy,' Marianne said despairingly. 'You are not still pining for the Marquis of Risley, are you?'

'No, that would be futile, wouldn't it? But I do need a change of scene. I have become very stale.'

'Nonsense! You are as good as you ever were.' She paused. 'But I do understand and I think you are probably right. If I can help, I will.'

And so it was, that when Major Donald Greenaway went to the theatre, a few days later, he was told she had left and no one knew where she had gone.

'Gone?' Duncan repeated when the Major found him the following afternoon, sitting alone at his club, brooding about his life and a future which seemed so empty. 'What do you mean, gone?'

'Exactly that,' Donald said. 'The play she was in has finished and she has not been cast in the new one. She has left the theatre.'

'With Valois?'

'No. I spoke to him. He affects to be distraught by her disappearance. And he did know the truth about the *comte*, though no more details than we already have. I could have kicked myself for not going earlier.'

'You did say it was a shot in the dark.'

'True. Now I am back to combing through records. Did you ask at the prison if they'd had anyone there by the name of Cartwright?'

'No luck, I'm afraid.' To please his friend he had approached one of the country's senior judges who had given him permission to peruse whatever records he chose. He had spent hours poring over lists, but to no avail. The search had served to take his mind off Madeleine for a few hours, but as soon as he was out in the street again, she was back in his head, tormenting him. And now she was gone. He felt as though he had received a blow to the body.

'In a way that's a relief,' Donald said. 'I would have hated to tell the old man his son-in-law was a criminal.'

'Newgate is not the only prison in the country, you know, not even the only one in London.'

Donald sighed. 'I know. What about the orphanage?'

'You must ask the Duchess. Now, if you will excuse me, I have to go home and change. It's the Bulford ball tonight. Do you go?'

Donald laughed. 'No, I am not fit to be seen in such exalted company.'

'I wish I were not. I have a feeling it is going to be a very uncomfortable evening.'

* * *

It was only a short step to Stanmore House and within five minutes he was in his room, being readied by Davison. His bath was filled and his evening clothes laid out on the bed. On his dressing table, beside his hair brushes, lay his fob, his pocket watch, his quizzing glass, cravat pin and rings. Several starched white cravats hung over the mirror. Sometimes they did not tie to his valet's satisfaction and became crumpled and he always insisted on having another ready to hand.

An hour later, complete to a shade, he went downstairs to join the Duke and Duchess and together they went out to the carriage.

He said little on the journey, his mind on the evening ahead of him. Somehow he had to make it quite clear to Annabel and her avaricious brother and his wife that he would not, could not, make an offer for her, and he had to do it without hurting her feelings. He rehearsed his words in his head over and over again, while he wondered how he had come to such a pass. He had never been more than polite to her, never even hinted that he had marriage in mind, so why did Society always jump to conclusions?

He tried telling himself that he was being conceited in thinking that they expected an offer, but after that conversation with his father, he knew that was a vain hope. Bulford and his wife were determined to fire Annabel off and her feelings would not be considered. Well, he intended to consider them. Marriage to him would be a disaster for her, just as marriage to his father had been disastrous for his mother. And the other way about too. And it had nothing to do with a certain lying kitchen maid. Nothing whatever!

They were a little late arriving, but that was no more than their host and hostess expected. Duncan could hear the music as he climbed the stairs to where Lord and Lady Bulford and Annabel stood receiving their guests. Annabel looked very young in a white gauze gown over a taffeta slip, a colour that did nothing for her complexion. She had white ribbon about her waist and another threaded through her fair curls and her blue eyes looked worried.

'Your Grace.' they said, addressing the Duke and Duchess in turn. Then to Duncan. 'Marquis.'

Duncan bowed. 'Ladies, your obedient. Bulford, good evening.'

'Please go in,' Lady Bulford said. 'We will join you directly.'

They passed on into the ballroom, leaving the Bulfords to continue greeting latecomers. 'My goodness, what a squeeze,' Frances said, looking round the overcrowded room. 'She has invited far too many. The world and his wife are here. Duncan do go and see if you can find a corner for us to sit.'

He made his way through the mêlée, looking for vacant seats, and came across his sister and her husband. 'Come and sit with us,' she said, pushing her skirt to one side to make room on the sofa beside her. 'We were just talking about the latest *on dit*.'

'I am sure you are,' he said smiling. 'But if you have spare seats, I will go and fetch Mama.'

'I can see her talking to Lord and Lady Graham and she won't want to sit down until she has heard all their news. And Papa has quite disappeared. Sit down, we will have no opportunity to talk when the dancing really begins.'

'We shall be dancing cheek by jowl, by the look of it,' James said. 'I shall probably go and play cards.'

'You will do no such thing,' his wife said, tapping him with her fan, as Duncan sat down beside her. 'Have you heard the latest?'

Duncan smiled. 'No, but I expect you are going to tell me.'

'Miss Charron has disappeared. One night she was on stage as usual, the next gone and the actress who came on instead of her was so bad, she was hissed off the stage. The audience threw orange peel at her.'

Duncan allowed himself a small smile at the memory of Madeleine's anger when orange peel had been thrown at her. 'I expect Mr Greatorex thought she needed to be rested.'

'Perhaps, but the newspapers are reporting the mysterious disappearance of Covent Garden's leading lady as if there were something havey-cavey about it. They say she would never have gone of her own free will when she has never missed a performance before. They say she had no reason to go; she was the darling of the London stage and earning hundreds of pounds a year. They say the Bow Street Runners are looking for her and hint that a certain well-known investigator has been asked to join the search. That must be Major Greenaway. Do not tell me you did not know?'

'I knew she had left, but as for the rest, that is pure conjecture.'

'You would say that, my lord, considering you are helping the Major with his investigation.' Startled by the voice, he looked up to see Annabel standing behind his seat. How long she had been there listening he did not know.

He scrambled to his feet to make her a bow. 'Miss Annabel, your obedient.'

'Is it not strange,' she said, 'Maddy appears from nowhere to be our kitchen maid and then she disappears for years, only to reappear as a renowned actress. And now she has disappeared again. I wonder what her next metamorphosis will be?'

'I have no idea,' he said, made uncomfortable by her look of innocent contemplation.

'It was a long time ago, to be sure. She was only a little thing, thin as a beanpole and pale with it, but look at her now. She is so composed and she speaks so beautifully. I never would have believed it if Hortense had not remembered who she was when I said her face looked familiar.'

'Was she called Charron then?' James asked, unaware of Duncan's discomfort.

'Yes. She came to us from an orphanage.'

'Which one?' Duncan asked, unable to stop himself.

'I do not remember, my lord. I was only a little girl, but when we spoke of it the other evening, Hortense said it was the one the Duchess is patron of, though she said it was not in Maiden Lane then.'

'How extraordinary,' Lavinia murmured, looking at Duncan.

Duncan could not bear to hear any more and turned to hold his hand out to Annabel. 'Miss Bulford, a dance is beginning, shall we take to the floor?'

'Oh, yes, to be sure,' she said, taking his hand and allowing him to lead the way on to the floor where the dancers were grouping themselves for a country dance. They joined a set and there was no opportunity to continue the conversation. When the dance was ended he offered her his arm to take a turn about the room before returning her to her brother and sister-in-law.

She had a very high colour, he noticed, and asked her if she were perhaps too warm. 'The room is very crowded,' he added.

'Yes, Dorothy was determined to squeeze everyone in. I wish she had not.'

'Why not?'

'Oh, my lord, can you not guess?'

His heart sank. 'They are expecting...' he paused, then went on '...someone to offer for you tonight?'

'Yes, I believe so.' She blushed to the roots of her hair. 'Surely, my lord, you know?'

He guided her out of the room and on to the gallery that looked down on the wide marble-floored vestibule. It was cooler out there and there was no one about, though he had no doubt their exit had been noted. Both were silent for what seemed a very long time, then he said, 'Miss Bulford, I am at a loss to know how to proceed...'

She gave a cracked laugh. 'Do not tell me you expect me to guide you, for I know even less than you do of how these things should be done.'

He smiled slowly. 'It isn't that I do not know the procedure. But I am of the opinion a proposal should come from the heart, and that if a man cannot in all sincerity lay his hand upon his breast and say ''I love you'', he should remain silent.'

'Oh.'

'You do understand what I am saying?'

'I understand, but I doubt whether Henry will. He told me it was all arranged, that he had spoken to the Duke and they had come to an agreement...'

That was not his understanding of the conversation of the two men, but he let that pass. 'Whether they came to an agreement or not is of no consequence, Miss Bulford. Do you really think that two men putting their heads together over a bottle of port should decide the happiness or not of two otherwise independent people?'

'You may be independent, my lord, but I am not. Henry promised to find me a good husband and I must bow to his superiority. He is my guardian and it is the way of things.'

'You do not sound very happy about it.'

'He says happiness comes later.'

Her face was scarlet and he began to feel very sorry for her. 'And do you believe that?'

'I have to or I could not endure it.'

'Endure it! What an extraordinary word to use about an offer of marriage. Endurance should not come into it. Joy, perhaps elation, delight at being loved, a desire to make another person happy, never unequivocal obedience, however one might esteem the person giving the direction. Miss Bulford, would you view an offer of marriage from me as something to be endured?'

She looked at her feet and remained silent.

He took her chin in his hand and tilted her face up to his. 'Come now, tell me the truth. The whole truth.'

'My lord...I...' She gulped. 'Yes, I suppose I would. I truly cannot see myself as the wife of a

Marquis, let alone a Duke, which is what it would come to in the end. Henry says I would have nothing to do but look pretty, but I know there is more to it than that and...'

'And?'

'I cannot put my hand on my heart and say I love you, any more than you can say it to me. But I am afraid.'

'Of me?' he asked, startled.

'No, my lord, of Henry. He will be so angry. He will blame me for not making a push...'

'Miss Bulford—Annabel—do not think about your brother, think of your own happiness. I will undertake to deal with Lord Bulford.'

'Oh, would you?' She sounded so relieved, he smiled.

'Now, let us go back, we have been absent long enough.'

He offered her his arm and guided her back into the ballroom. He was aware of hundreds of pairs of eyes watching their progress as they made their way to where Lord and Lady Bulford and Hortense were sitting. He bowed to them and Annabel took her place beside them.

'Well?' Lady Bulford said, shutting her fan with a snap. 'Are we to felicitate you?'

'I fear not, my lady,' he said.

Her ladyship turned to Annabel, hardly able to conceal her fury. 'You never were such a ninny as to turn him down, miss?'

'Do not blame Miss Annabel,' Duncan said. 'We agreed we should not suit. It was a decision mutually arrived at.'

'You mean you never offered!' Her voice was too loud and Duncan was aware that others had turned towards them, listening. 'Henry, do something. The man is a mountebank, a rake to lead an innocent, well-nurtured young gel into expecting an offer and then balking at the last fence.' She turned to Duncan, eyes flashing. 'Fie on you, sir!'

'Be quiet, Dorothy!' her husband commanded. Then to Duncan in a low voice, 'Risley, I think you have some explaining to do, but we are already attracting too much attention. Follow me, if you please.'

Duncan gave Annabel a reassuring smile and followed his host to his book room, where Henry turned to face him, his eyes cold with suppressed fury. 'I am waiting for an explanation, Marquis.'

'Explanation of what, Lord Bulford? I have already told you Miss Annabel and I agreed we should not suit.'

'You mean you convinced her of it and she is such a lily-livered chit she dare not stand up to you. But I will. I will tell the world you reneged on an offer.'

'The offer was never made, so how can I have reneged on it?' Duncan said. 'Not once have I hinted that I intended to do so. And I tell you at once that Miss Annabel was more relieved than sorry and it was only her fear of your bullying that led her to agree to receive an offer should one be made.'

'Bullying, my lord! I am the girl's guardian and it is my duty to guide her.'

'Then guide her. Do not force her. Or I shall be forced to believe her happiness is more important to me than it is to you.'

Lord Bulford looked as though he was about to have a fit of apoplexy. His rotund face became almost purple as he struggled to find the words to put Duncan down. 'The world shall hear of this,' he said at last. 'Your name will be reviled.'

'I do not think so,' Duncan said calmly, though not without a *frisson* of trepidation. If the man made good his threat, he would be cut by everyone. 'I think your reputation would be more damaged than mine.'

The man's reaction to this was extraordinary. He pulled a handkerchief from his pocket and mopped his brow, then sat heavily in a chair. His face was the colour of chalk and it suddenly came to Duncan that Lord Bulford had something to hide, something shameful, something he thought Duncan was privy to. For a moment it aroused his curiosity and he almost forgot the reason for their exchange of words. 'The brazen jade is a liar,' Henry said.

'You don't say so,' Duncan said, having no idea what he was talking about, but not about to admit it.

'I do say so. Whatever she has told you, you may be sure she has invented. 'Tis plain she wants to put an end to Annabel's hopes in favour of her own, surely you can see that?'

'Can I?'

'Are you being deliberately obtuse, Risley? She is an actress, after all, skilled in the art of pretence.'

So he meant Madeleine! What was Maddy supposed to have said to put his lordship into such a taking? He smiled slowly. 'You may be sure whatever she told me has no bearing on whom I marry, Lord Bulford,' he said firmly.

Henry mopped his brow. 'No, naturally it would not. We know her for a liar. All that nonsense about a French *comte*…'

This was a little too near the bone and Duncan was anxious to bring the interview to an end before he throttled the man with his own cravat. 'What is that to the point, my lord?'

'No, you are right, it is not relevant at all.' He seemed to pull himself together. 'We were speaking of your engagement to my sister.'

'We certainly were not, we were discussing the reasons why it could not and should not be.'

'Quite. I see I was mistaken in Annabel's wishes.'

'Good. Then no more need be said.' He turned to leave. 'And if I hear you have been browbeating Miss Annabel, then you may be sure I shall know what to do.'

And with that he left, having threatened a man without knowing precisely what he was threatening him with. Madeleine would know, but Madeleine was heaven knew where and probably would not tell him even if she were right beside him. And how he wished she was!

He went back to the Duke and Duchess, who were sitting with Lavinia and James. 'There you are, Duncan,' his stepmother said. 'You have been gone an unconscionable long time and the rumours are flying.'

'I'm sorry, Mama. I would not, for the world, embarrass you.'

'So you have not offered?'

'No, Mama. Annabel did not wish it any more than I did. She had been bullied by that brother of hers, but we have come to an understanding, Lord Bulford and I.'

'Amicable?'

'As amicable as it is possible to be with someone like him.' He paused. 'I came to tell you I was leaving, then everyone can gossip to their heart's content.'

'Perhaps that would be best. We will stay a little longer for appearance's sake.'

He left them and walked deliberately over to where Annabel sat with Lady Bulford and Hortense. He made her a sweeping leg. 'Your most obedient, Miss Annabel. Whatever you do, I wish you happy.'

She smiled bravely and stood to face him. 'I will walk with you to the door, my lord.'

He bowed to Lady Bulford and Hortense and offered her his arm. Watched by everyone, they made their stately way to the double doors that led to the gallery. 'I am sorry I brought this upon you,' he said.

'You did not, my brother did. And I am extremely glad you had the courage to tell me the truth.'

'On the contrary, you are the one with the courage.'

'What did he say?'

'Not a great deal. After I had explained, he agreed we should not suit.'

'He did not threaten you?'

'No, he did not threaten me.' He gave her a quirky smile. 'It is all over. But I shall not mind if you let it be known you turned me down. I intend to leave London shortly. There are things to be done on the family estate in Derbyshire. If the *haut monde* chooses to believe I am nursing a broken heart, then let them do so.'

They stopped at the door, he raised her hand to his lips and kissed it and then he was almost running down the stairs and out into the night air. He would find Madeleine. He could not live without her. Oh, there might be a little malicious gossip to start with, but he could endure that. He would have to endure the disapproval of his father and stepmother too, but nothing and nobody would stand in the way of his marriage to the woman he truly loved.

But where was she? Where to begin looking for her? Miss Doubleday would know. It was too late to go visiting, but tomorrow he would go to the theatre and ask. And wherever she was, he would go to her. He strode home on foot, determination in every step.

But Marianne did not know where her friend had gone. Or she pretended not to know. 'She simply said she wanted a change of scene,' she said. 'No doubt she will return in due course.'

'That won't do. I want to find her now.'

'Why?'

'Why?' He looked at her as if she were an idiot. 'Why would a man go after the woman he loved?'

'Do you? Love her, I mean.'

'Yes, I do.'

'I believe you, but unlike many actresses, she will not become anyone's *fille de joie*...'

'I know that, she told me so often enough. I cannot believe she has simply disappeared. Someone must know. Do you know the tattlers are saying the Runners are looking for her?'

She laughed. 'No? Oh, how droll! Though I must admit Major Greenaway came looking for her, but I thought you had sent him.'

'No, I did not. He is looking for someone entirely different and thought she might know something.'

'Yes, he told me. He had a portrait with him.'

'He showed it to you?'

'Yes, and though I give you a certain likeness about the eyes, it cannot have any connection with Maddy.'

'How do you know?'

'Because I know her story is true.'

'Not the *comte*?'

She smiled. 'No, not the *comte*, but you know that already, for she told me she had confessed her deception. But everything else is the truth.'

'You mean the orphanage and the place at the Bulfords.'

'Yes.'

'What happened there?'

'That is something you will have to ask Madeleine, my lord.'

'I would, if I could find her,' he said. 'But since she is not to be found, I need to know.'

'I believe she was turned off and before you ask why, she has not confided the reason to me, but I think it must have been something very dreadful. It gave her an aversion to all the aristocracy and a determination to revenge herself on them all. In her own words, she determined to make herself a lady of consequence, to be accepted in Society.'

'And used me like a flat,' he said bitterly.

'The trouble was, my lord, that everything changed when she met you. She discovered that not all aristocrats are rakes and tyrants…'

'I am glad to hear it,' he said drily, his mind in a whirl. Something had happened to Madeleine at the hands of Henry Bulford and he could easily guess what it was. Some men thought kitchen maids were fair game and he would not be surprised to learn that Bulford was one such. Had Madeleine succumbed? Had she been forced? But if she had, it meant… No, it did not bear thinking about.

'She fell in love with you, my lord, and was besieged by guilt and the knowledge that she had forfeited your respect. ''Hoist by my own petard'' I think were the words she used. That is why she left. And if I might be so bold, I think you should leave her alone to recover.' She paused and when he had nothing to say, added, 'Now, I have a rehearsal to go to, if you will excuse me.'

He left, utterly dejected. Was she right? Should he give up and accept that Maddy was lost to him? But how could he rid himself of this ache in his heart, this huge knot of longing that only she could relieve? He walked. He did not know where he was walking, nor did he care.

Chapter Ten

Arabella Cartwright took York by storm. Accustomed to having all the best actresses rushing off to London as soon as they had learned their craft, the theatregoers of that city welcomed her like a breath of fresh air. From her first performance in an indifferent tragedy by an unknown playwright, she was fêted and the theatre's takings took an unprecedented boost.

It pleased Madeleine that she was judged on her merit as an actress and not because she was Madeleine Charron, well known as one of Lancelot Greatorex's 'finds'. Everyone was singing her praises as the best tragedy actress the north had seen for years, but it was easy to play a tragic heroine when your heart was breaking. She had only to think of Duncan and how she had won him and lost him, for genuine tears to fall and her performance rose from good to superb.

Many, well versed in theatre lore, wondered where she had come from. She appeared not to have had the usual struggle to be recognised, but arrived already skilled and totally in command of herself and the role she had been given. Their questions were unlikely to be answered because she disappeared immediately after each performance and did not mingle with the other thespians and theatregoers who crowded backstage afterwards. It gave her a certain aura of mystery.

But she had learned her lesson. She told no lies, made no statements about her antecedents; she certainly said nothing at all about a French grandfather. She was, she told the theatre management when she applied for a job, simply a young woman who had come into acting because she had to earn a living and she had discovered she was good at it. She asked only for a chance to prove it. It was fortunate for her that one of their company had fallen sick and a replacement was needed and so, having given them a speech from *Romeo and Juliet*, her most famous role, as a taster, she had been offered a part as a temporary measure.

And just in case her fame had spread to Yorkshire, she had reverted to her real name of Cartwright and used her mother's given name. Not that she expected pursuit. Duncan was, by now, engaged to marry Miss Annabel Bulford, a young lady considered eminently suitable by his friends and family, and he evidently agreed with them. She tended to fall into hysterical laughter whenever she thought about it. Annabel Bulford was no more beautiful, no more accomplished, no more educated than Madeleine herself; indeed, she was probably less so. But she had the one thing that mattered: a pedigree.

Over and over again, she told herself that if a pedigree was all the Marquis of Risley was interested in, then she was well rid of him. Perhaps she should not have run away. It let him know how hurt she was and that would feed his...what did he once say to her? Prodigious vanity, that was it. But the thought of returning to London filled her with panic. She could not go. Not yet. One day, perhaps.

The London Season was drawing to an end, already some families had gone to their country estates and the knockers were off the doors. It could not come fast enough for Duncan. He longed for the peace and quiet of his Derbyshire home, to immerse himself in the affairs of the estate, being left more and more to his management because the Duke was involved with government affairs. There he could ride in the countryside, go hunting and fishing, help bring home the harvest on the home farm and amuse his cousin and young brother until both went back to school in the autumn. There, perhaps, he might find, if not contentment, then an easier mind.

Towards the end of July, the engagement was announced between Miss Annabel Bulford and Benedict Willoughby, something which came as a complete surprise to Duncan. He wished them happy with all his heart and gave his friend a lecture on the responsibilities he was taking on, which made Benedict laugh.

'You are a fine one to talk, Stanmore. What do you know of it?'

'I know she is a lovely girl and deserves the best.'

'You mean you. I am sorry you have been disappointed, my friend, but on this one occasion, I have bested you.'

'True,' he said. Henry Bulford had made sure everyone knew that Annabel had refused him and he had no intention of denying it. Let them think what they liked. 'And I felicitate you.'

'The ceremony is to be in London next April. Will you be my groomsman?'

'I will be delighted.'

He had never envied his friend before, but now he was filled with such unutterable despair, he was obliged to make his excuses and go off somewhere on his own. He did as he usually did when he was beset by problems, he set off for Newgate to talk to the prisoners and help them in any way he could; it reminded him how lucky he was. He had everything any man could possibly wish for, except the woman he loved. He was plagued by the notion that she had been violated by Henry Bulford and then his fury knew no bounds. He began to realise what drove a man to murder.

He spent two hours talking to the prisoners and arranging for extra food to be taken in to some of them and paid for the shackles of some others to be loosened and by then he had become calmer. As usual, he asked everyone he spoke to if they had come across anyone by the name of Cartwright and wondered as he did so, why he continued to worry about Viscount Armitage's daughter when there was another missing person nearer to his heart that he wished he could find.

Madeleine must have taken a coach to wherever she was going; he had made enquiries at every staging post in London but no one had recognised her, let alone remembered her destination. She seemed to have disappeared into thin air and he began to wonder if some of the rumours surrounding her disappearance might be true. Had some harm come to her?

Having done all he could for the prisoners and arranged for an inmate who had served his time to go to the house in Bow Street to be helped to find work, he set off for home, walking swiftly down Fleet Street and along the Strand to Charing Cross. Here he found himself outside the Golden Cross, one of the busiest coaching inns in the capital. The bustle of horses being harnessed and luggage being hauled out and strapped on the waiting coach made him stop to watch.

His previous enquiries about Madeleine had drawn a blank, but perhaps someone had remem-

bered something since his last call. He was pon-
dering whether to go in and ask again, when the
familiar figure of Donald Greenaway appeared at
his side, carrying a portmanteau and dressed for
travelling. 'Stanmore, what are you doing here? I
thought you'd gone to the country.'

'Not yet. My father still has some government
business to attend to before we leave. Where are
you off to?'

'I had word from one of my scouts that there is
an actress called Arabella Cartwright in York.'

Duncan smiled. 'Another long shot.'

'Perhaps, but that was her name, if you remember: Arabella Cartwright, born Arabella Armitage.
I have a feeling in my bones, this is the one.'

'Then good luck to you.'

'Since I spoke to you last, I have discovered
what happened when Mr and Mrs Cartwright left
St Albans. He was drafted to India and died there
of a fever in 1803, so that seems to rule out any
connection with Miss Charron. She said her father
was killed in the war with Napoleon, didn't she?'

It was in his mind to comment that if she could
lie about one thing, she could also lie about another, but decided to keep his own counsel. It did
not make any difference, especially now it looked
as though Donald was on the trail of the lady at
last. 'Yes, she did.'

'It means Mrs Cartwright was widowed very
early in her marriage and would have had to find a

way of earning her living. If the woman in York is
Arabella Armitage, it is strange she should choose
the same road as Miss Charron, don't you think?'

'Yes, I suppose it is, though if she were of gentle
birth, she would not have considered a menial job
like being a servant, would she? Nor, if she had
any spirit, being a companion at some elderly termagant's beck and call. At least acting would allow
her to retain some dignity.' He paused. 'I have a
mind to come with you.'

'Why?'

'Curiosity, I suppose.' He would not admit it was
anything else. 'And nothing else to do. London is
emptying by the day. Even some of those who stay
in town all the year round have drawn the blinds
on their front windows to make believe they have
country houses to go to. Lady Willoughby does it
every year and it fools no one, not even the cracks-
men who always seem to know when a house is
unoccupied.'

'In other words, you are bored.' The Major
laughed. 'I would welcome the company but the
coach is leaving in five minutes and I dare not wait
for you. She might disappear again.'

'Then I must not delay you. Besides, I have almost made up my mind to go to Loscoe Court
ahead of the family. But let me know what you
discover.'

Donald undertook to do so and the two men
shook hands and parted, the one to go on the coach

and possibly come to the end of his long search, the other to go home and add to his boredom by attending one of his stepmother's frequent musical evenings.

The crowd outside the theatre after the performance was thick as everyone called for cabs or called up their carriages and Madeleine had to force her way through. She had been asked to join a supper party, but had declined. Playing the tragic heroine had taken more out of her than she realised and she was anxious to go back to her lodgings, eat a solitary meal and go to bed.

If Marianne could see her, she would ring a peal over her for being such a ninny. 'You are not going to make a recovery if you do not make the effort to meet new people.' She could almost hear her saying it. But she was not yet ready to face the world. She had to learn to live for herself and not pine after someone she could not have and to face the knowledge that she would never have been in this coil if she had not told lies.

She was aware as she walked that there was one admirer who was more persistent than the rest and had followed her into the quiet streets behind the theatre where her lodgings were situated. She assumed it was an admirer, but it might be a footpad, and so she quickened her steps.

'Mrs Cartwright. Wait, please.' The voice did not sound like a thief; besides, a thief would not know her name. She stopped and turned and found herself face to face with Donald Greenaway.

'Major, what are you doing here?'

He had not been to the theatre and seen her performance and was as surprised as she was to find the woman who faced him was young and not the middle-aged one he had been expecting. 'Good God! Miss Charron, it is you.'

'Yes. Whom did you expect? Why did you call me Mrs Cartwright?'

'It is a very long story and cannot be told out here in the street. Will you come to my hotel and have supper with me and I will explain everything?'

She was wary. 'Did the Marquis of Risley send you?'

'Not at all. He does not know that Arabella Cartwright and Madeleine Charron are one and the same any more than I did until a moment ago. If he had known, I'll wager nothing would have stopped him from being here beside me now.'

She smiled crookedly. 'I doubt it. He is more than likely making arrangements for a wedding.'

'I know nothing of a wedding,' he said. 'What I have to tell you has nothing to do with the Marquis of Risley and, unless you wish it, I will not tell him of our meeting.' He paused, watching her face. Her violet eyes had lit briefly when he said he knew nothing of a wedding, but then became wary, as if he were about to trick her into something. He smiled reassuringly. 'So will you come?'

Curiosity won. 'Very well. But not for long. I am very tired.'

He led the way along several ill-lit streets until they emerged close to the magnificent Minster. Another turn and a few more yards and they were at the Star Inn. He ushered her inside and asked the patron for a quiet corner where they could talk undisturbed.

'Now,' he said, when a light meal and wine had been ordered and brought to the table. 'Why are you calling yourself Cartwright?'

'Because it is my name.'

'And Arabella, is that also your name?'

'No, it was my mother's name. Why are you quizzing me? You said you had something to tell me.'

'I wanted you to confirm what I believe to be true, that you are the daughter of Arabella and John Cartwright.'

'I never knew my father's given name. Are you quite sure you have not been sent by Lord Risley?'

'I am quite sure.' He bent down to a small case he had put on the floor beside him, opened it and extracted the portrait. 'Do you recognise who this is?'

She took it and studied it. The face that looked out on her was familiar from her childhood and she was at once transported to the little apartment over the dressmaking establishment where her mother sat at her sewing machine. She had a lovely smile, that was one of the things Maddy remembered most about her, the smile and the soft, cultured voice. 'It looks like my mother,' she said in wonder. 'Where did you get it?'

'From the Duchess of Loscoe. She painted it twenty-five years ago. When I said I was searching for Arabella Armitage, she remembered the painting and found it for me.'

The Duchess. So even she was determined to rake up her past and disprove the *comte* had ever existed. 'You said Arabella Armitage.'

'Yes, that was your mother's name before she married.'

'I never knew that,' she said, wondering how he could be so sure. 'She never spoke of her past, though sometimes she talked about riding in the country when she was a girl and a Miss Gunnery whom she had known and loved. I believe she was a schoolteacher, for Mama spoke of the things she had taught her.'

His face broke into a smile. 'You have just confirmed that I am on the right track, Miss Charron. Or should I call you Miss Cartwright?'

'Whichever you like, Major, but Madeleine will do.'

He smiled. 'Miss Gunnery was not a schoolteacher, your Mama never went to school, she was educated at home. Did she ever say where that home was?'

'No. In the country somewhere. It might have been Hertfordshire.'

'Now I am as sure as anyone can be that you are the person I have been looking for. Or to be more precise, the daughter of that person.'

'Looking for?' she echoed.

'Miss Cartwright, you told Lord Risley and others that your mother was dead. Is that true?'

She stared at him for several seconds. So he was out to prove her a liar, was he? But the only lie she had told was about the French grandfather and an exaggeration about her father's role as a soldier. She bristled. 'I would not lie about something like that, Major. My world fell apart when she was killed. She was all I had.'

'Not quite all,' he said softly. 'You had…you have a grandfather.'

She was confused and angry at the same time and answered him sharply. 'Oh, him. I invented him and if you have been talking to the Marquis of Risley, you must surely know that.'

'I am not speaking of the French *émigré*, I am referring to your real grandfather. He has been searching for his long-lost daughter, not knowing she was dead, but I am sure he will be overjoyed to meet her daughter.'

'Who is he?' she asked, leaning forward in her seat and forgetting all about the food congealing on her plate.

'Viscount Armitage.'

She sat and stared at him, unable to take in what he was saying. 'I don't understand.'

'No, I don't suppose you do.' He beckoned the waiter and asked for a glass of brandy for her and when she had it in front of her, he told her the story of the viscount and his search for his daughter.

'It was because Lord Risley thought the painting was so like you, that set me thinking,' he said. 'He told me you had been in an orphanage, but he did not know which one. Knowing the Duchess of Loscoe is a patron of more than one orphanage, I asked her if she could make enquiries. Her Grace always insists on keeping meticulous records just in case lost relatives turn up, you know. There was no information about anyone called Cartwright, though there were details of the arrival of Madeleine Charron whose mother's name, according to the neighbour who brought her in, was Bella. I began to wonder if they could possibly be one and the same, but before I could question you, you had disappeared.'

'How did you find me, then?'

He smiled. 'I have been pursuing these enquiries for a long time now and have a whole army of contacts and informants primed to tell me the minute anyone by the name of Cartwright turns up. I heard from one such only two days ago and came post haste, expecting to find your mother.'

She took a gulp of brandy. It did not seem to make any difference, she was still shaking and confused. 'I can't take it in. Are you telling me I have a family, a real family?'

'I believe there are aunts and cousins and suchlike besides your grandfather.'

'And he is really a viscount?'

'Yes. He is old and ill and worried about what has become of his daughter. News of her death will come as a shock, I have no doubt, but that will be softened when he meets you.'

'Does he know you have found me?'

'No, I did not know myself until an hour ago. But we must make all haste to go to him. His home, Pargeter House, is on the outskirts of St Albans, so we can take the London coach.'

'I'll have to get leave from the theatre.'

He smiled. 'Your life is about to change forever and you worry about your work. There is no need for you to earn your living, you know. Viscount Armitage is quite wealthy.'

She could not take it in. Why had this all happened now? For years she had longed for a family, any family. She had wanted to be loved and have someone to love, as she had her mother; she had even lied to try and bring it about. And now, when she had accepted that she was being punished for her deception and must rely on her own resources, this man had arrived and thrown her into confusion again. She did have a noble grandfather and she could, if she wished, take her place in Society. She was a lady of consequence.

Her thoughts flew to Duncan. Now she was acceptable. She began to laugh hysterically until he looked at her in alarm. 'Miss...Madeleine, I am sorry, this has been a shock to you.'

She stopped laughing as suddenly as she had started and took another mouthful of brandy. 'Yes, it has, but I am calm now.'

It was foolish even to think of Duncan Stanmore. Even if he did not marry Annabel Bulford, even if he came to her and begged her to marry him, she could not agree to it. He had not wanted to marry her as Madeleine Charron because she was an actress and too far beneath him. If he asked her now that she was a viscount's granddaughter, she would always know that status had been more important than love to him. She must put him from her mind and concentrate on what was happening now.

She wondered what her grandfather would be like. He might take an instant aversion to her, considering he did not like her father. 'You have not told me anything about my father,' she said. 'Was he a soldier?'

'Yes, but not an officer. He was an enlisted man, a foot soldier of no rank, but I imagine he must have had a certain amount of charm to have attracted your mother and made her defy her father.'

'What happened to him?'

'He was sent out to India, but your mother did not go with him. It was not long before you were born, so I expect she decided it would not be wise to travel. He died of a fever a year later.'

'I wonder why my mother did not tell me? Was she ashamed of him? Were they unhappy?'

'That, I am afraid, is something we might never know. But do not think of it. Think of the future.'

And that was almost as difficult as thinking of the past. What was her future? Would the Viscount allow her to go on acting or would he insist on her making her home with him? What if they disliked each other on sight? And if he had been hoping to see his daughter again and all he had was a grand-daughter, not even an heir, he might not wish to know her.

'Why are you hesitating?' he asked.

'Major, I am who I am. What you have told me does not change that. I like being an actress. I am good at it.'

'I do not deny it, but your grandfather is old, he will not live much longer. Can you not make his last days happy? After that, what you do is up to you.'

She could not deny him that and next morning, after a sleepless night, she asked the theatre management for leave of absence to go to Hertford-shire, while the Major obtained tickets for them on the noon coach.

* * *

'Duncan, whatever in the world is the matter with you?' the Duchess demanded. 'I have never seen such a Friday face. You are not pining over Miss Bulford, are you?'

'Good heavens, no, Mama, I wish her happy. And Ben too.' They were sitting together in the drawing room after an early nuncheon. The Duke had taken himself off to Westminster and later the ladies on the orphanage committee were expected for a meeting. He knew that before they arrived he was in for a roasting; his stepmother had that determined look on her face which he knew would brook no evasion.

'Then, dearest, what is wrong?'

'Nothing. I shall be glad when we go back to Risley and I can put my back into some work, that is all.'

'That is not all.' She turned to study his face. 'It's Miss Charron, isn't it?'

'Yes. Mama, I wish I knew where she was, truly I do. She might be in trouble, had an accident, be dead even...'

'I think we should have heard if that had happened. I wonder what Donald Greenaway discovered in York.'

He looked up startled. 'What should he have discovered? He went in search of Arabella Cartwright.'

'I know, but did it never occur to you that *le charron* is French for cartwright?'

He clapped his hand to his forehead. 'How can I have been such a dunderhead? I should have thought of that when I noticed the likeness in that portrait. But why Arabella?'

'You know the Major asked me to take a look at the orphanage records?'

'Yes. Did you find something, after all?'

'Something and nothing. Miss Charron was one of our children and her mother's name, according to the information lodged when she arrived, was Bella.'

'Mama!' He stared at her. 'Why did you not tell me before?'

'I am sorry, I thought you had put her from your mind. You said you had.'

'Never, Mama, never. I must find her. I have to tell her that I do not care who she is or what she is, I intend to make her my wife. If you do not approve…'

'Duncan, my approval is not needed. You are man enough to know your own mind, as I am sure your father has told you.'

'Yes, but he made it clear he did not approve of a kitchen maid.'

'You do him an injustice, Duncan. He is only concerned for your happiness, as I am, and the difficulties you would face, which would not be inconsiderable. But if she is really the Viscount's granddaughter…'

Duncan stood up, eyes alight. 'I must go to York at once.' He strode to the door, sent a servant to tell Dobson to have his travelling coach harnessed up and leapt up the stairs three at a time, shouting for Davison to pack his bag. He did not care if Maddy was the Viscount's granddaughter or not; he loved her and wanted her for his wife. He had to convince her of that.

Although his horses were the best money could buy and his carriage well-sprung with well-padded seats, the journey seemed unbelievably slow. Every change of horses seemed to take hours instead of minutes and it was all he could do to prevent himself shouting at the ostlers to stop dawdling and get on with it. Oh, how he wished he could fly.

He was in Grantham at breakfast time, though they stopped only long enough to buy a glass of ale and a currant bun while the horses were changed. After that he counted the hours as they rattled on through Newark, Doncaster and Ferrybridge and finally the tall towers of the Minster could be seen in the distance. He sat forward eagerly as the countryside gave way to streets and buildings and they were forced to slow down because of traffic. But at last they came to a stop at the Star Inn, less than twenty-four hours after leaving London.

He jumped down, too impatient to wait for Dobson to open the door and let down the step. Telling him to see that the horses were looked after, he did not even stop for refreshment, but strode away towards the theatre. He had no idea where Donald would be staying, but knowing Madeleine as he did, he was sure that she would never be far from a theatre. And hadn't Donald said Arabella Cartwright was an actress?

But he was too late; the stage door-keeper told him she had left only that morning. 'Might have known it,' he said. 'Arriving so sudden, it was odds on she'd leave sudden too. Something to hide, that one.'

'Where did she go?' he asked in dismay.

'Dunno,' he said. 'Went off with a military gentleman.'

Major Donald Greenaway. Had his search come to an end? If Arabella Cartwright had turned out to be Viscount Armitage's granddaughter, where would he take her? The answer was obvious and he lost no time in returning to the inn. Too keyed up to sleep in the coach the night before, he was worn out and decided to take a room and try to have a few hours' sleep before returning south.

It was while he was lying awake, unable, in spite of his exhaustion, to close his eyes, he began to wonder if hot pursuit was the right thing. He longed to see Madeleine again, to hold her in his arms, to tell her again that he loved her, to ask her to marry him, but how would she see his sudden arrival at the home of her grandfather? He could almost hear her. 'Oh, so now you have discovered I am of gentle birth, it is perfectly in order to make an offer, is it?'

How could he convince her that was not true? Why, oh why, had he not made a firm offer before all these revelations had changed everything? If she had found out about her real grandfather after their engagement, it would not have mattered.

He tried to imagine her at Pargeter House, getting to know her grandfather, becoming used to her changed circumstances, confused perhaps, but happy, because all she had ever wanted was a loving family. Going in with all guns blazing would not serve. Impatient as he was, he had to give her time. But he would not go back to London. Risley was nearer and to Loscoe Court he would go and he would write to her, put it all down on paper and ask her to see him. Once the decision had been made, he managed a few hours sleep and next morning, he set off for Derbyshire and Risley. Once there, Dobson could return the hired horses to the inn where he had left his own and bring them back. Suddenly he was looking forward to being home.

Madeleine need not have worried about her reception. Her welcome at Pargeter House could not have been warmer. The old man was frail but still very alert. He had once been very handsome, though now his hair was white and the hands that

grasped hers so firmly were thin and veined. 'My
child,' he kept saying. 'My child, home at last.'

She wondered whether he was confusing her
with her mother, but the notion was dispelled when
he said, 'You are so like your mother, it is uncanny,
but I believe your hair is not so dark; hers was
black as a raven's wing. You must tell me all about
yourself, but not now. I am tired with all the excitement and must rest. Mrs Danby will look after
you.'

She bent to kiss his papery cheek and left him
to sleep. Major Greenaway, his task done, was preparing to leave and she said goodbye to him with
some trepidation. He was someone familiar, someone from her old life, and she had felt comfortable
with him, but now she was on her own and was
not at all sure what to expect.

After he had gone, her days took on the quality
of a dream. They were a whirl of activity, meeting
the servants, some of whom had been in the
Viscount's service long enough to remember her
mother, being shown every nook and cranny of the
large, well-furnished house and hearing about her
mother from old Miss Gunnery, who had her own
apartment on the second floor, though she had long
ago ceased to do any work.

She was tiny and had the bluest eyes Maddy had
ever seen. She wore a black jaconet gown and a
lace cap, perched on the knot of white hair she had

drawn up on top of her head. She was sad when she learned that her former charge had died so tragically, but she did not dwell on it for fear of upsetting Maddy.

'Oh, it is like having our own dearest Bella home again,' she said. 'I do believe his lordship might make a recovery now you are with us. He has been so cast down, years and years and never a word from your mama.'

'I thought he had sent her away.'

'Oh, he did. I am sure he regretted it almost immediately, but it took several years for him to admit it and by then she had disappeared. They were both proud, you see. When he realised she was not going to come back on her own, he spent hundreds of pounds in the search for her. And here you are. I can hardly believe it.'

Madeleine could hardly believe it herself. Everything she had known and believed about herself had been turned topsy-turvy and her mind was in confusion. 'The Viscount is very frail,' she said. 'I wonder my sudden arrival has not quite overturned him and I am at a loss what to tell him about myself. I have not lived like a lady, nor always been honest about myself. I am afraid it will upset him…'

'Major Greenaway told me a little of your history while you were meeting his lordship,' Miss Gunnery said, laying a gentle hand on her arm. 'But I am of the opinion that nothing could upset him

more than seeing his daughter go off with that…'
She stopped herself. 'But there, he was your father
and what is past is past. I think you should tell the
whole, he is stronger than you think.'

And so she did. Everything, beginning with her
life with her mother and her mother's sudden death
and about the orphanage, which she told him was
not so very terrible, and her years as a servant.
From his reply she realised he assumed she had
been a ladies' maid, which was in his eyes, bad
enough, so she did not disillusion him, and she said
nothing of Lord Bulford's attack on her. That had
triggered everything that had happened afterwards,
but looking back now, she knew, terrible as that
ordeal had been, her long years of hatred of all
aristocrats had been wrong. She told him how she
had become an actress and even the story of the
comte, which made him smile.

'You are like your mother for that,' he said. 'She
liked to invent too. Why else think up an outlandish
name like Charron? But you are home now and
there need be no more invention. Whatever you
wish for, you may have, if it is in my power to give
it to you.'

But he could not give her what she most wanted
and that was the unequivocal, unencumbered love
of Duncan Stanmore, Marquis of Risley. The Major
had told her while they were travelling that Duncan
had not offered for Annabel Bulford and she had

accepted Mr Willoughby, which surprised her but did not change anything.

'There is nothing I need, Grandfather,' she said.

'Let me be the judge of that. Have you had a come-out? No, of course you have not. We must put plans in hand at once for next year...'

She was alarmed. 'No, sir, I beg you do not. I am four-and-twenty years old, far too old for that. And besides, everyone knows me as an actress. They would say I was puffing myself up and I would die of mortification.'

'But we must find you a husband.'

'That is just what you said to Bella,' Miss Gunnery put in, apparently unafraid to speak her mind. 'And look what happened; she rushed off with the first rake who bowled her over with flummery rather that accept your choice. You surely would not want to make the same mistake again.'

'Hmph,' he grunted, then to Maddy, 'You ain't got yourself involved with a redcoat, have you?'

'No, Grandfather. There is no one.'

'Time enough, then. I can keep you to myself a little longer.'

It was taken for granted she would stay at Pargeter House and, for the time being, she accepted it. Being cosseted and loved and exploring her new surroundings was as good a cure for her ills as she could think of. It would be time enough to worry about the future when his lordship no longer needed her. And best of all, when her grandfather found out she had never learned to ride, he arranged for her to have lessons from the groom on a quiet little mare. 'Your mama was an accomplished rider,' he said, which was something else she had never known.

Her mother had left her riding habit behind, knowing she would have no opportunity to wear it in her new life, and it fitted Madeleine perfectly. Although it would have been considered outmoded in London, it was beautifully made of heavy dark blue taffeta, with wide shoulders and a nipped-in waist. It was worn with a white lace cravat and a tall manly hat with a wisp of a veil. That costume, more than anything, brought home to her how much her life had changed.

She was quick to learn, which only went to prove she was her mother's daughter, her grandfather told her. He appeared to have been given a new lease of life, his eyes were brighter and his voice stronger, but he was still too weak to be dressed for more than an hour each afternoon and then he would send for her and they would talk of her mother, or she would read to him from the newspapers which were sent from London every day.

When he slept, she would scan the gossip columns for news of Duncan, but all she found was news of her own elevation and speculation on whether she would come to London and take her place in Society. Apparently the hopeful eligibles were already being lined up for her, which made her smile wryly. She turned to the theatre news, wondering if she would ever tread the boards again. She had written to Marianne, telling her about her changed circumstances and asking for news of her old friends, but as yet had had no reply.

But when the postman came it was not a letter from Marianne he brought but one from Duncan Stanmore. She took it to her room to read sitting on the seat by the window, so that the breeze from the open casement cooled her cheeks.

'My dearest love,' it began. 'Major Greenaway has written to tell me you have found your family and I write to felicitate you. I know we parted on bad terms, but that does not alter the strength of feeling I have for you and have always had. My greatest regret is that I did not convince you of it before your recent change of circumstances became known. I loved Madeleine Charron, the actress. I loved everything about her: her beauty, her talent, the way she made me laugh, her compassion and her independence, even when it came between us. I am equally certain I love the new Miss Cartwright because they are one and the same, the keeper of my heart. I beg you to write and grant me an interview and I will convince you of this. Your devoted slave, Duncan Stanmore.'

For a long time she sat gazing out of the window at the park that surrounded the house, the letter lying on her lap. He had said he loved her before, when they were in London, but he had made it

plain that marriage was not possible while she remained an actress and when he found out she had
been a kitchen maid and she had confessed the
comte was a fiction, his love had suddenly found
even more barriers he was not prepared to climb.
What had changed now? Only her status, her consequence in the hierarchy of the *haut monde*, and
what was that? Meaningless glitter, like the fake
diamonds she wore on stage. Worthless. It certainly
did not mean she had suddenly become a better
person. There was more meaning to her life as an
actress. And she was still an actress and could continue to be one.

But though her head debated, her heart was arguing a different line. She loved him and would
always love him, wherever she went, whatever she
did and she longed to see him again. So, should
she tell him to come, let him try and convince her
if he could? Where was the harm in that? And if
she still had doubts… Oh, those doubts, that stubborn pride, which would not allow her to let go of
her old prejudices without a fight. Why fight? Why
not accept that what he said was true? But could
she leave her grandfather when he had come to depend on her so much?

She looked up when she heard a knock at her
door and it was flung open before she could even
call, 'Come in.'

'Maddy, come quickly.' It was Miss Gunnery
with a worried look on her face and her cap all

awry. 'His lordship has taken a turn for the worse and is asking for you.'

The letter fluttered from her lap as she leapt to her feet and went to her grandfather's bedside. It was several days before she was able to give it another thought and by then she knew that, while her grandfather needed her, she could not leave him.

Riding had always been Duncan's greatest pleasure, but now it was the only thing he enjoyed. He rode for miles out across the moors with only his horse and the birds for company, until dark or rain sent him home again. And then he would hurry indoors and gather up the post from the silver tray on the hall table where the butler always put it when he was out. He would shuffle through the letters, looking for one from Madeleine.

'Martin, are you sure this is all the post?' he would bellow, as he went up to change out of his riding clothes.

Martin would appear from the kitchen or the drawing room, wherever he had been working. 'Yes, my lord. I asked the postman most particular.'

He had been asking about the mail ever since he had come home, but the expected letter did not arrive. Why did she not answer? Surely she could have written something, anything, even no. It would be better than nothing. But if she did not think enough of him to answer a simple letter, then he was better off without her. If he kept busy, he could forget her. He could and he would.

With the end of the Season and Parliament's recess, his parents and the boys returned to Risley, bringing Lavinia and her children for a little holiday, before she took them back to Twelve-trees and their autumn lessons. She found not the laughing easygoing brother she knew, but a morose, uncommunicative man who had nothing to say at all. After watching him for two days, she could remain silent no longer.

'Duncan, if you do not snap out of the dismals and do something about it, I shall have to box your ears.'

Her threat brought a flicker of a smile. 'What would you have me do?'

'Go to her. Have it out with her. I wonder you have not done so long ago.'

'Who?' He knew whom she meant, even though he pretended otherwise. 'I don't know what you are talking about.'

'Yes, you do. You and Madeleine. Your pride. And hers. I have no patience with either of you. You need your heads banging together.'

'That is not the case at all. I was simply giving her time to become used to her new family, which must make her feel very strange. I could not charge in like a bull in a china shop, could I?'

'No, but did you know Viscount Armitage had died?'

'No.' He was startled. 'Are you sure?'

'Yes, I saw it in the paper just before I left London.'

'Oh, my poor, dear Maddy. I must go to her.' And then he was gone, flying up the stairs to his room, shouting for Davison. An hour later, he was in his coach and being driven by the ever-patient Dobson towards the London Road.

The Viscount's death had come as a profound shock to Madeleine. She had known he was ill and made old before his time, but she had believed Miss Gunnery when she said she thought he might recover, simply because she wanted it to be true. She had only just got to know him and now he was gone.

'You must give thanks that his last few days were happy ones,' Miss Gunnery said, while they waited for the men to come back from the funeral. 'He is at peace and with your dear mama.'

She would have liked to have gone to the service of committal, to have stood beside the grave to say goodbye to him, but she was told it was simply not done, it was too distressing for sensitive female minds. And so they waited, Madeleine, Miss Gunnery and numerous female relatives who viewed her with deep suspicion. They had arrived in carriages from far and near, these unknown second cousins of hers, dressed in deepest mourning, each bewailing the loss in their own way. Madeleine had been introduced to them, but she had been so distressed she could not remember which was which.

One thing they seemed to have in common was a curiosity to know how his lordship had ordered his estate. There had been no son, no direct heir, and this new grandchild was a woman. She could almost see their minds ticking over in their eyes and the sharp way they looked about them, calculating the worth of the pictures and ornaments.

'I suppose I must, but I feel lost.'

'We all do. In spite of his pride, he was a good man. We shall miss him.'

'What shall you do?'

'I have a pension. It was awarded to me years ago and I have never spent it. I shall do very well. My concern is for you.'

Madeleine managed a smile. 'I can earn my own living, Miss Gunnery. I have been doing it since I was twelve years old, have no fear for me.'

This statement sent the good lady into paroxysms of weeping and Madeleine was trying to comfort her when the men returned, leaving their black-ribboned top hats on the table in the entrance hall and marching into the drawing room. She rose to act the hostess and offer them refreshment, which they accepted, ignoring her as if she were a servant. She did not blame them. She was an interloper. She slipped out before the will could be read, believing there was nothing in it for her, but hoping that whoever inherited the hall might allow her some little memento of her stay there.

She went up to her room where the portmanteau she had packed that morning stood by the door. It contained only those things she had brought with her with the addition of her mother's riding habit, which had been given to her. Sitting at the little desk, which had once been her mother's, she wrote a letter of explanation to Miss Gunnery, telling her she would write again when she was settled, and another to Mrs Danby, thanking the staff for making her so welcome, and then she slipped on her pelisse, tied a black straw bonnet on to her curls and, picking up the case, went down the stairs and out of the front door. No one saw her go.

It was only a short step to the village where she knew several coaches called on their way to London every day. Now she was once again Miss Madeleine Charron, actress. But there was a difference. She was no longer a liar, no longer embittered. She walked with a light step to meet the future.

As she approached the Peahen, she saw a smart coach arriving and watched as it swung into the yard and the ostlers hurried forward to see to the horses. A moment later its occupant alighted and stood looking about him.

The Marquis of Risley was the last person she expected to see and she stood rooted to the spot, staring at him. The noise and bustle of the coaching inn faded to insignificance. She saw nothing but his handsome face, looking rather more drawn than she remembered it, heard nothing but her own name on his lips. 'Madeleine!'

He was smiling as he came towards her. She did not know whether to fling herself into his arms or turn and run; her hesitation was her undoing. A horse snorted close to her, but she hardly noticed, did not hear the shout of the coachman behind her, felt nothing until Duncan flung himself on her and pushed her out of the way, as the great horse reared. She screamed as its hooves rose above Duncan's head. 'Duncan!' And then the sky went black and her knees gave way beneath her.

She came to her senses lying on a settle in one of the rooms of the inn and Duncan was sitting beside her, holding her hand. She struggled to sit up, but he gently pushed her back. 'Lie still, my love, you have had a nasty shock.'

She managed something very near to a laugh. 'Yes, seeing you get off that coach was shock enough to send anyone into a swoon.'

'I did not mean that, I mean nearly being trampled on by a horse. Did you not hear it behind you?'

'No, I was looking at you.' She paused. 'You saved me. I thought it had come down on top of you.'

'No, I managed to dodge it. But what about you? Are you hurt?'

'No, shaken, that's all.' She paused. 'What are you doing here?'

'I came to fetch you.'

'Fetch me?'

'Yes. I tired of waiting for you to send for me, so…' He grinned. 'If the mountain won't come to Mahomet, then Mahomet must come to the mountain.'

'I am sorry I did not answer your letter. I did not mean to keep you waiting, but my grandfather…'

'I know and I am most dreadfully sorry. But where were you off to? Surely you are needed at the house?'

'No.' She smiled wanly. 'My grandfather was buried today and the family are gathered like vultures. I could not bear it. It was lovely knowing him, if only for three short weeks, but it changed nothing. I am still Madeleine Charron, the actress. And before you say a word about being a viscount's granddaughter, let me tell you that it makes not one jot of difference.'

'No, my darling, not one jot.' He smiled, taking her hand in his and gently stroking the back of it with his thumb. The sensation it engendered was out of all proportion to the tiny movement. Her whole body tingled with a desire so great she hardly knew how to control it. 'You are what you are, forged by the hard life you have led, and are all the stronger for it. I love you for that. I love you for what you are, not whose child you are. Will you not be convinced?'

Her heart was hammering in her throat, making it difficult to speak. 'Are you sure?'

'Damme!' he exclaimed. 'Did you think I penned that letter to you for fun? It took hours to compose. I am deadly serious. I want you to marry me. All I need is for you to say you love me too.'

She was silent.

'Madeleine, put me out of my torment, I beg you.'

'Would you believe me if I said I did not? After all, how can you believe a word I say? I am an actress and a deceiver to boot.'

'Don't tease.'

'I am not. I need to know you forgive me for it. I should never have tried to deceive you.'

'No, but if you had not, I doubt you would be here now, talking to me like this. So, there is nothing to forgive. I understand.'

'You do?'

'Yes. Everyone needs a family. You did not have one and so you invented one.'

'That wasn't the only reason. I must tell you the whole truth.'

He waited, steeling himself to hear that Henry Bulford had ravished her, but when she had told her story, all of it, he breathed a huge sigh of relief. 'Oh, my love, I could run him through...'

'You must not think of it. It does not matter now because everything has come out right in the end. I found my grandfather...' She paused and laughed. 'The real one. And it would not have mattered to me if he had been the poorest labourer.'

'Nor to me. So what is stopping you from saying yes?'

'Oh, Duncan, there will be so many obstacles. How can a marquis, the heir to a dukedom, marry an actress? I could not bear to be the cause of a rift between you and your family. When I saw you in the park surrounded by all those children, I knew I could never take you away from them. That was when I decided to leave London...'

'And a merry dance you led me and none of it necessary, but you are found now and there are no obstacles that cannot be overcome and none of them put up by my family, I promise you. They will be happy for us. As for the wider world, who cares what the *haut monde* thinks when I have my heart's desire.'

Her tears were flowing now and she could not stop them. He lifted his hand and wiped them away with the back of his forefinger. 'Dearest one, why are you weeping?'

'Because, for the first time in my life, I am truly happy.'

'Oh, Maddy.' He bent his head and pressed his lips to hers, tenderly and gently, afraid to startle her, but she flung her arms about his neck and pulled him closer so that they were wrapped in each other's arms so closely they were almost fused as one. At last, too breathless to continue, they drew apart. 'May you never be sad again. And you won't be if I have anything to do with it.' He slipped from his seat and knelt beside her. 'See, I am on my knees to you. I shall not rise until you agree to marry me.'

She laughed. 'Oh, do get up, Duncan, that floor is very dusty.'

'Well?'

She hesitated briefly, but then gave in. 'Of course I will. How could you doubt it?'

'Oh, my love, we shall be so happy.' He rose to sit beside her and kissed her again and she kissed him back and it was only the light tap at the door that brought them back to their senses.

It was the landlord, ushering in a waiter with food and wine for them. They sat silently watching as a cloth was put on a small table by the window and the dishes and glasses set upon it. Duncan dismissed the men, saying they would serve themselves and then he held out a hand to raise her to her feet and escort her to the table. 'Now, we will eat and drink,' he said. 'And after that we will make plans.'

In the euphoria of the moment, practical matters were far from her mind and she did not feel like eating, but he coaxed her gently to taste a little of the delicious meal and by then she was quaking at the enormity of what she had agreed to and was full of trepidation. He seemed to understand, for he reached out and put his hand over hers. 'It will be all right, my love, I promise you.'

'I hope so. Perhaps—'

'No doubts now,' he said, attempting to sound severe. 'Where were you going when I came upon you? Back to London?'

'Yes. I thought I might take up where I left off. I hoped Mr Greatorex would take me back...'

'He would be a fool not to. But...' He paused, not wanting to introduce a jarring note, but needing to know the true state of affairs at Pargeter House. 'Did Viscount Armitage not make any provision for you?'

'I do not think so. I have no dowry.'

'I did not mean that and you know it.' His reply was sharp until he saw the twinkle in her violet eyes and knew she was teasing. He realised he would never be quite sure when she was being serious and when she was gammoning him.

'I know. I was thinking of my grandfather's great-nephews and -nieces, all looking at me as if I were an interloper who had no right to be among them. And I suppose they were right. In any case, it does not matter. Grandfather was ill when I arrived and had no chance to change his will before he died, so I decided to leave. It was such a short episode in my life, I never really had time to become used to it.'

'Madeleine, I am so sorry.'

'Oh, do not be. Nothing is ever wasted. As you said earlier, our experiences forge our character and I think I might have learned a little wisdom along the way.' She paused to chuckle. 'And how to ride.'

'You did?'

'Well, I had made a start under the tutelage of a groom, and I found I enjoyed it.'

He grinned. 'Oh, we shall have such great times, riding on the moors about Loscoe Court.' He paused. 'If you agree, we will go there first. My family are there and they must be the first to know.'

'Of course.'

It was not until they were in the coach riding north that she began to shake uncontrollably. He seemed to understand, for he smiled as he put his arm about her. 'Surely Madeleine Charron, the great actress who has entertained thousands and never turned a hair, is not quaking at the thought of meeting a handful of people who are already well disposed towards her? They will not throw orange peel.'

She laughed and settled her dark head against his shoulder and slept. He woke her when they passed through the gates of Loscoe Court. 'We are home, my love.'

Home. It sounded like heaven. She watched the enormous building come into sight at the end of the long drive, and began to shake again. This was the country home of the Duke of Loscoe, and she was about to be introduced as a prospective daughter-in-law.

The family must have heard the carriage arriving; before they had time to step down on the gravel, the door was flung open and the Duchess was on the step ready to greet her. She was drawn inside and was given such a welcome by the rest of the family she was overcome. But worrying her, like a gnat that would not stop nipping, was the question: would they have been so happy if she had not turned out to be the granddaughter of a viscount?

It was Lavinia who set her mind at rest. They were sitting in the morning room with the sun streaming in the window, waiting for Duncan to come and take her out riding. She was dressed in her mother's habit and Lavinia remarked how fetching it was and how it suited her and, when she did not reply, added, 'What are you thinking of?'

'What the world will say about it all. Whether they think I am puffed up and only accepted by

Society because my grandpapa was a viscount. Do you think Duncan—?'

'Good heavens, no! He does not care where you came from, he is only concerned that you have agreed to become his wife. And so are we all. His happiness comes first with us and it is clear to everyone that his happiness is with you. And it does not matter what the rest of the world thinks.' She paused, smiling. 'But there is no harm at all in using your new status to smooth his path, is there?'

'What do you mean?'

'When the engagement is announced, which Duncan is very anxious should be soon, you could agree to allowing yourself to be called the granddaughter of the late Viscount Armitage, could you not? For his sake?'

'What are you two plotting?' Duncan came in, dressed for riding in soft leather breeches tucked into shining boots, a brown riding coat with velvet revers and cuffs and a snowy cravat fastened with a diamond pin. Her heart leapt at the sight of him, as it always did, and she rose to take his hands. He bent and kissed her cheek. 'Well?'

'We were simply discussing the form the announcement of our betrothal should take.'

'A mere formality, my darling. Leave it to me.'

'And you are determined to tell the world you are marrying Madeleine Charron, the actress, are you not?'

'Naturally, I am. I am proud of her. I want everyone to know.' He knew better than to rouse her ire
by suggesting anything different. And besides he
wanted to prove that he had meant what he said;
he loved her whatever and whoever she was.

'But Madeleine Charron does not exist as a person, Duncan,' she said, watching his face carefully.
'The lady you are marrying is Miss Madeleine
Cartwright, granddaughter of the late Viscount
Armitage.' She paused and laughed. 'And, since I
have just heard that he left me a small legacy after
all, a lady of consequence.'

He took her shoulders in his hands and looked
down into her upturned face. Her eyes were shining
with love and he knew she was doing this thing to
please him as he was intending to please her, and
he smiled. 'Whatever you say, my dear lady.
Whatever you call yourself, you will always be a
lady of consequence to me.'

They did not notice Lavinia stand up and cross
the room, did not even here the soft click of the
door as she left them. He was too busy kissing her.

Six months' mourning was considered long
enough for a grandfather she had only just met and
they were married the following spring. They had
meant it to be a quiet wedding, but Lavinia persuaded them that a hole-and-corner affair would
only feed the gossips and they would do well to do
the thing properly. And they could not marry with-

out inviting some of their friends, and if some, then why not all? And so it became a grand Society affair.

Madeleine was dressed in a gown of heavy cream taffeta with dropped shoulders whose neckline was edged with ruched silk. The same ruched silk decorated the hem of her underskirt which peeped beneath the loops of taffeta of the top skirt. Her lovely hair was brought up into an Apollo knot over which was fastened a long Honiton lace veil, decorated with trailing silk ribbons. Duncan, handsome himself in a dove-grey superfine frockcoat and matching trousers, strapped beneath his patent leather shoes, thought he had never seen anyone so beautiful and her expressive violet eyes, looking into his as she joined him at the altar, told him clearly that she loved him. She had no eyes for the ranks of guests in the pews behind them as she was joined in matrimony to the tall handsome man at her side.

She did not think about them until the service was over and she walked slowly back down the aisle on her husband's arm and one by one the men bowed and the ladies dropped a knee in a curtsy. She was a Marchioness and they were acknowledging that. It was all she could do not to giggle. And among them were the cousins who had so disdained her and Benedict and Annabel with Lord and Lady Bulford, whom Madeleine had insisted should be included. She inclined her head graciously at their obeisance and moved on.

Duncan, smiling beside her, bent his head to whisper, 'Vengeance is sweet, is it not, my darling?'

None of them understood why she suddenly laughed up at him, but there wasn't a man among them who did not envy the handsome bridegroom who had everything, nor a woman who did not sigh with jealousy of his beautiful bride.

HISTORICAL ROMANCE™

LARGE PRINT

COLONEL ANCROFT'S LOVE
Sylvia Andrew

When Colonel John Ancroft is persuaded to escort an elderly widow to Yorkshire, he has no idea that the lady in question is heiress Caroline Duval. Her disguise is only revealed when he happens upon her, her widow's clothes discarded, swimming naked in a pool.

Suddenly his much-vaunted self-control is severely tested as he confronts this bewitching flame-haired beauty. But she's embarked on a dangerous family undertaking where scandal could bring them both down…

ONE NIGHT WITH A RAKE
Louise Allen

Beautiful widow Amanda Clare woke up in a strange bed, lying next to a tall, dark, very handsome *stranger*!

Knocked out in a stagecoach accident, they'd been rescued and it had been assumed that they were married – reason enough to put them to bed in the same room! Amanda had no idea who the man was – but, intriguingly, neither did he! The obviously wealthy gentleman had lost his memory, and was without two guineas in his pocket. Now Amanda felt obliged to take the gorgeous stranger under her wing – and continue the pretence that they were man and wife…

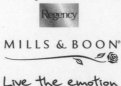

MILLS & BOON®

Live the emotion

HIST0204 LP